TRANSGRESSION

Rosemary Randall

About the author

Rosemary Randall is a psychotherapist who has been active in the climate movement for many years. She is co-founder of the Carbon Conversations project and a founder member of the Climate Psychology Alliance. She blogs at www.rorandall.org. This is her first novel.

Acknowledgments

Anyone familiar with the climate movement in the first decade of this century will recognise the real events – the actions, arguments, occupations and betrayals - which lie behind this fictionalised account. I have taken liberties with both time and geography in order to create my story and the characters are of course entirely fictional but I hope that the novel stays true to the dilemmas and difficulties of that time.

Thanks are due to all those who shared their experiences of this period with me and in particular to Andy Brown, Alex Randall, Tanya Hawkes and Tamsin Palmer who read and commented extensively on early drafts.

Contents

SUMMER 2009

Esther

When the doorbell rang at exactly three o'clock Esther thought that she must have forgotten someone. Ten minutes earlier she had waited with relief for the final click of the front door and retreated to the cool of the kitchen. There was time, she had told herself, to allow the clamour of the week's voices to subside. The children would not arrive for several hours.

The bell rang again, harsh and insistent. Had she changed an appointment? Failed to enter an extra session? Forgotten someone completely? She closed the patio doors and moved quickly towards the front hall, pausing briefly in front of a mirror to smooth her thick brown hair. Searching for some reservoir of compassion she turned the door handle.

A short, well-dressed, bullet-headed man stood on the doorstep. He was through the door before she could utter a word.

"Esther, I am so glad to see you, so glad to find you home. I felt sure you wouldn't mind..."

Esther stared at him in confusion. She had not seen Thomas Fortune for years. He was gesturing at the door of her consulting room and then at the passageway that led to the rest of the house.

"In here or in the kitchen? The kitchen maybe...more informal..."

"Thomas..." she began but he made his way authoritatively through her house and seated himself at her kitchen table before she could finish the sentence.

"I'm sorry to impose on you" he said. "I wouldn't normally arrive unannounced but I couldn't think of anyone else with your experience - or your discretion - and it is really quite urgent."

Thomas Fortune had recovered a touch of the charm that she remembered from her first meeting with him but beads of sweat stood out on his forehead and a slight tremor played around his thin lips. Esther resigned herself to the encounter, fetched him a glass of iced water from the fridge and sat down opposite him.

His eyes flicked round the room. "We are alone, aren't we?" he said, glancing towards the garden. "There's nobody else...?"

"We're alone," she replied.

"It's just that I'm anxious..." he said "...anxious about..." He paused, surprisingly lost for words.

"About confidentiality?" she suggested.

"About everything," he said, with a nervous laugh. "About confidentiality, about what you will think, about what people will say, about what could happen, about what I should do..."

She opened her hands in a reluctant gesture of encouragement. She had first met him eleven years ago through an email introduction. 'Esther,' an old colleague had written, 'Thomas has recently completed his training with us in London and is moving down your way for family reasons. We think very highly of him and hope you can introduce him to the local networks.'

He was then in his late thirties, a former public relations man who had found his way into psychotherapy through - as he put it - his own issues. He carried with him the bullish assertion of his previous profession but he was astute and appeared warm. His perceptiveness was too combative for Esther's liking. She had deflected his more intrusive questions and eventually he had explained that they were moving because his wife was unhappy with the London schools. He intended to maintain a small London practice and commute a couple of days a week.

"I like to be at the centre of things," he had explained smiling. She had registered his ambition and offered him the names of a few people who she thought would appreciate his style better than she did.

The suave confidence of that first encounter was completely absent.

"It's a problem with a patient," he began, "Not a big problem, not insurmountable, more that I'm worried about how it could be misinterpreted..." He stopped and then started again.

"You have to understand that my marriage is on the rocks – has been for a time..." Again, he stopped.

"Love," he said finally. "I need to talk about love. Is it right? Is it possible? Is it real?"

She raised an eyebrow questioningly and he laughed, "I can see you're not a romantic, Esther."

She bristled at his presumption but the put-down seemed to release him into speech and he began to talk rapidly, running through the pressures of a typical day as he rushed from home to London, from appointment to committee, from lecture to consultation.

"I've become a slave to the profession," he said. "There isn't a committee that doesn't want me, an enquiry that doesn't need me, they'll hardly release a press statement without referring to me."

She began to frame a question but Thomas had rushed on – his wife's inability to lose weight, something a patient had said, an exhibition he'd visited, an article she ought to read.

"The family don't need me, the sex is gone, the kids are almost gone, we share nothing, so why shouldn't I?" he was asking.

"Why shouldn't you what, Thomas?" she managed to ask but he had only stopped to catch breath and didn't reply, seguing into the story of an MP he knew who had been undone by an unwise affair.

"Thomas, it would help if you could tell me more exactly what has happened," Esther said in another of his infinitesimal pauses.

To her surprise he seemed to register this request and began talking about a patient. His speech was a little slower, his words a little more careful.

"It's an unusual piece of work, something I'm quite proud of. There's definitely a paper in there and in other circumstances I would have written it up."

When this patient first came, Thomas said, she could hardly speak, she stammered, stuttered and collapsed into silence.

"But I have a rug on my couch – a lovely, soft thing from Peru – and one day she pulled it up to her knees. She started playing with it, twisting her fingers in it, burying her face in it. Finally she pulled it over her head, so she was quite hidden from me. And we discovered, that like that, her stammer disappeared. When I couldn't see her, and she couldn't see me, she could speak coherently."

He felt they had achieved something quite special together and he was aware that she meant more to him than other patients.

Esther began to frame another question – what did he mean by special? But Thomas had changed tack and was talking theoretically, lecturing her, offering her the insights of his unwritten paper.

"Touch is one of the last taboos of course but I think we need to question it, challenge ourselves, interrogate our easy assumptions..." he was saying.

His story shifted again, to a meeting with a woman at an art gallery. He described his feelings as he waited for her – the trepidation, the uncertainty, the fear that she would not appear and the joy and relief when she did.

"I'd forgotten one could feel like this," Thomas said. "I'd forgotten what love is."

Gradually Esther pieced it together. The woman who sheltered beneath the rug and the woman he had met in the art gallery were one and the same. Thomas was contemplating an affair with a patient. He had met her outside the consulting room and was talking to her on the phone every day. Esther was aware that her face was freezing into an expression that did not quite reflect her feelings. She was appalled, yes. But beneath his angry braggadocio she caught glimpses of bewilderment and the confusion of a small boy.

"I think you are really in trouble, Thomas," she said.

"I know," he said. "I know." A bee buzzed at the window and she let her eyes move briefly past him to the hot, still garden.

"Have you spoken to your supervisor about this?" she asked.

He frowned. "I think it's important," he began "as one progresses in one's career, to free oneself of internalised authority or one can never truly be present for one's patients, never really authentic. One is always looking over one's shoulder, asking should I do this or should I say that, checking whether...whether..."

His voice was tailing away.

"The truth is," he resumed slowly "I'm not at the moment..." he tailed off again.

"You're not seeing anyone for supervision at present?"

"No," he said.

He was not engaged in that most fundamental part of therapeutic work, the weekly meeting with a more experienced colleague which kept you anchored to reality. She said nothing, fearful of what was coming next.

"It's one of the reasons I came to see you," he said eventually. "I wanted to ask if you might consider seeing me for supervision."

Thomas was looking at her now with the expression of a child who hopes to be forgiven. His hand, as he touched the glass of water, trembled ever so slightly. Esther watched the irregular rise and fall of his chest. "You do not need this," she said silently to her herself.

"It's so difficult," Thomas said "when you are in a public position like mine, to know who you can safely speak to."

Thomas Fortune's rise through the profession had been rapid. He had moved seamlessly from positions in his own small training organisation to positions on the National Association. He sat on committees and the boards of charities, wrote a column for a Sunday newspaper and gave numerous interviews to the press.

"I thought of you because you were so kind to me when I first moved here," he continued. "I've always been slightly in awe of you. I've always seen you as a model of integrity to aspire to." He was wheedling, pleading with her.

"I don't know what else to do," he said, "I don't know who else to turn to."

A moment longer and he would humiliate himself completely. He certainly needed help and his patients did too but she felt trapped. She had been manipulated. She reached slowly for the diary which lay at the corner of the table and flicked to the pages for next week.

"I can see you next Monday morning at 8.30," she said in a tone which offered no alternative.

Relief broke across his face and Thomas gave her a genuine smile for the first time in their encounter, agreeing instantly that he would make sure he was available.

"In the meantime I'd like you to make an appointment with your GP and get yourself signed off for stress."

"I'm not unwell and I can't possibly spare the time...I'm not someone who lets their patients down."

The brief moment of humility had vanished.

"I think you need a rest and time to reflect."

He held her gaze. She concentrated on the wall just behind his shoulder. They sat in silence for several moments, then he looked away. "OK," he said. "OK."

Esther gave him a slight nod of acknowledgment and continued: "When you come on Monday, could you bring a list of all the people you are seeing, both patients and people you are supervising?"

"Is that really necessary?" The bullish tone was back.

"It would be helpful to me."

"I'll see what I can do," he said. "But I do want you to know that the rest of my work is fine. There's nothing wrong with the rest of my work. And as far as Nicole is concerned, I'm not sure that there's really much to worry about either. She cares about me, she loves me, she's not going to make a complaint."

Esther observed that finally someone had a name and rolled the two syllables silently around her tongue but she cut him off. "We can talk about it on Monday," she said. "I suggest that you don't speak to her over the weekend."

Thomas protested again: "But she's expecting me to call, she's vulnerable..."

Esther paused, trying to recover some warmth.

"Try to take some time for yourself over the weekend and I'll see you on Monday." she said.

It was a dismissal. He recognised it as such but he could not quite allow her to have the last word. He looked at his watch as if in surprise.

"My goodness," he said. "It's twenty to five. I must dash. I've got patients to see."

He moved as if to embrace her but she had risen too and she pre-empted him by extending her hand. He smiled, acknowledging the move, took her hand briefly and hurried towards the front door.

Esther waited for the click of the latch, then she turned to the sink, took a packet of paracetamol from the shelf, filled a glass of water and swallowed two tablets. She wetted a cloth, walked through to the sitting room, lay down on the sofa, placed the cloth across her forehead and closed her eyes.

Clara

Clara sat perched in the window seat of her bedroom at the top of the house. She was carefully painting her nails, a look of intense concentration on her pale, freckled face. She glanced occasionally at Ruby who sat at the opposite end of the cushioned bench, her knees hunched to her chin, alternately checking her phone and peering down into the street.

Although she seemed to be concentrating on her nails, Clara's mind was on Ruby. Their conversation had stalled awkwardly and she was afraid for the moment to proceed. Ruby, rearranging her long brown legs, tried to lighten the mood by commenting on the passers-by below.

"Rooney passes to Giggs," she remarked as a group of ten year olds kicked a football across the road. "Justin Timberlake turning in at your front gate," she continued.

Clara shuffled her bottom on the seat in order to see. "Idiot," she said, observing her father pushing his bike round the side of the house. "We'll have to be quiet now." She picked up the remote, adjusted the volume on the music system and then held out her hands for inspection. "What do you think?" she asked.

The nails on one hand were deep emerald, those on the other electric blue. Picked out in delicate white letters on the left hand nails were the words 'No To' and on the right hand ones the word 'Coal'. Ruby raised her eyebrows slightly. "What will they say at work?"

Clara shrugged. "I'm not on the till tonight so it doesn't matter." She glanced at the old-fashioned watch she wore on her wrist. "I'll have to go soon, though."

Ruby pushed her hair back behind her ears and again opened the subject they had been skirting around for the last half hour.

"Mum needs to know about Greece," she said. "If you're going to come we need to book your flight."

"Can I let you know on Sunday?" Clara replied.

"Why?" demanded Ruby. "Why can't you make your mind up now? The villa's got its own pool and Mum and Dad won't bother us at all. I don't understand what this is about."

"There's this camp I'm thinking of going on," Clara said "and the dates clash."

"Camp!" expostulated Ruby, "You've not joined the Girl Guides have you? Or become a Christian or something?"

"No, no, nothing like that. But it's not just the dates. I'm not sure about flying either."

"What do you mean? Are you having panic attacks again?"

"No, no."

Clara hesitated. She and Ruby had known each other since they started secondary school. The friendship had happily supported them from the days when they ran unselfconsciously around the playground through their first encounters with cigarettes, alcohol, sex and drugs. They had listened, advised, loved and cried together for five years of intense, inseparable friendship but the last two years at Sixth Form College had seen their lives subtly divide. Emergent tastes had begun to push between them, creating fault lines in their easy sympathy. Clara was angry that Ruby would not talk seriously about the complicated world that was opening up in front of them. Ruby was perplexed that Clara no longer seemed willing to enjoy the straightforward pleasures and freedoms that were now within their grasp. Their quarrels were more frequent and the making up more protracted.

"It's political," Clara said eventually. "I don't think flying for holidays can be justified anymore."

"Oh, for Christ's sake," said Ruby. "The plane's going anyway. You martyring yourself won't make a blind bit of difference."

"Do you actually know what it does?" retorted Clara. "For everyone who steps on that plane a tonne of carbon dioxide goes whooshing up into the atmosphere and down into the oceans and sits there for the next two hundred years wrecking the planet for us and our children and our children's children. I don't want to be part of that anymore."

"So you're going to go to a camp and learn to be an eco-warrior instead? You're going to hang out with a bunch of blokes with face fungus..."

"They don't have face fungus."

"Mr Dawkins – that geography teacher you got all this from does. And I bet he's getting on a plane to go somewhere nice this summer."

"It's not to do with Mr Dawkins, Ruby. It's what I think. It's science."

"Science doesn't say you can't have a holiday."

"Science says this is important. It says there's this window where we can do something. And this is the year that the politics matter. This is the year when the pressure is needed, before they meet at Copenhagen..."

"I don't care about Copenhagen. I don't care about politics. I care about you..."

"And I care about you. I want you to wake up and see what's happening..."

"I'm awake all right. I can see all right. I can see that you need a holiday..."

"I don't want a holiday that means crapping on the planet."

"Clara, I want you to still be my friend and do things that are fun."

They had juddered to an uncomfortable impasse and they sat in silence, both staring out of the window. Thirty seconds passed. A minute. Clara could find no words to reply. Her heart

9

was with Ruby but it was battened down by conviction. She was hurt by Ruby's mockery and her easy expression of contempt.

Ruby broke the silence by returning to her jokey comments: "Look, it really is Justin Timberlake – there crossing the road – the guy with the dark hair and his head down."

Clara peered through the leaves of the acacia tree and laughed: "You idiot, Ruby – that's George."

"Gorgeous George? Your brother George?" The young man turned in at the gate, slouching towards the front door. "I didn't recognise him with his hair cut."

"It's George all right," said Clara with a sigh.

"But I thought he was meant to be on tour. I thought the band had a recording contract. What happened?"

Clara sighed again. "He was on tour. They did have a recording contract. But George got chucked out of the band. Months ago in fact."

"And...?"

"Mum got a phone call a couple of weeks ago from a hospital in Manchester. He'd got himself beaten up and fetched up in A and E. They'd kicked him out of the band because he was useless – drinking again – and they'd got all his songs anyway so they didn't need him. So Mum went and got him. He'd sold all his gear and he didn't have anywhere to live, so I guess she didn't have much option."

"Oh, Clar," said Ruby putting an arm round her friend's shoulders. "I'm so sorry. I didn't know."

When Clara and Ruby were eleven and George was sixteen he played classical violin and rock guitar, the one as easily and fluidly as the other and he moved amongst the coolest kids in the school. In line for a place at the Royal College of Music, he also wrote songs, had a band of his own and a neat line in making money by selling his course work and essays to pupils from another school. Invitations to Clara's house were gold dust to her Year Seven friends as occasionally George would deign to smile or ask one of them a question. But he also smoked a lot of weed, drank a lot of spirits and by seventeen he had crashed out of his 'A' level course in a haze of altered consciousness. His charm and politeness had evaporated in a miasma of debt and addiction. Some uncomfortable months in a private clinic had been followed by some equally uncomfortable cramming at a private college which resulted in some mediocre 'A' levels, a place on a music technology course and the end of his mother's dreams of his career as a solo violinist.

Charm and talent had not left him however and he was soon writing songs again, touring with a new band and seemingly on course for a recording contract. But it had not lasted. At the age of 23, he was back at home with his life unravelled once again.

"So what's he doing?" Ruby asked.

"Weed, spice, Dad's whisky, a few tinnies – anything he can lay his hands on really." Two small tears rolled down Clara's freckled cheeks. Ruby wiped them carefully away. "You should have told me," she said. They sat in silent commiseration for a few minutes and then Ruby asked: "What about your Mum and Dad – what are they doing about it?"

"Mum's all 'Oh you poor thing, you've had such a hard time, you just need some space to work out what to do'."

"And your Dad?"

"No-one can get a sensible word out of him at the moment. He's either in a foul mood or he's not here."

Clara could feel the incredulity rippling through Ruby. She shrank back into herself, fearing another of Ruby's angry lectures about her stupid, selfish family, sentiments which she agreed with, but which on another's lips only brought her furiously to their defence. Ruby retreated however.

"Are you worried about him?"

"I'm worried about all of them."

Any further conversation was interrupted by the sudden explosion of harsh, pounding music from somewhere lower down the house. Its vibrations thundered up through the fabric of the building. Clara was on her feet before the first bar had ended, pulling open the door and flying down the stairs. Ruby followed her and as she left, the draught from the open window caught the door and slammed it loudly behind her. Her footsteps clattered behind Clara's on the bare, polished boards.

In the living room Clara was shouting at George who sat slumped on the sofa, with his head nodding and a foot tapping:

"What the fuck do you think you're doing? Turn that off. You know Dad's working," she yelled. George responded slowly, gradually raising his eyes towards her but saying nothing.

"Where's the remote? Give me the remote...turn it off for Chrissake."

Ruby looked vaguely around the cluttered room, in a vain attempt to help. Ignoring them both, George picked up a pair of headphones, reached across and plugged them in, shrugging his shoulders.

"Chill," he said casually, as the door opened again and Clara's furious father stood framed in the unexpected silence. Closing the door quietly behind him, he hissed in acid tones, "How many times do I have to tell you that when I am working the house has to be quiet? If I have asked you once I have asked you a thousand times. I need silence. My timetable is on the kitchen notice board. I think you have been taught how to read," he finished.

"I'm sorry, Dad," said Clara.

"I'm sorry, Mr Fortune," said Ruby.

And he was gone, as quickly as he had appeared, padding back upstairs to his consulting room and the disturbed session.

George tapped his foot in response to the now private music, a disingenuous smile curling at the edge of his soft lips. He had a handsome, engaging face. The features which fate had arranged so carelessly on his father's face were refined in George to form a study in masculine beauty. The nose was less sharply defined, the lips were just a trifle fuller and the deep brown eyes peered out from beneath a regularly shaped forehead and a shock of thick, dark hair. He was indeed gorgeous.

Clara looked at him with contempt and distaste, Ruby with curiosity. Then Clara turned.

"I have to go to work," she said. Ruby moved to follow her but George roused himself suddenly from the sofa.

"Uh, Clara," he said, "You couldn't lend me twenty quid, could you?"

"No," said Clara shortly.

"Oh, come on Clar, just till tomorrow. There's a bloke in the pub owes me and I'll be able to give it back before you miss it."

"No," repeated Clara.

"Clar, you're not being fair, you know. You've got a job. I haven't. You should give me a hand. Ten quid then, ten quid till tomorrow."

"No," said Clara, opening the door.

George shifted his attention to Ruby. "What about your friend, then? It's Ruby isn't it? I remember you. I always liked you, you know." His smile was disarming and Ruby hesitated a moment. "You couldn't let me have a few quid could you?" he said. "I can give it to Clara for you tomorrow."

"Come on Ruby," Clara said, pulling at her friend's arm, and the two young women left the room and tip-toed through to the kitchen, glancing up the stairs at the closed door of Thomas Fortune's consulting room.

"I have to get my stuff," Clara said. "Have you left anything up there too?"

Ruby nodded: "My phone and my bag and my jacket."

"I'll go. Wait here." Clara crept back up the two flights of stairs, carefully avoiding the creaking boards, and retrieved their belongings. She knew that Ruby had only agreed to a last family holiday on the promise that Clara could come too. She knew how difficult it would be for Ruby to explain to her mother that three weeks before their planned departure she still didn't have a definite answer. She returned anxiously to the kitchen, guilty at her own ingratitude, ashamed of her dysfunctional family and fearful of Ruby's justifiable anger. But Ruby seemed to have recovered her equanimity and placed a comforting arm around her friend's skinny shoulders.

"Let me know on Sunday," she said. "It'll be OK if we know by then."

Relieved at her friend's generosity, Clara embraced her warmly. They left the house, Clara pushing her bike up the street till they reached the point where Ruby turned for home and Clara cycled off towards the supermarket and her evening shift.

Esther

Esther woke with her mother's injunction in her ears: 'Give not sleep to thine eyes'. It was six 'o' clock and the towels were still on the line, the beds unmade and the dinner unprepared. 'Consider thy ways', her mother would add sharply if Esther hesitated and Esther would quickly gather the knives and forks and place the Bible at the place of whoever was to read that day before grace.

She moved rapidly now, dragging the vacuum cleaner from the cupboard, changing her mind and running to the garden for the towels, hesitating in front of the vegetables spread on the kitchen counter. Thomas Fortune would not leave her thoughts. Why had she agreed to see him again? He had not wanted to expose his ordinary doubts and weaknesses to scrutiny, dressing them up in a spurious theoretical justification and a sense of his own importance. Why did she think she could help him? Wasn't that just another kind of arrogance?

She pulled out the chopping board and placed peppers, garlic and courgettes in front of her. Perhaps she could phone him, tell him she had reconsidered. 'Bear ye one another's burdens' countered another echo from the past. 'If a man be overtaken in a fault, restore such an one in the spirit of meekness.' She sliced effortlessly into a courgette, catching the tip of her finger, an act which brought tears of frustration to her eyes. Pressing a piece of kitchen paper against the slowly beading blood she retreated to the sofa and tried to clear her thoughts.

She was interrupted by the sound of a key in the front door, bags being dropped on the floor and a cheery call from the hallway: "Hey Mum, it's me."

"Felix," she called, giving the cut a last, hard squeeze, "I'm in here."

A spare, lanky young man pushed open the door and dropped himself into the armchair opposite her. Square, heavy-framed glasses dominated a serious face and a head of neatly cropped hair. Felix looked at his distracted mother, the vacuum cleaner trailed across the floor and the towels flung on the sofa.

"You OK?"

"Yes, yes, I'm fine. Just a long week. I'm a bit behind. I haven't even made up your beds."

"No sweat. It's only me and Jane – you don't have to put on a performance."

She didn't have to put on a performance and yet she liked to, longing for their visits more than she could admit.

"Shall I do the beds?"

"Please." She was relieved to have a few more moments to herself.

He disappeared back into the hall. She could hear him taking the stairs two at a time and the thud of a rucksack being dropped on the floor above. She moved back to the kitchen and the vegetables. Listening to Felix overhead, thumping heavily on the bare boards as he shifted the beds to tuck in the sheets, she gradually banished Thomas Fortune and the burdens of the week, repeating to herself the old words which strangely, still comforted her: 'Come unto me, all ye that are heavy laden, and I will give you rest.'

Felix reappeared, clean and damp from the shower, poured himself a glass of iced water and threw himself into a chair at the kitchen table.

"Don't do anything complicated, Mum," he said. "You know Jane's not going to be here till late." There was an edge to his voice, a familiar signal that something wasn't right. She turned towards him, disappointed.

"Didn't you get her text?" Felix asked. She pushed the hair back from her eyes, shaking her head.

"She thought you might not have," he said. "She's going to see the Haves this evening instead of tomorrow morning – they've got some horsy thing, so she can't go then. And she's booked you both in to some place to get your legs waxed and have a massage."

Esther's lips had tightened.

"It's all fixed and it'll be fine Mum. You get to spend the whole day with her tomorrow while I'm at my workshop and then we have Sunday all three of us before she goes back. And she'll be here by 9.30 – she's promised."

"Please don't call them the 'Haves' Felix. You know it upsets Jane."

"She's not here," he replied. "She can't hear me. And they are – Haves I mean."

Jane's childhood name for their half-siblings, twins Chloe and Lucy, had been 'The Halves' but it was Felix's angry translation that had stuck.

"Please, Felix."

"OK, OK. But it's true. They got everything." Felix's mood had switched from the cheerful good will of his arrival to resentment. The edge in his voice had become bitter.

"Your father loved you very much, you know."

"Oh yeah?" He was winding himself up in a familiar pattern.

Esther's relationship with Felix and Jane's father had not lasted beyond Felix's fourth birthday and he had died when Felix was eleven, his motorbike travelling straight ahead without braking at the bend of a country road. His blood alcohol had been 140 milligrams, he had recently re-married and he was the father of two baby girls. He was also heavily in debt and a diary found amongst his possessions recorded a stream of miserable invective about a life he seemed to judge spoiled beyond repair. The coroner had returned a verdict of accidental death.

"They got everything, didn't they? Because he'd married her and not made a will. That's how much he cared about us."

"Felix, she had three month old twins."

"Yeah, and parents who paid off her mortgage. And Mr Investment Banker hovering in the wings, just waiting for the lovely widow to dry her eyes long enough to say 'I do'."

Esther wanted to tell him that she was tired of hearing this over and over again but Felix's flushed cheeks spoke pain as well as bitterness and beneath the tightly drawn adult face Esther saw the soft contours of childhood confusion and grief.

"I'm sorry things happened the way they did," she said, wondering what had happened to set him off.

"It wasn't your fault Mum," he replied. "You didn't arrange for Dad to be a dickhead. You didn't make him a rubbish painter."

Esther's eyes travelled involuntarily to the portrait which hung above the kitchen table. Gordon had painted it when Felix was two and Jane four years old and she had always loved it. Felix sat in Jane's lap, his infant curls soft against her chest, his stubby legs pointing outwards between hers and his grey eyes constant towards the father whose paintbrush caught his serious gaze. Jane looked down at him with the devotion of a pre-school Madonna and the dominant blues and greens of the painting faded into abstraction around the edges, rescuing it from sentimentality. Contrary to Felix's invective, he had been very talented but it hadn't paid the bills.

"You didn't ask him to bugger off," Felix continued. "You didn't ask him to roll joints with his pupils."

Esther realised that she had miss-stepped. Felix was continuing to wind himself up, redirecting his antagonism to defend her. Loyal to her and angry with his father, Felix had refused to visit his stepmother and half-siblings. Jane, able to distribute her love more generously, had accepted the invitations. As an adult she had become an affectionate aunt figure for the little girls but Felix had remained angrily isolated, nurturing the past into a continual cause for rage and indignation.

Esther put down the knife and turned from the chopping board. "Please Felix," she said. "Let's not quarrel. It's been a long day."

"I'm not quarrelling," he said automatically but he met her eyes and seemed to reflect for a moment. He slapped his hands on his thighs and stood up. "Where's the gin?"

She nodded her head towards a cupboard and he busied himself with gin and ice and lemon and tonic water. Changing his tone he made a last stab at the subject with a recovery of his familiar, sarcastic humour.

"Anyway Mum, I behave like an adult now. I do birthday cards and Christmas presents and I visit once a year with Jane for about twenty minutes." He paused and grinned. "Just enough time for a glass of Mr I.B.'s excellent whisky."

"Mr I.B?"

17

"Mr Investment Banker – his full name's Ian Baker Sanderson – remember? – so Mr I.B. or Mr IBS if he's being a real pain in the arse. And mostly of course, he's not. He's charmingly polite: the ruling classes always are until you're uncouth enough to talk about taxation or fox-hunting."

He took a slug of gin. "And the twins are very sweet with their ponies and their piano lessons. And Mrs IBS is extremely hospitable." He imitated his stepmother's cut-glass accent: "'You're always very welcome to stay, Felix, there's plenty of room in our mansion, you know.'"

"She doesn't call it a mansion, surely."

"No. But it is."

Esther smiled: "Not in front of Jane – OK?"

"OK."

Later, they took supper out onto the patio. Sitting amongst the fragrance of honeysuckle and night-scented stocks, Esther began to relax. Felix lit a candle and talked about his work. He was at home for two weeks while he did a course on low-energy building techniques in London. It was the future, he told her. Esther loved to listen to him in this mood. His adult competence reassured her. Her pleasure in saying to her friends "Felix is finishing his architecture training..." was pride but it was also relief. Unlike Jane, she had never felt sure of him, never been convinced that Felix would arrive safely in the adult world. He had entered adolescence in a misery of self-consciousness. His quirky sense of humour had not always found him friends and a rapidly developing political conscience had made him scornful in a manner which reminded her uncomfortably of her brother Reuben.

But here in his professional role Felix was expansive and confident. The shadow of the difficult teenager had vanished. He drew his chair closer to hers and showed her sketches from his notebook. He had plans for how he would upgrade her draughty, Victorian terrace, plans for the house he would build for himself one day, plans for zero-carbon public housing. Esther looked with genuine interest at the dreams her clever son produced and thought herself blessed.

"And what about tomorrow?" she asked. "What are you going to do while Jane and I are at the spa?"

"I told you Mum, I've got this day event. I'm leading one of the workshops. I probably won't be back till late."

He had told her. She had obliterated it, muddled it with the course he would be travelling daily to London for, banished it from consciousness. She felt foolish. This wasn't an action, only the preparation, and she had irritated him already. She suppressed her other anxious questions. It irritated him to have to tell her again about the solicitors' phone numbers inked on the insides of their arms, the presence of the paralegal and paramedical teams, the training in talking to the police. It irritated him when she asked for details he could not give and irritated him when she said "Be careful".

He had tried to explain that it was exhilarating, that when you used your whole body - your physical, heart-pumping, muscle-straining body - to try and stop the emissions, you felt that you might actually be having an effect. "It's the only thing that stops the despair," he had once said and although she had believed him she could not feel it. All she could imagine was the terror at the sight of a police line bearing down on you, the crack of a truncheon on a defenceless skull, the chill of a police cell. "It's better when I don't know," she had said finally but still she could not stop herself from asking: "Are you still involved? Are you planning anything? Is it safe?" Afterwards, when she saw the photos of coal heaped on the steps of Downing Street, or the banners fluttering from the Houses of Parliament, she felt pride in Felix's principle but only until rumours reached her of the next action.

Felix was beginning to tap a finger on the table, the muscles of his jaw had tightened.

"Of course," she said. "I'm sorry. I'd forgotten."

Felix's finger hesitated, tapped once more and then paused. He nodded, acknowledging her acknowledgment. "I wanted to check with you," he said "I've offered a couple of spaces for the night – on my bedroom floor will be fine – it shouldn't disturb you. I'll make sure we come in quietly."

"That's OK," she said. "But no-one in my consulting room."

He grinned: "I'm not a teenager anymore," he said, remembering the drunken friend who had vomited on Esther's couch.

Felix went inside to make coffee and Esther checked the missed text from Jane. 'Going to Fairhaven first' it said. 'Will eat supper there. ETA 9.30. Want whole day tomorrow with you. Special things to tell you. Massage etc. booked.'

'Special things'. She was either pregnant or planning to get married. Probably the latter. Jane liked to do things in the correct order. Felix's outburst and the tension just below his skin explained themselves. Jane would have told Felix already, enjoining him to secrecy. Outwardly delighted, inwardly he would be brooding. Felix hated any alteration in the familiar constellation of the three of them. He professed to like – even love – Jane's boyfriend Adam, sharing a love of football and 1990s TV comedy, but he was often uneasy when Jane brought him home. He would pull Adam up for putting mugs away in the wrong cupboard, or argue provocatively with Adam's ill-considered political views. He stepped unconsciously into the role of the father who could not be satisfied with any of his daughter's suitors. 'Jealousy is cruel as the grave', whispered the irritating voice.

They watched the sun fade behind the trees at the end of the garden. They had managed not to quarrel, but somehow, Esther reflected, the sun always went down on Felix's wrath. Darkness hid it but it never vanished. Like her brother's wrath it never really weakened.

Felix

Felix was comfortably late. Activist meetings rarely started on time and he had no wish to appear eager. He had been enjoying a quiet cup of coffee, sprawled on the patio with his sister, surrendering with satisfaction to her practical good sense. Her beam of happiness had clearly included him and their mother seemed content. On this sunny July morning, the world felt surprisingly good. He was twenty-three years old and plans for the coming months of disruption were developing nicely. In six months' time international agreement would surely be reached at Copenhagen. Attitudes and policies would shift and perhaps he could take a small step back. Although he didn't care to admit it, direct action always alarmed him. The moments before they cut a wire, the snap of the D-locks as they attached themselves to the gates of a power station or the sight of the rows and rows of police in dark riot gear produced in Felix not a rush of righteous adrenalin but a sick fear in his stomach. It was why he had become an amateur expert in the legal rights of protesters. In the leather satchel slung across his shoulder a bundle of bust cards detailing what to do in the case of arrest rubbed shoulders with the pencils and sketch pad which he carried with him wherever he went. His role in today's meeting was to train his fellow activists in how to interact with the police, what their legal rights were and what to do if they found themselves charged with an offence. He had run this workshop many times in the last two years and he was good at it – calm, articulate and reassuring – the opposite of how he felt during an action itself.

He pushed open the gate of the community centre, catching his hand on the flapping sheet of A4 and its hand-scrawled arrow – 'Non-Violent Direct Action Workshop this way'. The main hall of the old school building was crowded. People were pushing their way in and out of the kitchen, calling across the room to old friends, embracing and gathering in small groups.

Felix stood for a moment quietly taking it in. There were one or two faces that he recognised but no-one that he knew. Although no two people were dressed alike, all were instantly recognisable as part of the same political subculture. There were dreadlocks and brightly dyed hair, heavy Doc Marten boots and delicate tattoos, flowered skirts worn over jeans and leggings, the occasional slogan on a t-shirt and piercings in noses and belly buttons. Most were people of his own age but there were a few who were veterans of the road protests of the nineties and a few older women with long skirts and hooped earrings who looked like they had probably been at Greenham thirty years ago. Felix knew that a moment's conversation with anyone would quickly turn up an acquaintance in common or memories of an action they had all taken part in. He felt happily at home. He made his way to a table where a woman with spiky orange hair was ticking names off a list and introduced himself.

She looked up. "Great. I'd begun to worry that you'd got lost or weren't coming. We'll get going in a couple of minutes."

The space looked chaotic but Felix's practised eye could see that everything was in order. The chairs were in a rough circle, flip chart paper and pens were laid out on a table, the catering collective who were organising lunch had fixed a large sign on the kitchen door 'All food today is vegan. Enjoy!'

"Is there anything I can do?" he asked.

She thought for a moment and then said "Actually, yes. There's a girl over there, come on her own who nobody knows. No previous connections as far as I can tell. Could you check her out? It's probably fine but I'd like to be sure."

Activist circles were simultaneously open to all comers and nervous about infiltration, welcoming and paranoid in turn. Felix remembered another meeting, after a power-station action, which had been attended by two young men wearing after-shave and newly purchased political t-shirts whom no-one had seen before. Their smart shoes and ignorance had quickly revealed them as energy company employees and they had been ejected. Despite the paranoia of a few on the fringes, it was clear to Felix that the police had neither the time nor the resources to send people to every obscure meeting.

He looked across the room at the young woman who was sitting on one of the tables that had been pushed to the side of the room. Her knees were drawn up to her chin and she was sipping from a water bottle as she carefully observed the melee around her. Her clothes certainly marked her out as different. She was dressed in neatly pressed blue jeans and a crisp white shirt. Soft brown hair fell in waves to her shoulders and there was a band of freckles across her nose and cheeks. Felix could not decide if the expression on her face spoke of self-possession or nervousness. He crossed the room and hitching himself up onto the table beside her asked "Anyone sitting here?" The girl shook her head and shifted her bag slightly.

"You look as if you don't know anyone either," he said smiling.

"I don't. It's my first time at a meeting like this."

"You've lots to enjoy then. Have you come from out of town?"

"No I'm local."

"Not part of the Activists' Network?"

She hesitated and he could see that she had not heard of the Network but she turned to meet his eyes and said, "No time. I've been studying and I'll probably be leaving town come the autumn." She was younger than he'd initially thought but there was a bright intelligence in her face that was attractive.

"So – you've just finished your 'A' levels and you're about to go to university?"

"That's my plan."

He liked the sharp certainty in her tone. "Where do you hope to go?"

"Sheffield. I've got a place to do Environmental Studies if I get the grades."

A smile of pleasure crossed Felix's face. "Cool course, great place and first coincidence – I live in Sheffield."

"First coincidence? What do you mean?"

Felix temporarily forgot his mission to check out the newcomer. "Don't you find that when you meet someone you're always discovering that you have things in common and that you keep going – 'Oh, isn't that a coincidence – I like that too, or I lived there once or I knew so-and-so.'"

She nodded, amused.

"But actually it's not a coincidence," he continued. "Statistically it's what you'd expect if you put a load of people from similar class backgrounds and education into a room together. So I like to count the so-called coincidences and that was the first one."

"So what's the second one going to be?"

It occurred to Felix that they were flirting. "Who knows?" he said. "We have to find out, don't we?"

"Why have you come all the way from Sheffield?"

"I'm leading one of the workshops this afternoon. And I'm visiting my Mum."

"Coincidence number two," the girl said. "We both grew up here. I'm Clara by the way."

"Felix," he replied.

Aileen, the organiser with spiky orange hair, was standing on a chair with one arm raised, looking round the room and trying to make eye contact with people. As they noticed, people were falling silent, looking for somewhere to sit and raising their arms too. Felix raised his arm and noticing the puzzled expression on Clara's face whispered, "We're about to start. That's what the arm raising means. It gets people's attention without being officious."

The girl cautiously raised her arm too. As the last voices died away Aileen got down from the chair and began to speak, welcoming everyone and running through the organisation of the day and its workshops – the basics of non-violent direct action, the buddy system and affinity groups, consensus decision making, communications and media, legal issues and handling the police. Felix tuned out as she ran through the details, quietly observing the girl next to him. She concentrated hard and took notes in a small hard-backed exercise book, sucking the end of her pencil. It certainly wasn't a police issue notebook. He raised his hand and identified himself as his workshop was announced.

Aileen was drawing to a close. "Finally," she said "we're still short of beds for people who want to stay over, three men and two women. Is there anyone else who's local who could offer some floor space?" A man in the corner raised a hand and offered to take the men. Aileen thanked him and continued to scan the room. "Anyone else?" No-one responded.

Felix nudged Clara gently: "I'm already down for two," he said. "What about you?"

The girl hesitated, looking slightly alarmed and then raised her hand tentatively.

"Brilliant," said Aileen quickly. "And you're...?"

"Clara."

"Thanks Clara. I'll hook you up with them later."

Felix watched Clara take out her phone and text. He could see the message. 'Mum. Two people staying overnight with me. No need for you to do anything.' It was unlikely that a police officer would take an activist home to stay with her mother. She was OK.

They swung into the morning's activities and Felix forgot about Clara, losing himself in the familiar arguments about direct action and non-violence, role-playing the provocations of the police and demonstrating the best way to protect yourself and others from the blows of boots or truncheon. He caught up with her in the lunch break, standing on her own in the old playground, balancing a plate of beans and salad in one hand and her phone in the other. He had been pleased to see that she had signed up for his workshop that afternoon.

"OK?" he asked.

She nodded.

"Want to find somewhere to sit?"

She nodded again and they squatted down with their backs against a wall. Clara looked at the white clouds scudding across the sky which opened between the vista of grey roof tops. "If people could see it," she said "maybe they would do something. If they could smell it or choke on it or touch it maybe they would react."

Felix smiled. She had the intensity they all had when it first clicked. You couldn't stop talking about it. You read every frightening statistic and every last snippet of prediction, waking sweating in the night with anxiety. He looked up at the sky and a blackbird singing from a rooftop. There it was, 385 parts per million, silently choking them, quietly altering the climate, stealthily making the world uninhabitable.

"Does it scare you?" he asked.

"No. It makes me angry."

Anger was good. It was what kept you going. It was what gave you courage.

"You have to get involved," he said. It was the only thing that helped, the only thing that stopped the nightmares. Once you felt you were having an effect, the issue dropped back into a more manageable space. "What is it you want to do?"

"Climate Camp for a start," she said.

In August, somewhere in the countryside, thousands of people would converge on a site as yet unknown and the fields would be squatted. There would be a week of workshops, celebrations, music and protest directed at some iconic piece of the fossil fuel industry. A power station, an airport or a coal mine were the most likely candidates but at this stage only a small central planning group knew the exact target.

"You need people to be with," he said. "If you give me your number I'll text you the details of the local group."

They exchanged contact details. Felix looked at the delicately decorated patterns on her nails as she rapidly entered his number. She had pretty hands.

"What I don't understand," Clara said, "Is why there's no information on the website about where Climate Camp is going to be. You'd have thought things would be a bit more organised by now."

"If it was on the website the police would know too," he said.

She blushed, embarrassed and Felix thought that this made her look even more appealing. "Where to go and how to get there will go up on the website the minute the site's been secured," he said. "You have to watch it from quite early that morning and get there as quickly as you can."

She had picked up a stick and was poking at the loose tarmac, dislodging small stones and lumps of tar.

"I wish I'd got involved in this a lot earlier," she said.

"There's time," he said, trying to sound encouraging.

"But that's just what there isn't," she replied. He recognised the angry despair in her tones. It was there always, somewhere in the background, for all of them. The scale, the enormity, the intractability could overwhelm you. "If we don't get agreement at Copenhagen, then what?"

"We will get agreement," he said, trying hard to believe his own words. "There has to be agreement. It's why this is so important. It's why it's good that you're here today. And it will make you feel better, once you're involved. Direct action's the only thing that really makes a difference – look at history – slavery, the suffragettes, Gandhi, Martin Luther King..."

"You sound like a preacher."

He laughed, thinking of the grandfather he had never met. "Maybe we have to be preachers sometimes," he said.

They picked up their cups and went back inside.

Esther

Esther stretched out her legs. The warm jets of the Jacuzzi bubbled around her.

"You must let me know what I owe you," she said.

"Nothing," replied Jane. "It's on me."

Esther looked at her assertive, self-possessed daughter. The dark hair and pale skin remained, but the elfin child had turned into a solid, imposing woman and the defiant pout had become a confident stare. Once Jane had made up her mind it was hard to shift her. Aged ten she had announced that she was going to be a primary school teacher, that she would get married by the time she was twenty-six and have four children. So far, her life was going pretty much according to plan. She had been teaching for four years, was head of years 5 and 6 and was the school's literacy co-ordinator. As Esther had thought, she had come home to announce that she and her long-term boyfriend Adam were going to get married.

"We're planning for May next year," she said. They would get married on the Saturday of half-term week and then fly to Crete for the honeymoon.

"Nothing posh," she assured Esther. "Nothing extravagant. Nothing religious." They had found the venue, she was making her own wedding dress and a friend of a friend had a company who would do the catering. The guest list was being finalised. Esther could see the Excel spreadsheet in her daughter's head.

"One thing I do need to talk to you about," Jane continued "is the twins and Ian and Sofia." Esther steeled herself. They would have to come of course. And Ian would doubtless make a generous financial gift to the young couple, something that would dwarf whatever she could manage. For a moment she hated them as fiercely as Felix did.

"The thing is, that it's also Ian and Sofia's wedding anniversary and I happen to know, because he told me, that he's got tickets for Glyndebourne, which means that they won't be able to come."

Esther's heart lifted.

"But the twins would love to be bridesmaids. I know they'd just love to do all that holding bouquets and following me down the aisle in pretty dresses stuff."

Esther, panicking, thought to herself, 'She's about to ask me if the twins can come to stay, she's going to ask me to look after them'. "Will there be an aisle?" she asked irrelevantly. "In a secular wedding I mean?"

Jane laughed. "Yes – I'll show you the photos of the place." They emerged from the Jacuzzi and sat down at a poolside table. A neatly dressed waitress delivered herbal tea and Jane pulled brochures from her capacious bag.

"My plan," Jane explained "Is that the twins will stay with Adam's parents so it will just be you, me and Felix the night before."

Esther felt humbled by her careful, organised daughter. Her practicality concealed a surprising sensitivity. Jane had known how difficult Ian and Sofia's presence would be for her and had chosen the date deliberately. No doubt Jane would make things right with Ian and Sofia on some private occasion that she would not have to hear about.

Esther was sometimes slightly afraid of Jane. Her own cautious ability to see all sides of a question could appear as moral wavering in the face of Jane's certainty. Where Esther saw an impossible conflict, Jane imposed a solution with such confidence that everyone followed her, their objections and arguments forgotten.

"So all we have to decide," Jane finished triumphantly "is who is going to give me away – you or Felix?"

"Can a woman do that?" Esther asked in surprise.

"Of course she can. For a feminist you're sometimes so old-fashioned Mum."

Esther hesitated. She had no idea what she wanted at all. "What does Felix think?" she asked. "What would you like? And Adam – what would Adam like?"

"We all want to do whatever feels right for you." Jane paused. "You don't have to decide now."

Esther collected herself, realising that she had scarcely congratulated Jane. "I think it's lovely that you're getting married," she said. It was true. Jane looked so happy. She loved to arrange, to organise and to give others pleasure and her wedding would undoubtedly do so. Whether marriage could bring permanent satisfaction, Esther would not open a book on.

"Tell me about your wedding," Jane demanded.

Unlike Felix, Jane had always wanted to know about the past. Her childhood questions had been incessant. "What did you like to eat when you were little? Did you have a 'My Little Pony'? Why don't we see Nana and Granddad?" Esther had tried to be open but she had rarely elaborated. Over the years Jane had wormed the details out of her. "Poor Mum," she had said affectionately aged nine on hearing that Esther's family did not have a television. "He was a bully," she had announced definitively aged fourteen, on hearing that Esther's brother Reuben forbade her from walking to school with a friend who was not a Member. "You'd have been taken into care if anyone had known," was her verdict aged twenty-two on hearing about her parents' ideas of discipline.

"I've never seen the photos of your wedding," Jane continued. "What happened to them?"

"There were only a couple," Esther replied. "They're in a drawer somewhere."

She remembered her wedding day perfectly. It had marked the final break with her family. It was the act that confirmed her expulsion, not just from the small Protestant sect she had grown up in, but from her family itself. She had met Gordon at a bus stop during her second year at university. It was unusual for someone from the Assembly to have been allowed to attend university, but her quiet conformity and the need for qualified teachers in the tiny independent schools that the Assembly ran, had finally brought agreement from the Elders. For the first year, she had endured the long, daily commute into Leeds but in the second her parents had found her lodgings with an elderly Assembly member. On this occasion, the bus had not come and she was standing, panicking, at the bus-stop, fearful of her landlady's disapproval, her long plait swinging behind her as she peered into the distance, willing it to arrive. Gordon had stopped and spoken to her. It turned out later that he had been observing her for days, in the library, outside lectures and in the canteen but this time he had merely said: "No bus?" and offered her a lift on his motorbike. Relieved, Esther had accepted. A few days later, she had met him for coffee.

"I want to paint you," Gordon had said. And that had been the beginning of her secret life. He took her to the cinema, where she struggled to follow its conventions but was entranced by the stories. He played music to her and she gradually learned to understand how, unlike the solid hymns of Assembly meetings, its rhythms and harmonies could dance through your body. He took her to the theatre, lent her novels and political pamphlets and laughed as she cautiously sipped her first glass of beer in her first visit to a pub.

He filled a notebook with sketches of her and used them as the basis for a series of engravings, illustrating a poem by Apollinaire.

"You are my muse," he had said romantically and the paintings which he made of her formed the basis of his degree show.

The life which Esther's parents had tried to protect her from, the worldly, sinful existence of those who were damned, began to open up to her as a place of joyous excitement and a different kind of love. She began to buy clothes with her grant money, a second private wardrobe of jeans and bright Indian cotton prints which she kept at Gordon's flat.

She began to invent evening lectures and weekend field trips and her elderly landlady, ignorant of the demands of university life, did not object. Esther's faith, never particularly strong, began to fade, though her conscience attacked her mercilessly, every time she accompanied her landlady to the Meeting Rooms for the evening prayer meetings or the long Sunday services.

At the end of her second year, Esther had told her landlady that term ended two weeks earlier than it did and her parents that it ended two weeks later. In the stolen four weeks Gordon had taken her to Rome, Florence, Venice and back across Europe to Paris and Amsterdam in a dizzying tour of European art.

"So, tell me about the wedding," Jane demanded, interrupting Esther's reverie.

"It was a bit of a mistake really," said Esther remembering the confusion that had surrounded it.

"But you were in love, weren't you?"

"Oh yes, totally, absolutely, but we wouldn't even have thought about marriage at that point if it hadn't been for your Uncle Reuben finding us."

It was just after Finals, when she was waiting for the results. Walking through Leeds market she had suddenly come face to face with her older brother Reuben. It was a hot day and she was dressed in shorts, sandals and a skimpy t-shirt. Unknown to her, the family were expanding their fruit and vegetable business to Leeds and Reuben had come to make arrangements. He had written to tell her that he would be visiting but courtesy of another series of lies to her landlady, she had spent the last two nights at Gordon's flat and had not received the letter.

Reuben had stared at her in open-mouthed astonishment and she had run, run as if for her life. Her split-second reaction had given her a momentary advantage as she dodged between the crowds but she was hampered by the sandals and he had caught her in a side street, leading away from the stalls. He had manhandled her bodily into his van, driven to her landlady's house, packed up her belongings and driven her back home.

"They locked you up?" Jane asked in amazement. She had not heard this part of the story before.

Esther nodded. "They call it being 'enclosed.' It's so you can think about what you have done and repent."

They had locked her in the room she shared with Ruth. She was not allowed to eat with the family and Ruth was banished to a bed on the sofa. Her mother had wept and shouted, threatened and entreated. Her father had simply prayed, his silent reproach more painful than her mother's rage. The Elders had visited and there were exhortations, Bible readings and more prayers.

Esther had wavered. She had loved her family deeply. She knew she had betrayed them. Caught up in the joy of knowing Gordon she had not considered the consequences. The thought of never seeing her mother again was torture to her. The pressure of her father's silent grief ate at her soul. The wide-eyed witnessing of David, Philip and Ruth brought her again and again to tears but they were tears of sorrow, not repentance.

Back in Leeds, Gordon had been desperate. No-one knew where she was. He had checked the hospitals, scoured the streets and gone round to her lodgings. The landlady would say nothing. He had returned with her Tutor and a police officer and the woman had admitted that Esther was back with her family. Gordon wrote and the Tutor wrote but there was no reply. He had called, dressed in the suit hired for his graduation, but they would not admit him and he had returned, depressed and hopeless, to Leeds.

"But they kidnapped you," protested Jane. "Surely it was illegal. Surely the police could have done something."

"The police wouldn't have made any difference. The police wouldn't have changed their beliefs. It wouldn't have changed the choice I had to make."

"But their beliefs were crazy."

"They were desperate. They knew that if they couldn't persuade me to come back to the community, then we could never see each other again."

"Why?"

"Because they believed that if they did, they would be complicit in evil. They wanted to save my soul. They believed they were rescuing me from damnation. They did it out of love."

"I don't call that love."

In the end it was Reuben who had decided her. He had stormed and threatened. He had shouted and reviled her. He had railed at her, "Do you believe? Do you believe?"

He was a large man with furry eyebrows that met across his forehead and at the end of one particularly bruising altercation, he had shoved her across the room, slamming her against the wardrobe.

"You will awake to disgrace and everlasting contempt. Is that what you want? Is it? Is it? Do you want God to say to you 'Depart from me, ye cursed, into everlasting fire'?"

She had longed to say that she believed. She had longed to be accepted back into the loving circle of community. But she did not believe and the community now appeared increasingly strange to her. She had long known that the Assembly was unusual but without the certainty of salvation its strictures began to seem peculiar. Without the promise of grace, its practices lost all purpose. The drab house without pictures or adornment depressed her. The interminable reading of the Bible stifled her. The rejection of simple pleasures like dancing or the cinema or television seemed to offer an eternity of joyless labour in the service of a delusion. The fear of contamination from those outside smacked of paranoia and she could see the violence beneath the surface. Reuben frightened her.

One morning, three weeks after her forcible return, when Ruth was at home with hay fever and the rest of the family were at work or school, Esther had called out from behind the locked door that she needed to go to the lavatory. Ruth had unlocked the door. Esther had taken the money that her mother saved in jam jars on the mantelpiece for the gas and electricity bills. Tucked behind one of them were the letters from Gordon and her tutor and a brown envelope with notification of her successful degree. She had slipped them into a carrier bag, written a short note to her parents, hugged Ruth in a long, trembling embrace and slipped out of the house. It was the last time she saw any of her family. In ten minutes she was on the bus to Leeds.

"But the wedding – I wanted to hear about the wedding." Jane was visibly distressed now and a tear had formed at the corner of one of Esther's eyes. Jane looked in guilt as it rolled slowly down her mother's cheek.

"I'm sorry, Mum. I didn't mean to upset you."

"It's OK. It's a long time ago but you never really finish with grief like that. There are some things you never completely get over."

Jane took her hand. "What about some more tea?"

Esther smiled. "More tea would be lovely," she said.

Sipping tea by the pool, Esther tried to present her wedding in a cheerful light. She had been too shocked to know whether or not she wanted to get married but Gordon had insisted, in the mistaken belief that even a secular, Registry office wedding might appease her parents and bring reconciliation. It had been a minimal affair followed by lunch in a nearby pub. She had bought a new dress. Two of Gordon's friends had acted as witnesses. His parents, on holiday in Spain, had not attended and in the confusion of the hurried arrangements his two brothers had somehow not been informed. Her Tutor, in a final act of pastoral responsibility, had made a speech.

Esther described the long, flowing outlines of her Indian cotton dress, the Victorian splendour of Leeds town hall and the white suit which Gordon had borrowed from a friend in an ironic reversal of convention.

"We were happy you know. For at least ten years we were happy."

Jane seemed satisfied.

Clara

It was six 'o' clock. A barbecue was being set up, crates of beer had appeared and speakers were being dragged out into the old playground. Aileen introduced Clara to the two women who would be coming to stay with her. Nell wore a colourful printed frock, leggings and converse trainers. Becca was dressed in dark cargo pants and a singlet. She stood with an arm draped casually round Nell's shoulder and there were two tiny butterfly tattoos dancing down towards her wrist. They laughed a lot, capped each other's jokes and finished each other's sentences. Clara tried to imagine Ruby standing beside her at an event like this and felt momentarily sad. She checked her phone. There was still no reply from her mother. She resent the text, shoved the phone back in her bag and moved away, looking for a quiet place to sit and think.

One phrase repeated itself again and again in her mind. "There is power over, power with and power within," the workshop leader had said. When she had talked about learning to access the 'power within' - the strength they each had but might not be aware of – Clara had seen for the first time that her fruitless anger might be transformed into something useful. When they had discussed building 'power with', from the collective strength in the room, Clara had felt a fierce warmth towards the people around her. And when they had moved on to learn how to challenge and subvert the 'power over' - the power of class, gender, institutions, corporations, governments and the dominant culture - which acted only in the interests of the few, Clara felt that she had arrived home.

She could suddenly see power everywhere, from the smallest row at home to the sweep of corporate hegemony. Her father's self-importance, her arguments with her mother, her spats with George and Ruby all appeared subtly altered. School, politics, friendships and society were rewritten in front of her. And somewhere – which she located physically in the pit of her stomach – she felt a determination that connected her deeply to the group of strangers around her. For the first time in her life she had met people who talked seriously about the things which concerned her, people who thought politics mattered and believed they could do something about it.

Only Felix puzzled her. He had claimed to know no-one but he moved easily amongst the assorted company. When he caught up with her in breaks, half of his conversation seemed flirtatious but the other half was intrusively probing. Why was she interested? What had got her into this? Why had she come on her own? She looked across the playground at him, considering his spiky hair, his heavy framed glasses and his idiosyncratic leather satchel. He was attractive in a geeky sort of way. Catching her gaze, he left the group he was with and came across.

"OK?" he asked.

"Really OK," she replied. "I just needed some space."

"Glad you came?"

"Really glad. This is where I want to be. This is where I belong."

He drew her across to the barbecue, introducing her to people from the local network who she could travel to Climate Camp with and her heart lifted again as the discussion batted backwards and forwards – the emissions from meat, the role of the Chinese, the shortcomings of the government. She found she had something to say and that others listened. Her own eloquence surprised her. She forgot about her mother, forgot about Ruby and forgot her reservations about Felix.

Gradually the chat became jokier and more personal until it was drowned out by the thumping bass from the speakers and people began to dance. Clara realised she was enjoying herself in a way she rarely did on a night out with Ruby. But by ten 'o' clock the neighbours were complaining and Aileen was fussing about the smell of dope. Nell and Becca grabbed Clara.

"Some of us are heading out for a smoke..."

"...up on some hill..."

"...over that way, somewhere..."

"...are you cool to come...?"

She joined a small group of people, straggling after Felix who led them under the railway and out onto down-land that overlooked the town. They headed up towards Gravely Wood, an area that Clara barely knew. It lay on the opposite side of town from her home. Pushing her bike over the rough ground she reflected that it would be a long trek back. She checked her phone again. There was still no reply from her mother. A vague unease swept through her, remembering the morning's row. Gail Fortune had stood in the kitchen doorway in her dressing gown, blocking Clara's exit.

"Do you think," she had asked slowly, "that George is..." she had hesitated, as if searching for the appropriate words "...you know, all right?"

Clara had looked at her with a blank expression that bordered on contempt.

"If you mean, is he still doing drugs, then yes – he is still doing drugs."

Her mother had blinked and swallowed. Clara had slammed her cereal bowl angrily into the dishwasher and continued: "And if you mean does he have a purpose in life or a goal other than living off you and Dad, then no."

Relenting slightly, she'd added "I'm sorry Mum. I've got to go." Pushing her mother out of the way with a perfunctory half-embrace she had left the house. Now, standing amongst strangers, on an unfamiliar hillside, disquiet pricked at the edge of consciousness. She pushed it away.

Some of them lit a fire, pulling brushwood and fallen branches from among the trees. Clara found herself sitting next to Felix, gazing out over the lights of the town beneath them, listening to the clatter and rattle of passing trains.

"Do you come here often?" he asked jokily.

"I don't know it at all. I live way over on the other side of town."

"It was one of my favourite spots when I was a kid."

The joint came their way and Felix handed it to her. She passed it on without taking a puff.

"You don't smoke?"

"You wouldn't if you knew my brother George."

He raised an eyebrow as if asking why but he said nothing more and Clara chose not to elaborate. The conversation around the fire drifted between weary discussion of the G8 and gossip about mutual acquaintances.

Clara lay back and looked up at the sky. Clouds were beginning to obscure the stars but she could still make out some of the constellations. Felix lay back beside her.

"Cassiopeia," he said.

"The Plough."

"Pegasus – just disappearing behind those clouds."

"Venus."

"The fault is not in our stars, dear Brutus, but in ourselves..."

"Literature graduate?"

"Nope. Mother who liked Shakespeare."

It began to spot with rain and as the drops became heavier the group got up to leave. Clara checked her phone again. There were no incoming texts, no missed calls. She moved away and called her mother. The phone rang and rang but her mother didn't pick up. The guilt of the morning returned. She began to imagine a car slewed across a dual carriageway, a random knife attack, a terrorist bomb, her mother's pale face and lank hair against a hospital pillow. She called the landline. It rang with a deeper note, on and on and she imagined it echoing through the empty house.

George's voice came on the line, mumbling "Hello?"

"George – is Mum there?"

"Is that you Clar? Really mean of you, you know, going out, not leaving me any money."

"George, I need to speak to Mum."

"She's not speaking to anyone. You've missed one hell of a dust-up here, y'know. Shit's really hit the fan."

"Why? What's happened?"

"Dunno. Tears and shouting. Best not ask I reckon. Least said soonest mended and all that. "

"George, put Mum on."

George yelled into the background "Mum – Clara on the phone for you," and there were sounds of doors banging and raised voices.

Her father came on the line. "What's wrong?"

"I wanted to talk to Mum. I'm bringing a couple of friends home for the night and I just wanted to check..."

"You're not bringing anyone home. Not Ruby, not anyone. It's not convenient."

"But Dad, I've promised,"

"Then un-promise. They've all got homes to go to. Tell them."

She said nothing, her heart fluttering.

"Do you understand, Clara?"

She swallowed hard.

"Is there a problem? Do you need to get a taxi?"

"No," she said, "No."

"Then get back here. On your own. And be quiet when you come in. We'll be in bed."

She cut the call. The rest of the group were several hundred yards ahead of her, down the hill, pulling on jumpers and waterproofs. She picked up her bike and slowly moved towards them, the back wheel bumping awkwardly on the tussocks of coarse grass. Felix was moving slowly back towards her.

"Problem?" he asked. Humiliated, she told him. He was silent for a few moments, not looking at her, tapping the fingers of one hand against another. The success of the day ebbed away from her. His irritation was palpable and she could see herself uncomfortably through his eyes: a flaky schoolgirl who made promises she couldn't keep.

"They'll have to come back to mine," he said shortly. "You'd better get yourself home." He turned away abruptly and strode rapidly down the hill.

Clara slithered after him on the wet grass and pulled her bike lights from the bottom of her bag. She wasn't at all sure where she was. Nell helped her push the lights onto their brackets.

"It was good to meet you," she said cheerily.

"You take care," said Becca, "we'll see you at Climate Camp."

Felix and the two men were already walking on ahead. Nell and Becca hurried after them. Clara stood alone, scanning the dark, unfamiliar, streets. If she headed for the centre of town she should be able to find her way home. She scooted her bike a few yards and swung herself into the saddle. The back wheel bumped hard against the tarmac, she braked, the bike slid sideways on the wet road and she landed awkwardly in the gutter with a clatter of metal. The back tyre was completely flat. Nell and Becca turned and ran back the few yards that separated them.

"You OK?"

"What happened?"

They helped her up. Becca leant the bike against a wall. Nell retrieved her bag.

"I don't think you can ride that..."

"Have you got far to go?"

Becca shouted to Felix and the two men to wait. Tears of humiliation mixed with the rain on Clara's face as she struggled to reply. Once more Felix turned back, silently taking in the tableau in front of him. He looked angry but then something changed in his face and he shrugged his shoulders.

"Come on," he said. "Three people in my Mum's consulting room won't be any worse than two. We'll fix your bike in the morning." He touched her arm in an awkward gesture of reconciliation. "It's OK," he said. "Really." She looked up at him and gave him a weak smile of gratitude.

Felix pushed her bike. Nell and Becca joined arms behind her and they stepped out through the rain, enclosing her in a sisterly embrace. As they walked the quarter mile to Felix's house she texted her mother 'Staying at Ruby's. See you tomorrow', and texted Ruby, 'Told parents I'm staying at yours.' Ruby replied, 'Where are you? Are you OK?' 'All OK,' she replied. 'Speak tomorrow.'

Thomas

Thomas looked with distaste at the small, terraced house and rang the bell. The neighbourhood was mean, too near the station and the new retail park. Esther's consulting room had a pleasant neutrality however and she had placed a vase of summer flowers on the small table, alongside the usual box of tissues and carafe of water.

He was regretting his decision to see her again. He had found her cold, and her barely concealed disapproval had unnerved him. He sat down in the chair she indicated and tried to regain control.

"I need to clear up one or two things about Nicole, Esther. I think you have the impression that this is some kind of mid-life crisis, some kind of folie..."

Esther interrupted him. "We can talk about Nicole in a moment, Thomas."

She handed him a leaflet about her services and charges and a form on which to complete his contact details. Glancing at the leaflet, he attempted a joke:

"I don't think this is going to break the bank."

Esther didn't smile.

"When I begin supervision with somebody," she said "I like to hear something about their personal background and what drew them to become a psychotherapist. I think it helps if I can understand a little about the experiences that shape your approach to the work."

"Of course," Thomas said quickly. This at least was a game he could play.

He told her briefly and selectively about his conventional, middle-class family, the younger brother he never got on with and the escape to university. He skated over the early, painful attempts at relationships, concentrating instead on his discovery that he had a gift for persuasion. This had taken him first into student politics, then into public relations and, when he changed career in his thirties, had driven his rapid rise through the profession.

"I like to think," Thomas said smiling, "that I have been of some service."

Esther's face remained neutral. "And relationships?" she asked.

His mind turned awkwardly to his wife, Gail, and the sour atmosphere at home. Reflecting on Gail's dull conversation, her preoccupation with their son George and her solid, spreading body, he could not remember what had attracted him, beyond the fact that she would have him.

"I married young," he said baldly. "I was twenty-two and Gail was pregnant."

Esther looked at him, expecting more. He offered her some anodyne details about his experiences of youthful fatherhood. She had a way of tightening her face which unsettled him.

"Psychotherapy," he said abruptly. "I should explain how I got into this business, why I changed career."

Thomas had been taken by surprise when Gail had announced her second pregnancy. George was five, Gail had been back at work for three years – a job in a museum archive if he recalled correctly - and they had settled into what seemed to be a tolerable accommodation. His own work was exhilarating. He had moved from a post in the House of Commons Press Office to a post as special advisor to a member of the shadow cabinet. Working long days and late nights he had discovered how proximity to power could make you attractive and that his gifts of persuasion were not limited to political expression. He had not agreed to or wanted another child.

"I became acutely depressed and anxious after our daughter was born," he said. "Seriously depressed, time-off-work depressed. Gail was fine – people always think it's the mother who gets postnatal depression, but that's not true. Men suffer as well."

Esther's face softened briefly into sympathy and, against his better judgment, Thomas took the path of co-operation, selectively elaborating on a period of his life which had felt like a life sentence. Ignoring the affair with an intern who had turned out to be a Minister's daughter, he spoke instead of how Gail's continual demand for his presence, the incessant crying of a colicky baby and the foot-stamping protests of a five year old had brought him to a place he didn't know existed. Sleep had eluded him. Uncontrollable sweats and a racing heart convinced him repeatedly that he was about to die. The weight of domestic drudgery had been punctuated only by the terror that his affair would be exposed and finally by the humiliation of explaining to colleagues that he had become incapable of summarising the simplest report.

"My GP suggested psychotherapy. And that was it," he said. "It opened my eyes. Made me realise that there was a whole world I knew nothing about. An inside world as well as an outside one. And having been helped myself, I wanted to give something back. That's how I got here, I guess." He spread his hands in an affable gesture, neatly avoiding the necessity of disclosing that the affair with the Minister's daughter had made his position impossible.

"Is there a similarity between what you experienced in that period of depression and what you are feeling now?" Esther asked.

"I recognise that something needs to change," he said.

"And you imagine that Nicole might be the change?" Esther's voice had sharpened a fraction.

"I'm sure of it," he said firmly, taking a brief sip of water. "I know that what I'm doing seems unusual," he continued. "I know it appears to break all the rules but believe me, I've thought and thought and thought about this. The problem isn't in the relationship with Nicole, it's about how to negotiate it, how to make sure it doesn't become a subject for gossip, or the means for someone to further their own agenda. I'm no stranger to envy. I know how the world works."

A slight frown appeared on Esther's face.

"I've agreed with Nicole," he said, "that we need to wait. We're going to meet on Wednesday as arranged but we've agreed that we should leave a little time between ending the therapy and starting the relationship properly."

"I think we need to go back a step, Thomas," Esther said. "I need to hear more about the therapy. I need to understand how it has come to this."

She was being obtuse. The therapy was in the past. It was irrelevant. He controlled his anger and tried again.

"The therapy was effective, there's no doubt about that. It was when we tried working towards an ending that we ran into difficulties. We couldn't do it. She couldn't bring herself to finish but neither could I. I interpreted our relationship again and again, talked about her lack of secure attachment figures in the past, suggested she was ready to do without me now, encouraged her steps towards independence – all the usual stuff - but nothing changed."

He took another sip of water. Esther's face was impassive.

"The truth is that there was something I'd been blinding myself to for months. The reason nothing shifted is because the attachment was real. She wasn't in a state of unresolved, childhood dependence. It wasn't that I was being flattered by her uncritical adulation. The love between us was real and it remains real. We love each other as two adults, two ordinary, responsive, mature adults."

Thomas paused again, trying to judge Esther's reaction. He could not read her.

"This presented me with an extraordinarily difficult ethical problem as I'm sure you realise," he continued. "But in the end, I decided that I wouldn't – couldn't – let therapeutic convention stand in the way. We want to be together. We need to be together. When I spoke to Gail on Saturday, when it was clear that my marriage is as dead as I thought, all my doubts fell away. This feels right. I just need to make sure that I effect the transition responsibly and without damage."

He looked directly at Esther, willing her approval. Her face was grave and she seemed to be looking at a point just past his shoulder. She shifted her gaze slightly in order to meet his eyes and said:

"I have to tell you that in spite of everything you have just told me, that I think there is something terribly wrong here. I think you are at risk of harming your patient and harming yourself."

He should have anticipated this. Esther Dunn, paragon of integrity, patron saint of rectitude. His mouth set in a hard line. "I was afraid you would say that."

"I am not your enemy Thomas. I would like to help you, if I can." The clock's hands stood at twelve minutes to the hour. "I think the only thing we can do, is try to explore this further," Esther continued. "If it would help, we can meet again later in the week."

"Not possible. I'm in London till Thursday."

He snapped his briefcase shut. He had no desire to subject himself to Esther Dunn's scrutiny again. But if he didn't return – what then? He could not speak to anyone in his immediate circle. For all its vaunted confidentiality, psychotherapy was a leaky profession when it came to the indiscretions of its practitioners. And if he continued to avoid supervision he breached the conditions of his registration and his insurance. Esther Dunn – private, discreet, irreproachable - was maybe the best option. If he could just get the measure of her, he could surely manage her.

From somewhere, Thomas found a smile. From somewhere he summoned some warmth into his voice. "I'm sorry," he said "I didn't mean to be abrupt. I'll see you next week, Esther. It's been very helpful talking to you. I appreciate it. I really do."

They fixed the appointment, he shook her hand and he got himself out of the door.

Clara

Clara had spent Sunday evening composing what she would say to Ruby. She had finished her shift at the supermarket at 5pm and cycled slowly home. The house was coldly quiet. George had vanished. Her father was secluded in his consulting room. Her mother had greeted her in her usual, vague manner and then complained that she had cooked a chicken for Sunday lunch which no-one had turned up to eat.

"I'm a vegetarian and I was at work," Clara had said, edging her way through the kitchen.

"Well," her mother had said "I don't know what I'm supposed to do. I don't know what's going on." There was an unusual pallor on her already pale cheeks but she either did not remember or was not bothered that Clara had not come home the previous night. Clara had escaped with relief to her room.

She had stood in front of the mirror rehearsing phrases, none of which seemed to come out right. She had tidied her desk, rearranged her make-up and stood, staring out of the window, tossing her phone gently from hand to hand, as if it were a coin. "Heads I call, tails I wait for her to call. Heads, tails, heads, tails." It was always tails. She re-read the chapter in George Monbiot's *Heat* about flying, googled the emissions from the tourist industry and fantasised about Felix who had kissed her as she left. She made another speech to the mirror. At ten 'o' clock, surprised that Ruby had not called, Clara had picked up her phone again. The battery was flat. She had put it on to charge, switching it to silent, and gone to bed.

At ten the next morning Clara found herself sitting in Starbucks opposite a furious Ruby.

"You promised, Clara. You promised you would let me know on Sunday and you couldn't even be bothered to pick up the phone."

"The battery was flat. I didn't get your calls."

"We were supposed to meet. You should have called me. How do you think I felt? I'd told my Mum you were letting me know yesterday. She kept asking me 'Have you seen Clara yet? Has Clara called?' She's been waiting for weeks to know."

Clara stared at the table, drawing patterns in the spilt sugar. The words wouldn't come.

"My Mum was sitting there all day, checking the flights for you, worrying about the prices going up, wondering if my Dad would mind if she subbed you part of the ticket. You are the most selfish, ungrateful friend I've ever had."

Clara said nothing.

"So what's the answer then? Are you coming? Can I call Mum and tell her to book the flight?"

"No."

"Just no? Is that all?"

"Ruby, I can't."

"You can. If you weren't so stupid and so pig-headed and so self-righteous, you'd say yes and we could have a wonderful last holiday together before Uni."

Clara longed to say yes, and she longed to find the words that would persuade Ruby that 'no' was a better answer. Last night in front of the mirror she had convinced an imaginary Ruby to come to Climate Camp with her. They had attended the Activists' Network meeting together, marched in solidarity like Nell and Becca, D-locked themselves to power-station gates, been arrested, bailed and made impassioned speeches in court. But now, faced with the real Ruby slamming her empty latte on the table, she recognised it for the fantasy it was. And she longed to talk to Ruby about what was happening at home. She longed to tell her more about George, to share her suspicions about her parents' argument, to be invited back to Ruby's house where Ruby's mother would offer words of comfort and tell her that she was always welcome, any time.

She froze under the power of Ruby's attack. Her arguments vanished and all she felt was the injury she had caused. If she started to apologise she would cry. And if she cried she did not believe she could stop. And the shame of it would swallow her up.

"Ruby, there was something else I wanted to talk to you about..."

"If it's about your precious brother or your ditzy mother you can tell it to the birds." Ruby's voice was quieter now but it was determined. "I'm going." She picked up her bag and walked out of the café.

Later Clara texted Ruby "I'm sorry," and Ruby texted back "I'm sorry too" but Clara knew that something had broken between them. She spent the rest of the morning drifting round town and checking her phone until it was time to go to work.

As she stood in front of the mirror in the 'Colleagues' room, adjusting her uniform, her phone buzzed. She pulled it eagerly from her pocket but it wasn't Ruby. She didn't recognise the number and she put the phone away without checking the text. Mechanically swiping customers' shopping, she began to tell herself that she didn't care.

During her break she turned her phone back on again. There were no new messages. She suppressed her disappointment and opened the one from the unknown number. It was from Felix. 'Would you like to meet tonight? I get back on the 7.15 train.' She tossed the phone from hand to hand, heads, tails, heads, tails and then quickly replied, 'Working till 8 tonight. Later in the week better.'

She met him in the bar of a quiet pub near the centre of town. It was old-fashionedly eccentric. There was no food, no coffee and no cocktails, just beer and piles of board games stacked lopsidedly on a shelf.

"The parents of an old school-friend of mine run it," Felix explained. "They used to serve us free beer after closing time."

They talked about themselves, with the tentative and surprised pleasure common to all early encounters in relationships.

"What do your parents do?" Clara asked after the second drink.

"My dad's dead," Felix replied "and my mum's a psychotherapist."

"Ah," said Clara. "Third co-incidence. So is my dad."

"Dead or a psychotherapist?"

"Psychotherapist." And they both laughed. Then she said, more seriously, "I'm sorry about your dad," and he told her part of the story, factually, carefully. Clara's eyes lingered on the smooth, dark hairs of his browned forearm and the neat fit of his jeans and she realised that she found the way he carefully cleaned his glasses endearing. They left the pub arm in arm.

Esther

Esther found that she saw less of Felix during his two week stay than she had hoped. He left on an early train for London and was rarely back before seven. He would eat his supper quickly and then either retreat to study coursework for the following day or disappear to meet a friend. She had forgotten that he still had old school-friends who lived locally but she suspected that he was in fact meeting one of the young women who had unexpectedly stayed the weekend. He shaved before going out and he whistled as he got ready.

"It's going well," he said in answer to her enquiry about the course. "Lots of Maths. I have to concentrate."

He showed her the fat course book and the equations that helped you calculate energy use. Esther loved his quickness and intelligence and his belief that the world could change.

Part way through the second week, he admitted that he had been seeing the freckle-faced girl with the bike.

"Do you remember Clara?" he asked, "One of the women who stayed here after the Direct Action training day? Turns out we know each other from years back. We last met when she was seven and I was twelve and we played Connect Four together."

"How come?"

"It wasn't that long after Dad died. You dragged me off to lunch with someone you knew – a bloke who'd recently moved here and I was supposed to get on with his son because the son was starting at Gloucester Road in the autumn. Only I didn't – get on with him I mean – and I ended up playing board games and Connect 4 with the little sister. She was obsessive about it and she beat me every game. Anyway, it turns out that was Clara."

Esther struggled to keep her reaction from her face. Felix was going out with Thomas Fortune's daughter. She could think of nothing more problematic. This was the blurring of boundaries that all psychotherapists who worked in small towns dreaded and which their London colleagues could not understand. If you exploded at your children in a moment of supermarket rage you looked anxiously over your shoulder in case your loss of temper had been witnessed by a patient. You worried about joining a gym in case you encountered the person you had been seeing an hour before, sweating on an exercise bike. Esther had over the years abandoned several dinner invitations in order to maintain the confidentiality of her consulting room and the privacy of her personal life.

She remembered the lunch well. Thomas Fortune had ended that first, awkward encounter eleven years ago by insisting that she come to lunch and bring her son so that the boys could meet. She had dragged an unwilling Felix across town to a large, fashionable house where Thomas had played the expansive host, pouring her unwelcome glasses of wine while his wife prepared lunch with excruciating slowness. Thomas had tried jovially to introduce the two boys to each other but the streetwise George was in the process of disappearing out of the side gate to meet some new-found friends. "Go with him," Thomas had said. "Boys should be outside." Felix had half-heartedly followed George to the corner of the street where, in the company of two older lads, he was twisting the mirrors off a row of parked cars. As Felix approached, they had whooped in derision and run off down a footpath towards the common. Felix had returned to the house, where the little girl had instantly colonised him.

"Why Connect 4?" Esther asked, swallowing her anxiety and trying to show some interest.

"Don't know. She just always liked it I guess."

This was not strictly true. Clara had confided, in one of those moments of sudden intimacy which delight the early days of a relationship, how the game had become an obsession. After the family had moved from London, Clara always had to play with the red counters, because the door of the old house in London had been red. And she had to get her four counters in the winning line because they represented the members of her family. The first was her mother, the second her father, the third her brother George. If she didn't win, then it meant that the fourth counter – Clara herself – had been left behind and she would be consumed by hysterical crying, a piece of bad behaviour which confused her mother and which her father had no time for. Felix was afraid that his mother might raise an eyebrow in professional interest, or make a comment that would spoil his sense of a private, precious gift.

"I'll see you later Mum," he said, grabbing his coat and leaving Esther to her difficult thoughts. There was nothing she could do. Saying anything would be a breach of trust. At least Felix was going back to Sheffield at the end of the week. And the girl would be going away to university somewhere. Perhaps that would be the end of it. Perhaps it would be like all the rest of Felix's relationships she thought sadly, another short-lived and anguished affair.

A few days later Esther faced Thomas Fortune once again in her consulting room. She was regretting agreeing to see him. He had ducked her questions and answered in clichés. It was clear that his caseload was impossibly large and that his attention had long been reserved for his public persona. He was proud of his media presence: he wrote a column for one of the Sunday newspapers, had a regular slot 'Talking with Tom' on one of the London radio stations and was attracting an increasing number of patients with wealth or celebrity status as he'd made clear in the neatly typed sheets of A4 he'd provided, detailing his caseload. And now Clara.

Quarantining the freckle-faced girl in a distant part of her mind she began with a sentence which she had carefully rehearsed.

"I know you feel there's no need to talk further about Nicole," she said, "but I think it would be easier for you to move beyond the therapy if we discussed what actually happened."

"I take your point," Thomas said slowly as if searching for a valid objection. Then he smiled and said with a touch of his old charm, "Let me gather my thoughts."

Esther was relieved to find him calmer and more co-operative, though she was unsure what it meant. Nicole had been twenty-four when she first came to him, Thomas explained and he had been seeing her for five years.

"She was depressed, she didn't really know what she wanted to do with her life, she came from one of those messy backgrounds where there's always a child who slips through the net and in this case it was Nicole."

Thomas described the mother whose troubled, serial relationships with unreliable men had led to Nicole's neglect, the half-brother ten years older, the father who left when she was two, the step-father who had arrived when she was six and lasted till she was twelve, the succession of increasingly problematic boyfriends whom her mother had entertained alongside the beginnings of a dependence on prescription drugs. There had been little opportunity for Nicole to develop a reliable relationship with a responsible father-figure.

Esther calculated rapidly that Nicole was almost twenty years younger than Thomas.

"What's remarkable," Thomas was saying "is how together she was, given her background."

She had been a pretty child and her mother had supplemented her income by registering Nicole with a modelling agency. By sixteen she was making her own living.

"Hands were her thing," Thomas explained. "She has lovely hands. They're in all those ads for nail varnish and cuticle cream."

But what Nicole had always loved was animals. Shortly after starting therapy she had begun working in a dog-grooming parlour. Three years later she had set up her own business. And now, Thomas said proudly, she was about to start 'A' levels so she could go to university and become a vet. They had plans for the house they would share in the suburbs, the paddock she would need for a pony, the room he would use for his work.

Thomas was talking easily and confidently. Esther risked a trickier question.

"When did you first have physical contact with Nicole?"

Thomas hesitated for a heartbeat but replied. "About eighteen months into the therapy. We weren't really getting anywhere. She'd told me that she'd been sexually abused but she wouldn't talk about the details and she wouldn't really talk about anything else."

He recalled again how she had hidden beneath the soft blanket on his couch and begun to talk more freely.

"What did she say?"

"It wasn't always coherent. She'd talk about herself in the third person, sort of free-associating. She'd say things like 'She's afraid of the dark but she mustn't be,' or 'They're coming, they're coming, they're coming,' or 'Dark clouds, big skies, all on top of her' –that's one I remember particularly - but mostly it didn't really make sense. And then one day, she was talking like this and she started to shake, just shake and shake."

"Still under the blanket?"

"Still under the blanket, and then she said 'Hold me, hold me, I want you to hold me.'"

"And did you hold her?"

"Not at first. I tried to speak to her but she became more and more distressed."

That was when Thomas had climbed onto the couch and sat behind Nicole, cradling her between his legs, her head leaning on his chest, his hand stroking her hair. She had calmed down, relaxing her body against his and they had sat there in silence for the rest of the session.

"Did this happen again?" Esther asked.

"It went on for quite a time."

"Months? Years? Every session?"

"Maybe a year. Maybe part of every other session for a year."

"And what came out of it?"

"She seemed to trust me more. She began to talk about what she wanted to do with her life, hating the modelling, wanting to work with animals."

"Was there other physical contact?"

It had become a habit, Thomas said, to end each session with a hug. He would hold Nicole gently in his arms. She would rest her head on his shoulder and he would stroke her hair. It felt parental, paternal, he said defensively.

"Not stimulating?"

"What do you expect? I'm a man. She's a beautiful woman. But no. I felt it was therapeutic, corrective, offering her something she'd never had before."

"Did she talk any more about the abuse?"

"No."

"You don't know who the abuser was?"

"It could have been the stepfather, or one of her mother's boyfriends or someone from the modelling world."

"You never found out?" Esther was aware that she had raised her left eyebrow by a millimetre or two and that her lips had hardened again. Felix as an eight year old would yell at her, "Mum – not that face, not that face, I can't bear that face, I haven't done anything," and would fling himself sobbing on the sofa.

Thomas's voice tightened. "Nicole didn't want to talk about it and I felt I had to respect that. If I ever tried to return to it, it would set us back for weeks. She'd go back to the silences, the retreats, the sitting under the rug. So I decided to concentrate on other things."

Esther forced her features to relax. "When did you become aware of the attraction between you?" she asked.

"I think it was always there. There'd always been something special about her."

Esther had heard this before, usually from trainees captivated by their first experiences of the transference – psychotherapy's name for the complex relationship that developed between therapist and patient as powerful feelings from the patient's past swept the room. A patient's admiration could make the novice feel uniquely lovable, unusually gifted and dizzyingly important. At worst, he or she could indulge their own needs in a fatal dance of mutual attraction with a vulnerable patient. Despite his experience, this seemed to be what had happened to Thomas. His own desires and fantasies had entered the therapeutic space.

Instead of carefully dispensing with his patient's illusions, he had added to them with desires of his own.

Thomas described how Nicole had become difficult, petulantly demanding reciprocation for all she had told him about herself. "You know everything about me," she would say "and I know nothing about you." It had taken little to make him give up interpreting. After a few, feeble attempts at explaining the boundaries of the therapeutic relationship, he had given up, releasing himself into the pleasure of what seemed to be a special and precious bond.

The therapy had limped along for a while but his heart was no longer in it. They had begun to talk about starting a new relationship, a real relationship as Thomas put it. "You mustn't think I took this lightly," he assured Esther. "I tormented myself over it. I lost sleep over it."

"This is around the time that you gave up supervision," Esther said.

"It's not connected."

They sat in uncomfortable silence. I cannot undo what is done, thought Esther. All I can do is try to limit the damage. She tried once more to soften her features.

"How far has the sexual relationship gone?" she asked.

Thomas remained silent, a soft blush spreading from his collar to his neck. The supervision is reflecting the therapy, Esther thought. Thomas is not allowed to know what happened between Nicole and her abuser. I am not allowed to know what has happened between him and Nicole.

"I don't need to know the details," she said. "I just want to have some idea of what you might be accused of, should this result in a complaint."

"There won't be a complaint. That's not where this is going." He took a breath. "In the last month, after we'd agreed that we would end the therapy, there was one occasion when we did have...when we began to...to have more contact of a sexual kind."

"In your consulting room?"

"Yes. It developed out of our farewell embraces. But it was only once. I thought it best to wait. Nicole was disappointed, but she agreed."

"I see," said Esther gravely.

The hands on the clock had just passed ten minutes to the hour. Esther got up and picked out a book about the erotic transference.

"You may have read this already," she said "but I think it might be worth revisiting."

"This relationship is real," he replied. "I'm going to get a divorce. I'm going to marry Nicole."

Esther forced herself to meet his eyes.

"You've been honest with me today, Thomas, which is helpful. I have a much clearer picture of what has happened. Take a look at the book and we can talk more next week."

He accepted it and left.

Clara

In the pub, Felix and Clara talked quietly about Climate Camp.

"I'll meet you there. Travel down with Aileen and the local group if you can. I'll be with the Yorkshire lot."

"As early as possible?"

"Yes. Keep your eye on the website from five or six in the morning."

"What do I need to bring?"

"You can share my tent if you like but you'll need a sleeping bag. Travel light. Don't bring anything that you would mind losing. And nothing that could be construed as an offensive weapon."

Clara said goodbye to him at the station on the Sunday afternoon and returned home to wait out the ten days till they would meet again. His absence brought Ruby increasingly into her thoughts. She had heard nothing from her since their quarrel and each passing day made it feel harder to repair the damage. She spoke to no-one about what had happened between them.

The atmosphere in the house was tense and distant. When her father was not in London, he hid himself in his consulting room. When her mother was not at work, she spent her time wandering round the house, making lists and then losing them, and tidying things which were already tidy. Whenever George could persuade his mother to give him money he disappeared and returned spaced out or incoherent. The rest of his time he spent asleep or beneath his headphones. Clara's repetitive job in the supermarket was a relief and she signed up for extra hours. Finding her mother drifting purposelessly round the kitchen when she returned from work one day, she talked guardedly to her about her plans.

"Did I tell you I was going on a camp at the end of next week?"

"I don't know dear. Maybe you did." Gail Fortune tried to pull her thoughts into a coherent pattern. "Is it a sort of Glastonbury thing again?"

"Not exactly. It's not music this time but I'll need a sleeping bag and stuff. It's something Mr Dawkins – my old geography teacher – told me about."

"Something for your course?"

"Yeah – it's an environmental thing."

"Will you let us have the details so we know where you are?"

"I'll have my phone with me. You'll be able to talk to me any time."

"Oh, of course you will. I forget we all have phones now." Gail Fortune laughed apologetically and then added "I expect your Dad and I will just stay here. It's hard to go away with George like he is."

Clara felt guilty about her evasions. Relieved to feel her mother's attention return to its usual focus she allowed herself to sit down at the kitchen table. "What's going to happen with George?" she asked.

"Your Dad's found a rehab place in America that he wants to send him to but I'd miss him, I don't know if it's a good idea..."

"Why can't he go to Alcoholics Anonymous like anyone else?"

"Your father's afraid of who he'd meet there, afraid that if people knew he'd got a son with problems it might affect what they thought of him, affect his work. And anyway, I do think it's important that George gets the best help there is."

"Won't it be terribly expensive?"

"Well yes, I suppose it will. But if they could get George playing his violin again..."

"But why not something in the UK?"

"I don't know dear. You know what your Dad's like once he's got an idea in his head." There was an unusual annoyance in her mother's voice.

Clara drew patterns on the table, her finger moving in swirls of figures of eight. "Have you and Dad been quarrelling?"

Her mother waited a long time before answering. "I wouldn't say quarrelling exactly," she replied eventually. "Just the little differences that married people have."

Clara persisted. "You don't seem to be talking to each other much."

"Well you know how busy your father is. And he doesn't like to be bothered when he's busy."

"George said you had a really big argument a couple of weeks ago."

"Did he?"

"Yes."

"Well, I'm sure it will all blow over," Gail Fortune said. "Nothing to worry about." She got up and busied herself with the dishwasher.

A week later Clara went back to school to collect her 'A' level results. It was the first time she had seen Ruby since their quarrel. They were friendly but distant with each other, easily separated amongst the crowds of excited students and relieved teachers. Both had done well. Ruby would be going to Liverpool to study accountancy, Clara to Sheffield for her environmental studies course. "I'll see you when I'm back from Greece," Ruby had said and Clara had replied "Of course," wondering whether they would actually manage to or not.

Thomas

Thomas Fortune sat in a cramped, overcrowded train, rattling his way to London, sweating and angry. He was trying to write a conference paper - *Boundaries and Space in the 21ˢᵗ Century: what Facebook Means for Psychotherapy* - but the air conditioning was not working and the man next to him spread his bulk annoyingly across the seat, restricting Thomas's ability to type. His thoughts kept returning to Esther's cautiously raised eyebrow as he had suggested that enough time had elapsed for him to pick up his relationship with Nicole. "Did you look at the book I lent you?" she had asked and he had evaded the question, politely he hoped, remembering how he had flung the book contemptuously to a corner of his London flat.

He felt he had behaved responsibly. As Esther had suggested, he had visited his GP, although he had binned the prescription for anti-depressants and ignored the two-week sick-note. The only good outcome from seeing Esther had been her suggestion that he should talk to Gail.

Gail had not stormed and shouted. She had not wept. She had simply demanded to know exactly what he had been doing, whom he had been doing it with, where it had taken place, and how long it had been going on. He was the one who had slammed doors and raised his voice in frustration at her asinine persistence.

"Who is she?" Gail had asked and he had responded evasively that she was someone he had met through work in London.

"Younger than you, no doubt," Gail had said and he had been forced to admit that this was the case.

"And pretty, and flatters you I expect."

He had told her that he wanted a divorce and she had said, "I don't see why," and then, "You'll probably have changed your mind by next week."

At the end of it she had told him he was a 'silly, silly man' and gone to bed with chilly silence in the spare room. The silent, subdued atmosphere in the house confirmed to him that the relationship was dead. He would sort out some rehab for George, make sure Clara's university fees were covered and put the house on the market. He had a date in his diary to speak to a lawyer. Gail had a good job as an archivist and he was sure she would have no right to maintenance or his pension.

He texted Nicole: 'Love you. Thinking of you.' She replied to him less promptly than she had two weeks ago and though they spoke every evening on the phone, he missed the quick thrill of her instant messages. As the train hurtled into the London terminus he texted again: 'Let's meet. How about this weekend?'

Fighting his way along the Euston Road, he was surprised by a voice calling from behind him. Someone he had just passed was shouting: "Thomas! Thomas Fortune!" He turned to see John Williamson, wheeled suitcase in tow, extricating himself from the stream of pedestrians rushing in the opposite direction. He had trained with John Williamson, nearly fifteen years ago now. John was a few years younger than himself and at that time had been a bright young psychiatrist, looking to extend his skills with a training in psychotherapy. Thomas had not known him well and had been a little in awe of his medical status. He tried to remember what John had gone on to do and had vague memories of him moving up north somewhere. At any rate he knew that it was years since they had met.

"Fancy running into you, man." John clapped him on the shoulders, pulling him into the relative calm of the British Library forecourt. "How's it going? How are you doing?"

Thomas focused and found his public voice: "Very well. Very well."

"You pop up everywhere you know. I keep seeing your name in the Sundays. And I heard you on the *Today* programme the other week. Good stuff – very good stuff. Remember how I always said we needed someone like Tony Blair to speak up for us? Someone who could do the sound-bites? I never thought it would be you."

"Thank you. Thank you." Thomas could feel himself expanding in the man's cheerful flattery and began to frame a suitable reply but John Williamson was rattling on.

"I'd love to stop but I'm late for a meeting at the Royal College and then I've got to head out to the suburbs for a family party.

I didn't realise you were still in London. We must meet up for a coffee next time I'm down."

They exchanged email addresses and Thomas headed off through the side streets towards the tiny one bedroom flat that served as his consulting room. It was a long walk but he preferred it to the sweaty intimacy of the tube. The flat felt quiet, private and safe. Double-glazing protected him from the noise of the street below. The pale walls and the single, carefully placed pot plant reflected back to him a sense of his professionalism - careful, neutral and responsible - while the muted hubbub of the street below reminded him of the infinite possibilities of the city. Lowering himself into the consulting room chair, the relief of being back in London spread physically through him. The ideas for his paper began to return. He checked the latest email from the producer of his radio show, running through the possible candidates who might present their problems to him on air. An idea for a future Sunday column occurred to him and he made some notes on his laptop. In the moments before his first patient of the afternoon arrived, he checked his phone. There was no message from Nicole and it wasn't till he had finished with his last patient that a text finally arrived: 'Weekend no good. Boring family do. Next week any time.'

The extent of his disappointment unnerved him. He went and stood in the bathroom, staring with distaste at his face in the mirror. The light reflected off his bald head and he noticed that his jaw muscles were becoming slack. There was a droop to his chin that had not been there before and his ears affronted him. They always had. Cries of Dumbo, Big Ears and Mr Spock had followed him through the playground and still echoed in his memory. He turned away from his reflection with irritation and slumped onto the bed, flicking through the TV channels, ignoring the piles of papers that demanded his attention.

When Nicole finally called it was past ten 'o' clock. She recounted a breathless story of losing a client's dog on a walk and a giggly story about a night out with girlfriends. They arranged to meet on Monday. "I love you," he said. "I love you too," she replied. His spirits rose sufficiently for him to answer the outstanding emails in his inbox but it was not till the following morning during his radio programme - skilfully eliciting the details of some domestic tragedy from a distressed caller and offering his usual blend of sympathy and commonplace advice - that he began to feel himself again. The presenter signed off: "You've been Talking with Tom, our resident psychotherapist. If you have a problem you'd like to air you can call us on..."

Seguing into the next record he pressed mute and turned to Thomas: "Brilliant as always, Tom. You have a wonderful voice for radio."

Clara

Clara emerged from a small, suburban railway station in the wake of Aileen and others from the local network. It was raining, with a light persistent drizzle and there was a police van parked opposite with two officers standing beside it, one talking into his phone, the other staring across at the straggling groups of activists emerging from the train. Behind them, a man who might have been a journalist but was more probably another police officer, was taking photographs. They stopped to pull on waterproofs and then set off through side streets towards the country lane that would take them to the camp. About half a mile from the entrance they rounded a bend in the hedge-lined road and found police vans pulled up on the verges on both sides. Officers in riot gear milled around, their radios crackling.

"Christ," said Aileen, "This is heavy. Keep walking and don't make eye contact."

Clara found it difficult not to look at the officers: curiosity and indignation pulled her eyes first towards their shields propped against the vans, then to the helmets dangling from their hands and finally towards the eyes of the men observing her as she walked. Aileen took her arm. "Look at your feet, or focus on the middle distance."

Round the next bend they caught up with a group of twenty or thirty activists waiting at a police barrier. A stream of people were being funnelled slowly through a checkpoint. At tables set up in the road, the police were searching bags and conducting pat-downs. A hundred yards head of them Clara could see the entrance to the camp, and the power station itself which loomed heavily against the grey sky about half a mile away. A huge banner, suspended from a construction of scaffolding poles, hung across the entrance to the field. "Welcome to Climate Camp."

"They'll ask you lots of questions," said Aileen as they were waved towards separate tables. "You don't need to tell them anything other than your name and address and why you're here. Just say No Comment to anything else."

Clara watched in silence as a policeman emptied out her small rucksack, rummaging through her toiletries and underwear. Staring straight ahead, she held out her arms as a policewoman patted down her body, feeling for a knife or other offensive weapon. Airport checks always left her feeling anxious and humiliated but this encounter made her feel proud to belong to those considered a threat. As she left the checkpoint she felt she had passed another test.

A small village had sprung up on the squatted fields. The tents of the different geographical regions were arranged round the central space, where marquees for meetings and workshops had been erected, alongside a large cooking tent and the tents that housed the medical, legal and media teams. Composting toilets and waste systems were being set up and solar panels, small wind turbines and bicycles were being organised to power lap tops and music. Clara found Felix helping to construct a waste water treatment system, using straw and old baths. He broke away from the work to greet her and she was glad to see him. His eager smile was more endearing here amongst a field full of strangers and whatever became of their relationship, it was clear to Clara that he was her best route into the action. He seemed to know everybody.

Over the next two days the camp prepared. Clara quickly learned the silent hand signals that showed agreement or disagreement, asked a speaker to hurry up, or indicated that you wanted to clarify what was being said. She got happily involved in chopping piles of vegetables for vegan meals and found herself surprisingly able to laugh and joke with people she had met only the day before. There was a warm inclusiveness quite different from the pushy competitiveness of her school life.

She texted Ruby: 'Having great time. Learning loads. Hope Greece fun. You'd love it here.' This wasn't true. Ruby would hate it. It was Glastonbury without the music and Ruby, were she present, would hate the toilets, hate the food, mock the seriousness and argue with everybody. Nonetheless Clara still longed for her presence and tried to believe that when Ruby returned she could at least convince her of the importance of what she was doing, if not persuade her to join in.

But then she quarrelled with Felix, not a blazing, shouting argument but a quiet, intense stand-off. It took both of them by surprise. Clara wanted desperately to be one of the group who would occupy the power station itself or at least be one of those who locked on to the gates outside. She could not accept that the groups undertaking these tasks had been preparing for months and that she lacked the experience to take part.

"They're really tight groups, you can't just join at the last minute, you'd hold them up, you'd get hurt..."

"So it's a hierarchy."

"No, it's about preparation and experience."

"You mean exclusion." She could hear the unfairness in her voice but disappointment made her continue. "You pretend there's this flat structure but actually there are people at the centre like you and people on the fringe like me."

"Another time, next time, you'll be able to do whatever you want."

"It's this time that matters." The urgency would not leave her and she pushed on. "Introduce me to them. Let them decide."

"They'll say no. Listen Clara, the main demonstration is just as significant. It's where I'll be, with the legal team. It provides cover, it occupies the police, it shows how much support there is. You'll be an important part of things just by being there..."

"Don't patronise me," she said.

"I was just trying to explain," he said sharply before faltering to a halt. She felt momentarily sorry but something stubborn in her had met something persistent in him. Neither knew how to continue and it was several hours before she accepted his awkward peace offering of coffee and flapjack. She could not bring herself to apologise but she moved to sit beside him and allowed him to place an arm around her shoulders.

The morning of the demonstration was bright and sunny. Sipping tea from an enamel mug, Clara watched the sun rise behind the mass of the power station, filtering through the smoke and steam which billowed across the lightening sky. Felix appeared at her elbow with muesli and fruit and they sat in companionable silence, listening to birdsong and the sounds of the camp awakening.

"What are you thinking?" he asked.

"That in a few hours' time, all that will be quiet. All that smoke will be gone."

"Maybe. Hopefully."

"Definitely." Her disappointment had lifted, her optimism had returned and she felt warmly towards him again.

By seven-thirty the demonstration was snaking its way out of the camp. It was light-hearted and celebratory. A samba band led the way, there were families with children and a contingent of people dressed in polar bear suits. The advance groups had managed to evade the police cordons by dodging across the fields in the dark. There was no news of those who planned to occupy the power station itself but twenty or thirty people were locked on to the main gates, hoping to prevent the shift change that was due at 8 'o' clock. As the demonstration moved onto the road that ran past the gates they encountered waves of angry employees whose cars had been turned back. Police vans with their sirens blaring pushed their way slowly through the crowds of people and by the time the front of the demonstration arrived at the gates there was a police cordon across the road, separating the march from the people who were locked on.

People began to sit down in the road and to sing. A heavily pregnant woman displayed her bare belly with the message 'Here for my future' inked across it. A group started face-painting, turning their own faces blue and decorating the faces of children with polar bears, trees and tigers. Dancing down the police line, two young women humorously asked the police if they'd like a make-over too. Clara recognised Nell and Becca whom she had met at the training day and joined them. They painted her face as a tiger and she danced along beside them, growling cheerfully at the impassive officers.

For an hour or so, little more happened. News was filtering back that the attempts on the perimeter fence had failed. Police officers had been stationed in advance inside the site and had arrested the demonstrators shortly after they had broken through. The blockades on the back gates and on a pedestrian entrance had also given way and the shift change had taken place. By twelve 'o' clock the mood amongst the crowd had begun to alter. The families began to retreat and as they did Clara found herself packed tighter and tighter against the other demonstrators.

"What's happening?" she asked a man she was shoved up against.

"They're kettling us. There's a line of police behind us, moving forwards to shut us in against the line in front."

"Why?" she asked.

He shrugged. "Because they can. To provoke us. To make things uncomfortable for us."

Clara looked around for Felix but he was nowhere to be seen. She was aware of her heart beating faster. She could just glimpse Nell and Becca further towards the front, battling to stay on their feet as the crowd was suddenly pushed backwards by a surge from the police.

"Sit down," the man beside her said. "Link arms. It makes it harder for them to move forward on us."

Gradually the crowd sat down struggling to find space on the hard tarmac and Clara could see, over people's heads, the lines of police in riot gear blocking both ends of the narrow lane. The shouts and taunts of young men facing the police line carried across the clear air and were punctuated periodically by the wail of a child and then by the throb of the police helicopter passing backwards and forwards over the demonstration.

Clara gradually managed to still her beating heart, quietening her fear by counting the number of people she could see, losing count and counting again. As she regained control, her old feeling of angry determination returned. She told herself that she could see this out, she would see this out, whatever it turned out to be. Half an hour passed, then an hour. The man beside her stood up. Something was happening behind the police lines. The helicopter swung across the demonstration again and as the noise of its blades retreated Clara became able to hear the distorted orders being issued through police loudhailers. "Disperse now, or dogs, horses and long-handed batons will be deployed. Officers will be moving in to make arrests. Disperse now."

People turned to each other in confusion. There was nowhere to disperse to. The police line was solid. Some people got up, scanning the dense hedges for an exit. Others tried to pull them back down. Another line of police, some with dogs, was beginning to edge along the side of the road and in the distance mounted police were visible. Close to the police line the mood had become instantly uglier. A group of young men began throwing lumps of turf pulled from the roadside, shouting and taunting the police, darting towards them and retreating back to the cover of the crowd. The turf bounced pointlessly off the police shields and the line took another step forward.

From the other direction Clara spotted the yellow tabards of the march stewards and the legal team moving through the crowd, stepping over those who had remained seated, squeezing round those who were standing. They were repeating the same message over and over, fighting to make their voices heard above the noise of the helicopter and the police loudhailers. "They're opening a gate into the field over there. You'll be allowed to leave if you get up now."

Felix, stumbling through the seated people, caught up with Clara and grabbed her arm.

"Go back," he said. "This isn't going to end nicely."

She demurred, determined now to hold out.

"Please go. This is going to get violent. They're looking for excuses to make arrests. There's always a group of police who are looking for a ruck and some of our lot who are happy to oblige. There's no point in getting arrested in that kind of skirmish. You're likely to get hurt and the bail conditions will mean that you can't take part in anything else for months."

All around her, people were heading in the direction of the exit. Reluctantly, Clara joined them. As she passed through the narrow defile she was searched and her photograph was taken again. A woman in front of her was pulled from the crowd for questioning, her companion raised her arms in protest and was herself wrestled to the ground and dragged across the bumpy field. Clara hesitated but seeing the yellow tabard of one of the legal observers, allowed herself to be swept on by the momentum of the crowd, feeling both cowardly and terrified.

It was several hours before Felix returned, angry and exhausted but exhilarated too. The group at the gates had unlocked themselves and escaped arrest but there had been serious scuffles with the police, several people had been injured and several more charged with assault and obstruction.

"I've never seen the police so heavy before," he said. "Never seen them so determined, so completely out of order."

"So we failed," said Clara.

"No. It's a sign that the authorities are worried, a sign that they're taking this seriously."

"But we didn't manage to shut the power station down."

"No, but there were more people than on any previous action and the publicity so far has been fantastic. They've shot themselves in the foot behaving like that. There were journalists – regular journalists – caught up in the kettling."

"But we've made no impact on emissions."

Felix seemed unable to understand her disappointment and Clara could not explain it. She could not tell him that she had been frightened, could not admit to the anxious beating of her heart stuck in the kettled crowd, and could not speak of the shame she had felt at her failure to help the woman who was dragged helplessly across the field.

Esther

Esther picked up a folder of papers and left the house, heading through the side streets and across town towards Martin Tischbein's house. She was editing a collection of papers published in honour of his eightieth birthday and she had the cover illustration to show him, along with her own Introduction. Tisch – as he was called by those who knew him well - had been her own therapist, over thirty years ago, when she and Gordon had first come south, taking up their first permanent teaching posts. Two years into the job, overwhelmed by curriculum changes and a difficult class, she had collapsed in tears in her Head of Department's office and found herself unable to stop crying. It was months before she could accept that she was not crying about the job and years before she properly understood the effects of the break from her family. Esther had written regularly to her parents but had received no reply. After a year her letters had begun to be returned. Shortly before she collapsed in her Head of Department's office she had received a brief note from her brother Reuben. It had told her to stop writing, that she was damned and would never be welcome in the family again: there was to be no further communication between them.

In the month's following Reuben's letter Esther had felt as if the isolation would kill her. Martin Tischbein was the man who had helped her survive the loss of everything that had previously given meaning to her life and who had eventually encouraged her to use her unusual attunement to others to make a new career. Gradually Esther had found friends amongst her colleagues and when the children were born she had discovered a shared joy of motherhood with the people she had met through toddler groups and at the school gate. The sense of being an outsider had never entirely left her however and Esther remained cautious in her connections to others. The loss of Gordon, first through divorce and then through death had confirmed to her that it was risky to allow yourself to become wholly dependent on another.

It was unusual to retain the kind of connection Esther still had to Martin Tischbein. In a world where the boundaries of relationship were strictly arranged it was rare for there to be any contact, other than of the most formal kind, once therapy had ended. But Martin Tischbein was a man who made his own rules. He thought that many of psychotherapy's cherished but rigid norms were a pompous and damaging defence against the anxiety that the work produced. He was interested in the ordinariness of the therapeutic relationship, the points where it became coterminous with human kindness. The books he wrote, with their emphasis on common wisdom and the therapist's capacity to heal, remained subversively popular.

Martin Tischbein and Esther maintained a careful, respectful friendship, meeting once or twice a year and occasionally collaborating in criticism of the managerialism which had colonised the profession. She could never quite forget that he had been her therapist. He never quite stopped seeing her as a patient. Supposedly retired he still supervised a small number of people and occasionally took on another patient. He was one of the few people whom Esther felt had a true vocation for the work. He would not know what to do if he stopped working entirely.

As Esther walked through the quiet streets she could not stop thinking about Felix. "No news is good news," Jane had said firmly on the phone but the pictures from Climate Camp had alarmed her. She had played and replayed the news footage on her laptop, trying to spot Felix's yellow 'Legal Observer' jacket amongst the crowds of police and demonstrators. "Stop," Jane had said, "Just stop. You'll hear soon enough if he's been arrested." She tried, but when she did, angry thoughts about Thomas Fortune flooded in instead. He had finally settled down to some sensible discussion of his work but she sensed that this was tactical and that he was just waiting for the moment when he would surprise her with another move in his pursuit of Nicole. This morning, as he left, he had revealed that he intended to arrange another meeting with her.

Esther dropped down the hill and crossed the centre of town, passing through the market. The striped awnings, piles of vegetables and racks of cheap clothes never failed to return her briefly to childhood. Every Wednesday lunchtime her father had stood on the steps of the Market Cross of her home town and preached. "Friends," he would start, "If you were to die today, are you sure that you would not go to hell? Do you know what the Bible says will happen to those who die unrepentant and unreconciled to the word of God?"

During the school holidays Esther and her siblings were made to stand silently in front of him, holding a placard which said 'Return to the ways of the Lord' and which gave the address of the Meeting Rooms. Occasionally the lower lip of Ruth, the youngest, would begin to tremble and she would break into a wail of distress as week by week she became able to understand more of what her father threatened. His voice would rise to a crescendo: "Before the anger of the Lord come upon you, before the day of the Lord's fury come upon you, seek you the Lord."

And he would finish, exhausted, on a hissing outbreath: "Wash thine heart from wickedness, that thou mayest be saved..."

So far as Esther knew, no-one had ever been recruited through her father's sermons. The children were not permitted to talk to the passers-by, who for the most part ignored them. Her father himself would hurry back to work, his eyes fixed to the pavement, the moment he had finished and her mother would escort the children home. Her father was a shy, quiet man for whom these weekly performances were an agonising test of his belief and a necessary submission to God's will. Esther had gradually become aware that he did it only because of his own fear of damnation. When Reuben turned eighteen, he took over the responsibility for preaching as it became apparent that he had a facility for terrifying an audience that far surpassed his father's and was not afraid to respond to the taunts of hecklers and drunks who occasionally interrupted him. To the relief of Esther and the rest of her siblings he preferred to brave the market day crowds on his own and the school holiday ordeals slipped into the past.

She dismissed the memory and set off up the hill on the other side of town, towards an area of wide suburban streets and comfortable 1960s houses, lined with flowering cherry trees.

The door was opened by Laura, Martin Tischbein's wife. "He's in the conservatory," she said, showing Esther through the neat, detached bungalow.

Laura Tischbein's grey hair was gathered behind her in an old-fashioned bun and she wore an artist's apron, smeared with clay. "There's coffee and biscuits on the side," she said as they walked through the kitchen. "I'll be in the studio." Since the ending of her therapy with Tisch, Esther had observed their relationship with curiosity. They lived deeply connected but deeply separate lives. The house, the garden and her work as a potter were Laura's domain. The consulting room, the intellectual life and the quiet public acclaim belonged to Tisch. And yet they knew every inch of each other. Each turn of the other's mind or quirk of feeling could be responded to almost before it had happened. Esther wondered sometimes whether, if she and Gordon had survived together, they would ever have achieved this serene, respectful affinity. It was hard sometimes not to feel envy.

Tisch was sitting in the conservatory looking out at the garden, which was a work of art in itself. The detached bungalow occupied a large plot and a mixture of paved and grassed paths led from the vibrant colour of herbaceous borders into areas of wildflowers, fruit trees and vegetables.

He stood up easily and they shook hands. He was physically confident with few of the afflictions of age. Esther sat down beside him and spread the proposals for the cover on the table in front of them. It had taken a long time to arrive at the title and she was pleased with the design.

"*Elaborating Ambiguity: a Celebration of the Life of Martin Tischbein,*" he read aloud. "It makes me feel like I'm dead already."

"You said you were happy about it last time we talked."

"It looks different, written there in big print."

"We could say 'work' instead."

"Still makes me sound dead."

"Or we could say: essays in honour of Martin Tischbein."

"Yes. That's better. That will do."

"What about the design?"

"Yes, yes, it's fine. It will do fine."

"And the introduction?"

He rummaged amongst the papers, flipping over her carefully typed sheets. "I have one thing...here..." He had found a typo.

"That's all?"

"That's all."

She felt deflated. She gathered up her papers and stacked them neatly, wondering if he wanted her to leave. Looking sideways at him, she said as lightly as she could: "You're in a bad mood, Tisch."

He laughed. "That's what Laura said. She said to me 'You're in a bad mood. Don't take it out on Esther.' This morning I got a letter increasing my car insurance because I've passed eighty. Tomorrow I have an appointment for a new hearing aid. And now you turn up with a book that tells me that my life is over." He looked directly at her, a smile playing around his eyes. "I've never dealt well with the promise of mortality and I don't like to be told what to do. I apologise."

He stood up. "Come. We will make some coffee." And he led the way back to the kitchen. Esther had never quite got used to Tisch's abruptness. The subject of the book which she had spent so much time preparing was finished. She knew he was pleased about it because Laura had told her so but there would be no prolonged examination of its merits and no extravagant gratitude.

When Esther had first met Martin Tischbein she had imagined a tragic history for him as a Mid-European, Jewish refugee and had used this to excuse his sometimes peremptory manner. When she had finally confessed to her fantasies he had been amused. He had questioned closely why she needed him to have suffered so deeply, the origin of the pain she wished upon him, her desire that his empathy should spring from adversity. And then, later – when they had worked through the aggression and the envy which lurked in the fantasy - he had explained that although his family were indeed Jewish and had originally come from Austria, they had arrived in the 1920s, courtesy of his father's medical career and marriage to a woman of impeccably English descent. He had been born and educated in England and the only trace of his religious and family history resided in his name. His manner he had once explained, owed more to a background of English privilege than to a life of sorrow and defeat. "I've been lucky," he had said "And I shouldn't be so arrogant."

Esther told him about her dilemmas with Thomas Fortune and he laughed at the entanglement caused by Felix and Clara. "So the daughter unconsciously finds her way to your house as well. How long before the wife and son arrive too?"

"Tisch, don't be ridiculous," she said crossly. "This isn't a Shakespearean comedy."

He became more serious. "Is he a bad man?" he asked. "Or a foolish one?"

"Foolish, I think."

"Manipulative?"

"Very. How do you think I agreed to supervise him?"

"With your kind heart, I expect. It has got you into a lot of trouble over the years." He was referring to the paltry maintenance Gordon had paid after the divorce, her sympathy for Gordon's second wife and her difficulty in refusing to see needy but indigent patients.

Esther sighed. "The first time I saw him I thought he genuinely wanted my help in understanding what had happened. I thought he was in the grip of an unexamined erotic transference and trapped in an unhappy marriage and needed help to get himself out of it all. But now I'm beginning to feel that he might be using me to condone his determination to pursue an affair with his patient."

"And you're afraid he'll succeed?"

"There is something ruthless in him, something that makes me afraid."

"You don't need this work, Esther. You could tell him that you can't see him anymore."

"But what about his patients? If I dismiss him I don't think he'll go to someone else. Don't I have a responsibility there?"

"Your responsibility is to do your job as well as you can. If you can't do it, or if he prevents you from doing it, you must tell him so and suggest he finds supervision elsewhere." He paused. "The rest is an inflated superego."

"You think I'm trying to rescue him? That it's vanity? Narcissism?"

"The pleasures of being the rescuer are very seductive. None of us is immune."

"You make it sound so straightforward."

"No. No. It is not straightforward. Maybe you will turn him around. Maybe you won't. But I think that you will find your own way. You usually do."

They sat in a companionable silence for a while, surrounded by Laura's garden. A swathe of old-fashioned flowers, lupins, delphiniums, hollyhocks and geraniums, was covered in hoverflies and Esther felt suddenly hopeful about the future, despite Felix's gloomy predictions and her anxiety about his safety.

She got up to leave. As she stepped out onto the road she glanced at her watch and saw that she had been there for exactly fifty minutes. She smiled to herself and returned across town to her next patient.

Clara

The evening news and the next morning's papers carried pictures of the march and of the demonstrations outside the power company's headquarters where coal had been tipped across the doorway. There were interviews with demonstrators, a comment piece criticising the police action and a front page picture of a banner that had been unfurled from the top of Tate Modern, bearing the message 'Art is the only future for coal'. Clara and Felix were sitting in an open area of the field that looked down towards the camp entrance, flicking through the newspaper coverage. The sun shone weakly through clouds that threatened more rain.

"Do you feel it's more successful now you see all this?" Felix asked.

"Maybe." Clara had been enjoying the camaraderie of the camp and some of her good humour had returned.

A tall, good-looking man with his dark hair tied back in a ponytail flopped down beside them.

"Felix."

"Jay! How are you man?"

"Cool - just sorry to have missed all the action. I couldn't get away from work."

"Still lots to do."

"There certainly is. And who's this?" He was smiling at Clara. He had a strong face and the weathered skin of someone who worked outside. Felix introduced them. Jay had an easy, direct way of talking and Clara warmed to him instantly, telling him how she would be in Sheffield soon, about the course she would be doing and the demonstration she had taken part in.

"A few of us are going to have another go at getting through the perimeter," Jay said, addressing himself mainly to Felix. "Do you want to join us? There's a way through from the housing estate on the Eastern side and we reckon we've got a good chance of getting into the control room through a side door. The staff come out for a smoke fairly regularly so we reckon it's unlocked."

Felix looked concerned. "It was agreed at Spokes Council last night that we weren't going to make any more attempts on the building. We decided we should concentrate on the education side and creating a good experience for people who are newcomers. We've got some great workshops lined up and we don't want the police invading the camp in retaliation."

Jay shrugged. "Difference of opinion I guess. There's a small group of experienced people who really want to have another go but if you're not up for it that's fine."

Toiling across the field from the gate was a small, dark-haired woman. She had a day pack on her shoulders and a roll of flipchart paper in one hand. She was looking around perplexedly, as if trying to locate someone in particular amongst the small groups of campers dotted around the field. Felix jumped up and started waving energetically.

"Anusha! Hey – Anusha – over here!" She didn't see him and turned towards the main marquee. Turning back to Jay, Felix said "Just a sec. We can finish this conversation in a minute," and he took off across the field in an easy lope towards the dark haired woman.

Jay stood up to go.

"Wait a minute," said Clara. "I might be interested."

"Really?" He sat down again.

"Yes. I was really disappointed that we didn't get in on Monday."

"Yeah?"

"I thought shutting it down was the whole point so I'd really be up for another try."

Jay looked at her critically. "I'm looking for some experienced people," he said. "Good runners and climbers, people who know what's what inside a power station, people who've done this kind of thing before. I'm not being sexist but you don't look..."

"I may be small but I can run."

He laughed. "You're cool," he said.

She admitted that this was the first action she'd ever taken part in but Jay was encouraging. The shame that she so often felt at not knowing exactly how things were done left her as she listened to Jay describe the plan. He seemed to treat her as an equal in a way that Felix was reluctant to do. Finally he said, "Listen. I need another two people and because this is a tricky action I'm going to look for people I've already worked with but if I can't find any, then I'll come back to you. Is that OK?"

She nodded.

"You're disappointed, huh?"

She nodded again.

"Listen, when you're up in Sheffield, we can get together and do some stuff. I can see you've got grit and that's what we need. But we need to get you started on something where there's been more planning. These ad hoc actions are risky and I wouldn't want to see you getting hurt. Is that OK?" He lifted her chin so she had to look straight into his eyes. They were a beautiful deep brown with tiny crows' feet just beginning to appear at the corners.

"That's OK," she said smiling. "I'll look forward to that."

They exchanged mobile numbers and he moved off across the field. Felix was walking towards her carrying Anusha's roll of flipchart paper. He had one arm comfortably round her shoulders and Clara felt a stab of jealousy at the easy comradeship expressed in the gesture. Anusha sat down beside her and held out a hand.

"You must be Clara."

Clara smiled back. "That's right."

Anusha had one of those warm, interested smiles that was irresistible. She leant herself against Felix and pulled out her water bottle. "What a journey," she said, shaking her head.

"Have you come far?" Clara asked politely.

"I work in Birmingham and I was staying with a cousin in London last night. That was fine. It was this last bit that was grim. It's a lot heavier than I expected."

"They searched you?"

"They were really rude. Asked me for identification. Asked me where I came from, how long I'd lived in the country, shit like that."

"You could complain," said Felix.

"It was really upsetting but no, no. I just want to get on with what I've come here for and have a good day. And catch up with you and meet Clara properly."

She turned to Clara again. "We go back a long way, Felix and me. Reception class? Nursery?"

"Nursery. And then we were in the same class all the way through till you abandoned me in sixth form."

"I abandoned you? You abandoned me, going off to study difficult subjects like Mathematics and Art."

They had an easy familiarity.

"By the way, Mum says how come you were home for two whole weeks and you didn't call round to see her and Dad?"

Felix groaned. "How did that get back?" he said. "I was going to but..."

"You were too busy hooking up with Clara."

"Our Mums have been talking?"

"Of course they have. What do you expect?"

Their mothers were friends and Felix and Anusha had grown up in nearby streets and gone to the same schools, playing in and out of each other's houses. Like Felix, Anusha had moved away for university and then for work but they were still in touch, bound together by a mesh of shared memories and the friendship between their two families. It occurred to Clara that her own mother didn't really have friends and for a brief moment she wondered why.

Anusha looked around the field. "So where are all the brown people?" she asked. "Where are all the black faces?"

Felix groaned again. "Anusha, it's not my fault."

She laughed. "I'm teasing you," she said. "I always have a go at Felix about this," she explained to Clara. "But I'm serious too. This space is exclusively white, middle-class, educated and under thirty. You guys don't realise how off-putting you are to anyone who doesn't come from your particular tiny slice of the community. I love you dearly but you're shit at diversity."

"That's why I asked you to come and do the workshop," Felix said in exasperation.

Anusha had come for the programme of workshops and talks that made up the second half of Climate Camp. That morning she was due to run one on Power and Privilege, exploring the subtle and unconscious ways that activists maintained established systems of power amongst themselves. She was a natural communicator, a woman who moved easily and with generosity amongst everyone she met.

"It was good of you to ask me," she said, giving him a quick hug. "Is there any coffee in this place?" she continued, stretching herself out more comfortably on the grass. "I've got half an hour before I start."

Felix headed off towards the catering stall and Anusha turned to Clara: "So tell me about yourself. Felix tells me you're going to be moving up to Sheffield with him." Clara baulked at the phrase 'with him', wondering what Anusha had been told, but she explained about her course and then to her surprise found herself talking about her family, about George and his problems, about her falling out with Ruby and about the half-truths she had told her mother about where she was. The pent-up anxiety of the last few weeks came tumbling out of her. Anusha said little, but listened encouragingly. "You're in the middle of a big transition," she said eventually.

Clara felt there was something reassuring about the idea. Maybe it was natural to feel at sea. "What do you do?" she asked shyly, feeling that she needed to reciprocate.

"I work on an inter-faith project about climate change in Birmingham."

Clara swallowed, feeling out of her depth once more but Anusha filled the space for her, explaining the delicacy of the relationships between the different groups she worked with and the importance of her work. "I'm so lucky to have a job I love," she said.

Felix returned with the coffees, breaking the sudden intimacy that had sprung up between the two women. Clara was aware of a feeling of disappointment, almost as if she were jealous, but whether of Anusha or Felix or both of them she could not have said. They chatted inconsequentially till Anusha checked the time and left to prepare for her workshop.

Felix turned back to Clara and asked, "What did Jay say to you?" There was a tension in his voice.

"Nothing much. I said I'd join the break-in if he couldn't find anyone else."

"Don't, Clara."

She bristled. "Why not?"

"Jay's a great guy but he's hot headed. He gets people into trouble unnecessarily. I've seen him do this before. He sets up an unthought-through action, attracts a bunch of boneheads and ends up in a confrontation with the police. These things are a gift to them and get us a bad name."

"I liked Jay. I don't think that's what he was planning."

"Not what he was planning – no. But it's what will happen. They haven't got a hope of getting in there now. The place is crawling with private security as well as with police."

"But surely we ought to try – the whole point was to shut the place down, wasn't it?"

"There was consensus last night that we weren't going to make any more attempts, that there were other things to do now, like the workshops that Anusha's come for."

"You mean he's not allowed to?"

"No. No-one will stop him but they'll be going in on their own. The legal team won't be there. The first-aiders won't be there. People will get hurt."

"It doesn't have to be like that surely. If you do NVDA properly it won't be like that."

"Jay personally is fine. He's not into violence. He's a lovely, lovely guy but I've seen him make the same mistake over and over again, putting volatile, inexperienced people into a standoff that he can't control where someone gets hurt and loads of people get arrested. For what? They end up with fines and restrictions and we lose them for months because if they take part in anything while they're on bail they'll go down."

Clara fell silent.

"Clara, it's you that I'm concerned about. I just don't want you to get hurt."

Clara sat staring at the ground, twisting the end of her scarf round and round her finger. When Jay had told her he didn't want her to get hurt, she had felt cared for and protected. When Felix did so she felt like a small child being told off. Felix looked at her in puzzlement, confused by her sudden change of mood. He stretched out a hand.

"Come on," he said. "You were going to do Anusha's workshop and I wanted to hear the panel on biodiversity loss."

She got up reluctantly and they walked across the field together.

Two days later the camp ended quietly. As Felix had predicted, Jay's attempt on the perimeter fence had been short-lived and had ended in several arrests, though not of Jay himself who had returned to the camp, upset and indignant, and with heavy bruises all down one side of his body where he had fallen awkwardly from the fence. Clara had listened to his angry stories, half-wondering whether Felix was right but finding herself captivated by Jay's willingness to put himself physically in the way of danger.

Clara helped to decommission the composting toilets and watched as the marquees collapsed into forlorn heaps of white canvas on the grass. Her mind was full of Anusha's workshops. The first one, on power and privilege, had unsettled her. The realisation that she belonged to an educated, self-entitled elite did not square easily with her feelings of personal powerlessness. The second one on 'The Story of Self, Us and Now' had inspired her however. It had introduced her to the idea that she had something to say which would speak to other young people like herself, something that could fire others up to share her urgency. She had discovered to her surprise that she was good at it too. Once she centred herself in her own experience, the words came spontaneously and fluently and Anusha had been warm in her praise. To Clara's surprise, Anusha had invited Clara to shadow her when she ran another workshop in Sheffield for Freshers' Week. "You'll be great," Anusha had said. "The idea is to pass the skills on."

As she pulled her rucksack onto her back she texted Ruby 'Best week of my life so far' but did not share this feeling with Felix. Jay came up to say goodbye. He had an old white transit van and was driving back to Sheffield with some of the Yorkshire area's equipment. He and Felix clapped each other on the shoulders in a blokeish way, with promises to see each other soon. He held Clara in a big bear hug: "We can be in touch once you're up in Sheffield," he said releasing her, "We'll get you more involved." And then, as Felix turned away to talk to someone else, he briefly kissed her, full on the lips, before walking away towards his van and the piles of scaffolding poles and trestle tables that were being stacked up beside it. Clara wiped her lips with the back of her hand in confusion.

Clara and Felix set off towards the road and the long trek to the station. She had not realised how tired she was. Felix too seemed exhausted. He placed an arm around her as the creaky suburban train rattled into London and she allowed her head to rest on his shoulder. He was heading for St Pancras and a train North.

"Good week?" he asked.

"Brilliant week," she said. Away from the camp, the crowds and the excitement she felt more kindly towards him. There was a sweetness in the way he tried to look out for her.

"I won't be down South again before the start of term," he said. "I've got drawings to get out for a big job we've got on and I've got a coursework submission and a presentation for my Part Two to complete."

Clara felt a pang. When they were in the company of others she was not at all sure that she wanted Felix as her boyfriend. But when she was about to part from him and would not see him for several weeks he suddenly seemed more attractive. "We can talk on the phone," she said. "We can text."

"Every day?" he said.

"If you like," she replied. "But you're not to be cross if I don't instantly pick up."

"It's a deal," he said. "I don't always pick up either."

They said goodbye in a small café near St Pancras. "I'll let you know when I'm arriving," she said. "I'm still waiting to hear about where I'll be living but I'll let you know."

"I'm looking forward to you being in Sheffield," he said. "Really looking forward to it."

"Me too," she said, uncertain how absolutely she meant it. They kissed and parted.

AUTUMN 2009

Thomas

Thomas Fortune glanced sideways at his daughter. She sat silently, her new phone in her hand, staring out at the motorway slipping past them. He had been wrong-footed. He had arranged to spend this weekend with Nicole and now here he was driving his daughter to Sheffield to start her university course. Gail had been adamant. She was taking George to London to meet a friend of a friend who might have an opening with a recording company. She had batted Thomas's protests aside, citing his infidelity, his responsibilities and his absences: he would have to take Clara. She had a new-found hardness that surprised him.

Thomas had hardly seen Nicole since the day he had burst into Esther Dunn's house and poured out his complicated story. There had been the tearful meeting when they had agreed they should wait a month or two before starting their relationship. Some weeks later, they had snatched a brief supper before she left for a two-week holiday in Ibitha with a girlfriend. Nicole had been excited and giggly, chatting about friends who had never featured in her therapy sessions and whom he was not sure he would particularly like to meet. Thomas had become uncomfortably aware that there were dimensions of her life that he knew nothing about. Nonetheless, she had been flattering and affectionate and they had arranged to spend this weekend together. He had continued with his plan to retreat to the London flat, re-organising his schedule so that he only spent one night at home.

He looked again at his daughter.

"OK?" he asked. "Looking forward to it?"

"Fine."

He tried again. "Big step."

"Yeah."

"You'll miss Ruby I expect."

She shrugged.

He gave up and concentrated on the traffic, realising that he hardly knew this daughter. She had changed without him noticing. It was what happened in adolescence, he reassured himself. The sweet prince became a monosyllabic lout. The little princess turned into a moody drama queen. Then they emerged at some point in the future as fully-fledged, useful members of society. You could not control their lives. He wondered briefly whether she was upset about the impending divorce and then dismissed the thought. She had to find her own way. She was independent. She would be all right.

Thomas found the Hall of Residence without difficulty and carried what seemed an extravagant number of bags and boxes up to her room. Her tight, withdrawn expression had not changed and it was hard for the two of them to manoeuvre in the tiny space.

"Well," he said finally. "Got everything you want?"

"Yes thanks Dad."

"Shall I be off then?"

"Yes. Thanks for bringing me." Clara managed the shadow of a smile and gave him an awkward hug.

"We'll be in touch," he said. "Your Mum will be in touch – she'll check how you're doing."

"OK." She closed the door quickly behind him.

In the car park Thomas watched other families making affectionate goodbyes. 'All families are different,' he told himself, starting the engine and slipping the car into gear. If the traffic was OK he should make it to London in time. The planned weekend away had turned into a dinner date with the promise of a lazy Sunday to follow, though he was unsure where they would spend the night. His tiny flat, with the living space given over to his consulting room, felt somehow out of bounds and he had no idea what Nicole's place was like, apart from the fact that she lived in Enfield.

He had chosen the restaurant with care. Up-market but not too flashy and somewhere he was unlikely to meet anyone he knew. He picked Nicole up outside Enfield station and they drove into London. She wore a black sheath dress, high-heeled platform shoes and a short, pale bolero jacket. As she slipped her long legs effortlessly into the passenger seat Thomas could not help comparing her both with the daughter he had just left and with the wife who was probably now spread heavily across the seat of the train home following a futile attempt to persuade someone to employ George. Clara's new Doc Marten boots and oddly layered t-shirts offended him as much as his wife's shapeless tops and ill-fitting trousers. Settled in the restaurant, the food ordered, he smiled expansively across the table at Nicole.

"See the couple in the corner?" she said. "That's Ryan O'Connor and that's not his wife."

"Who?"

"You know – East Enders and then Dr Who."

Thomas didn't know and previously he would not have cared but he obliged Nicole by raising a quizzical eyebrow.

"You don't know anything, do you?" she laughed. "He's married to Estella York and they've got a baby but that's definitely not Estella York."

Nicole talked as if she knew these minor soap stars personally and Thomas was aware once again of a distance between the world he inhabited and the preoccupations of the dazzling young woman opposite him. It was interesting though, and he wondered momentarily whether there might be an article in it – *'Oedipal Re-enactments through the Imagined Lives of Others'* perhaps. But Nicole had moved on.

"Do you want to see my holiday pics?" She had a smart phone, like the one Clara had just bought with the money she'd earned from her holiday job, and she was passing it across the table to him.

He took it awkwardly and looked at an image of Nicole in a bikini, brandishing a large wine glass amongst a group of other bikini-clad young women.

"Swipe right," she said and then, as he fumbled clumsily with the device, she laughed again. "It's a touch screen, swipe the screen."

He got the hang of it and looked quickly at a succession of images of young people whom he did not know, in bars, on beaches and in night-clubs, posing drunkenly for the camera. He knew that Nicole was almost thirty, but here she looked younger and he felt unsettled by his stupidity with the device. He smiled at her again. "Looks fun," he said.

The food arrived and he managed to change the subject.

"How's the 'A' level course going?" Nicole had been due to start evening classes in the subjects that would allow her to apply to university to study Veterinary Medicine and Thomas felt proud of having helped her to this decision.

"Didn't I tell you? I decided not to do that after all." She elegantly finished a small mouthful of sweet and sour beetroot and continued. "I realised that although I love animals, I don't like seeing them when they're sick. And that's what it is when you're a Vet. You only get to see the animals when they're ill and then some of them die and also you have to put them down sometimes. I don't think I could do that. I couldn't kill an animal, even to put it out of its suffering."

Thomas could not conceal his surprise. Nicole had seemed so enthusiastic when they had discussed this possibility together. She had agreed with him that it would play to her strengths, develop her unexplored intelligence and make up for the missed opportunities of her teenage years. It was also, in Thomas's eyes, an important part of the new life they would forge together. It would make her his equal and allow her to share fully in the world that he inhabited.

"But I thought..."

Thomas found himself unexpectedly tongue-tied. In the consulting room he could have met her eyes with an expression of serious concern, allowed himself a weighty pause and carefully articulated the single word 'Really?' before explaining that her destructive impulses were inhibiting her natural ambition. But here, such gestures were lost in Nicole's bright enthusiasm and the clatter of the other diners. It was a while before he could get a single word past the mackerel pate or his own disappointment.

"I really think you should reconsider..." he began, aware that he probably sounded pompous.

She reached across the table and tapped his wrist teasingly. "I'm doing what you always encouraged me to do," she said. "I'm thinking for myself. You should be pleased."

He was silenced once more.

Over the main course, she became more serious. "I realised I'd agreed to it because I wanted to please you," she said. "Really I'm very happy doing what I do. I've got a nice little business. I love the dogs. I've got lovely customers."

Thomas poked at his duck with black garlic and tried to imagine introducing Nicole to his colleagues. Perhaps he could say she was an animal behaviourist. Maybe he could suggest she put that on her business cards. He pulled himself back to the pretty face opposite him. She was asking him what he thought.

"I'm actually rather disappointed," he said. "I thought we'd agreed that this would be an important part of our lives together." The tone wasn't right. He sounded plaintive, on the back foot.

"Everything's so different outside the therapy room, isn't it?" she said. "When we talked about it I really thought it was what I wanted to do but now – I can see it was a fantasy. It's not me. I don't like studying. I don't like illness. I don't want to turn out in the middle of the night for a sick horse."

Nicole pushed her spelt risotto round the plate and said: "When I was in your consulting room with you, I used to feel really confused, really unsure who I was. But now, now

I'm not seeing you any more – for therapy I mean – I feel like I know myself better, know what I want."

"Well," Thomas said stiffly, "That's a good thing, of course." He was alarmed. She claimed that she knew herself better but he was beginning to feel that he didn't know her at all.

She gave him one of her most winning smiles. "I've been wanting to talk to you about this Thomas," she said, "because I've begun to think that this isn't such a good idea – you and me I mean. We're so different. You read loads of books and you're serious and weighty and clever and I'm not. I like stuff that you think is crap like *East Enders* and *Hello* magazine. And you're older than me – really a lot older than me. I think maybe we both got caught up in an illusion."

He was shot back to all those early university encounters, all those pretty girls who had said 'I really respect you Thomas but...' or 'We're just different kinds of people Thomas...' All the kind attempts to let him down gently because his ears stuck out and his jeans didn't fit and he sweated uncontrollably whenever he was the least bit nervous. He was sweating now. He could feel a flush on his forehead and a stickiness beneath the collar of his expensive shirt. Was she telling him it was over?

"This time apart has been good for me. I've been able to think. Seeing John helped, too."

Thomas looked blank.

"You know John – my cousin. He was at my Nan's 80th - that family do I went to a few weeks ago."

Thomas still looked blank and Nicole laughed, an affectionate laugh but a laugh nonetheless.

"You do know John. He's the one who gave me your phone number in the first place, persuaded me I needed to talk to someone. John Williamson. Your colleague. He's a second cousin on my Mum's side."

Thomas's stomach turned over. How could he have forgotten? Nicole had been referred to him by John

Williamson, the old colleague he had run into three weeks ago on the Euston Road, the psychiatrist down from the North, rushing off to a meeting at the Royal College and then on to a family do. He was Nicole's cousin. He remembered the phone call, suddenly, with perfect recall, John's careful medical tones saying "I wondered if you could see a young cousin of mine. She's not someone I know well, so there isn't a boundary issue. I'm not entirely sure what the problem is but I know you're fully capable of making your own assessment." Thomas had been flattered and happy to get the referral. And then, in the years of therapy that had followed, and the falling in love, and the hopes and dreams of the last few weeks, he had quite forgotten how Nicole had first arrived in his consulting room. How could he have been such a fool? He swallowed.

"What...what did you say about us?"

"We didn't talk about you, silly, we were talking about me. I was telling him about enrolling for 'A' levels and he asked me why when the dog business is going so well and when I talked about it with him, I realised I didn't want to."

"You didn't say anything about us? You didn't talk about our plans?"

She shrugged. "No. Not really. That's not any of his business."

He felt a momentary relief but as he looked across the table at her toying with her food he felt sure she was lying. She smiled at him again, her beautiful, curved lips revealing the tips of her perfect, white teeth.

"Let's have a nice evening together, Thomas," she said. "I like you very much you know. I've never known anyone quite like you."

Perhaps she hadn't said much. Perhaps John would be discreet.

"I don't think we should meet again," Thomas said, determinedly wresting back control. "These things happen sometimes and I wouldn't want it to spoil all the good work we achieved together. I think that's what we need to concentrate on. That's what you need to remember."

"I'll always remember you. I'm very, very grateful for everything you've done for me." Nicole was looking at him directly now. She seemed sincere.

Then she abruptly changed the subject, as if there was nothing more to say, chatting to him about friends of hers whom he didn't know, customers of hers whom he would never meet, plans for the flat he would never see. Somehow he got to the end of the evening and they left the restaurant behind the couple Nicole had remarked on earlier.

As they stepped onto the street a camera flashed, once, twice and then again and a voice shouted "Ryan! Ryan! How's Estella and the baby? Any comment for your fans?" The man in front of them put up an arm in an attempt to shield himself and the woman from the photographer's lens, and hurried her into the waiting taxi. Thomas blinked, confused. Nicole, quite unabashed however, slipped across the road to speak to the photographer. When she came back, she was clutching the photographer's card.

"I wanted to know what magazine he was from," she explained. "So I can look out for the picture when it comes out."

Nicole was excited, exhilarated by the brief brush with fame. Thomas escorted her numbly to the car and drove her home. She leaned across and kissed him chastely on the cheek.

"Goodbye Thomas," she said. "Thank you for everything. I'll never forget you." And she was gone.

He hesitated. He could not face the flat. Its tiny bedroom, the anonymous walls of the consulting room, the galley of a kitchen – all pressed in on him in a reminder of his folly. He pushed the car into gear and headed for the motorway. At home, he found Gail and George in the kitchen. It was a quarter to midnight and Gail was cooking.

"Well," Gail said, "we weren't expecting you." She slid steak and onions and chips onto a plate which she placed in front of George. "We've had a very successful day – haven't we George?"

George grunted and Gail continued to fuss around him with offers of ketchup, pepper and salt. Thomas looked at them with distaste and said: "Clara's fine by the way."

Neither replied. Thomas retreated to his consulting room and opened his laptop. He would email John Williamson. Arrange a meeting. Get things straight. Move on. It would help to know more about him – congratulate him on his career or comment on a paper he had written. He googled John Williamson Consultant Psychiatrist. The details came up quickly. He had a post in York. He specialised in borderline states and complex personality disorders. There was a long list of academic papers, and a list of professional bodies and committees he served on. At the bottom of this list were some initials Thomas didn't recognise. Special Advisor to APPA. He clicked on the link and found himself on the site of the Association for the Prevention of Psych-Abuse, a patient-led network that campaigned against compulsory treatment, the overuse of anti-psychotic drugs and inappropriate relationships between professionals and their patients.

Clara

Clara closed the door behind her father with relief. The journey had been a nightmare of silent, anxious questions. What if she couldn't find the lecture theatres or the library? What if her room was occupied by someone else? What if she wasn't on the list of new students? What if she hadn't really got a place at all? She hated her father to see her anxiety. His stupid, therapist's questions left her feeling humiliated and the effort of blocking him out had been exhausting.

She carefully unpacked her belongings. The rhythm of sorting, deciding and arranging began to settle her and she looked at her tiny room with quiet satisfaction. She had a view out over the city from her fourth floor window and she was a comforting two hundred miles from the troubles of home. Her kettle and two mugs graced the wide window ledge. Her clothes hung snugly in the wardrobe. Her pens were arranged neatly on her desk beside the second-hand laptop which her earnings had paid for. The books she had ordered and read in advance stood on the shelves beside the battered travel set of Connect 4 which she could not bear to leave behind. Her breathing was quieter now and she noted that there was a text in from Felix. She read slowly through the Welcome Pack for new students and ventured out to find the communal kitchen.

Over the next few weeks Clara settled into a routine that suited her. The frenzy of fresher's week had not interested her. It suited her to look down on it as immature and frivolous. She was polite but distant with her fellow students and quickly gained a reputation for being studious and possibly dull. She rang her parents dutifully, one call a week to her mother and one to her father. Her mother was distant and vague, her father distant and jovial. She assured them that she was working hard and told them little else.

She had located the student environmental societies – People and Planet and the Youth Climate Coalition – and been introduced by Felix to the open meetings of the Climate Action Network. She was frustrated that she could not penetrate the inner circle of people who were involved in direct action. A big action, six months in the planning, was due to happen at the end of November. It was aimed at bringing maximum pressure on the UK's negotiators at the Copenhagen summit but it was wrapped in secrecy. The affinity groups of six to eight people were long established and meeting separately.

"Where's the action happening?" she asked Felix. "When is it going to be?"

"I can't tell you. It's on a need-to-know basis."

"I'm not going to tell anyone. I want to be involved."

"It's really important that this comes off. The fewer people who know about it the better."

Felix was always nervous in the run-up to an action and the precautions surrounding this one were intense. Each meeting was held in a different house or out in the woods if the weather was fine. They suspected the police of electronic surveillance and before the meetings they removed the batteries and Sim cards from their phones. On the actions themselves they kept in touch with a collection of cheap devices that could be disposed of afterwards. With six weeks to go the atmosphere was tense.

Clara persisted: "Why can't I join one of the groups?"

"You have to be asked. People have to be sure of you. They have to be confident that you're capable, they have to trust you not to talk."

"Of course I wouldn't talk."

"If I hear of anyone dropping out I'll suggest you but as far as I know all the groups are complete."

Clara's relationship with Felix stumbled. She felt that he did not respect her. She became stand-offish and in response he alternately withdrew or pursued her with a renewed and passionate energy that irritated her.

Her involvement with the Youth Climate Coalition was another matter. She had discovered in Anusha's workshop at Climate Camp that she had a talent for public speaking. Far from increasing her anxiety, the exposure seemed to bring her confidence and the phrases she had written herself rolled easily from her lips: 'I realised this was bigger than my own sadness,' 'I discovered my story was also the story of other young people' and 'I found that with others I have strengths that I had not imagined.'

She co-led workshops around the city and found herself speaking to young people at Further Education Colleges and to small groups of sixth-formers as well as to large student meetings. She was invited to speak in Leeds and Manchester and helped organise a flash dance demonstration outside the offices of a big power company. Come December she would travel to Copenhagen to be part of the youth demonstrations.

"You're a star," Felix said fondly as he listened to her presentation yet again. Clara warmed in his praise but she could not give up the desire to be part of the action that he was involved in.

"What's the point in mobilising all these people if we're not drawing them into direct action? What's the point if we're not actually shutting down the infrastructure?" she demanded.

Then she and Felix would go round and round the arguments again. Direct action was valuable because it prevented emissions. No - it was symbolic. Direct action was actively preventing a greater crime. No - it produced publicity and pressure. The most important thing was preventing emissions. The most important thing was drawing people into the wider movement. Felix felt increasingly that he was winning the arguments but losing Clara. Clara raged at his calm reasoning and his secrecy about the plans. He was bewildered by her storms and the way they alternated with a sudden crisis of confidence or a tearful lament that it was all too late. He rang his sister Jane. She listened carefully but when Felix had finished she had no hesitation in giving her opinion:

"She's too young for you and she sounds neurotic. Back off."

Felix did not wish, and could not see how, to follow her advice.

One night, at the end of a workshop she had helped to run in Leeds, Clara noticed a familiar figure leaning against the wall at the back of the room. He had not been there at the start. In fact, it looked as if he had only just arrived. It was Jay, the man who had kissed her as she left Climate Camp. She had not seen him at any of the meetings she had attended since her arrival and had given up all hope of his promises to involve her. As the assembled crowd dispersed he came over.

"Fancy a lift home?"

"Jay! I'd quite given up on ever seeing you again."

"I've been working away. Should I have let you know?"

Clara flushed in embarrassment but Jay's smile disarmed her and she replied "I'd love a lift. But what are you doing here?"

"I came to hear you. You're making quite a name you know. Everyone's talking about you."

"Really?" She was flattered but not seduced.

"OK – my route back was through Leeds but I did want to hear you too."

"But I don't think you did – hear me I mean – you weren't here for the workshop."

"I didn't make it in time. I just caught the end. I'll come to another one."

Clara was glad of Jay's offer. The train journey back to Sheffield was slow at that time of night. He steered her out through the dwindling groups of stragglers and they crossed the road to his van. His manner was as easy as she remembered it and he had a warmth that Felix lacked. Just as before, Clara found her words coming spontaneously. She talked about her course, her arrival in Sheffield, what she thought about the Action Network and the students and young people who were getting involved through her workshops. She explained how she crafted her short speeches, how she helped people construct their own and how she intended to join the demonstrations at Copenhagen. Where Felix was angst, Jay was confidence. Where Felix was serious Jay was humorous. He praised her intelligence, told gossipy stories about the people in the Network, and listened thoughtfully to her frustration at not being part of the upcoming action.

"I'm sure there's an affinity group you could join," he said.

"Felix is supposed to be listening out for me but he says none of the groups need an extra person."

"Are you sure you want to take part?" he asked. "It's going to be arrestable and one of the bail conditions will be that you can't leave the country. You wouldn't be able to go to Copenhagen."

Jay had none of Felix's caution and paranoia. He let slip hints of what the action would be – a co-ordinated attack on an open-cast coal mine, a coal-fired power station and the transport systems that connected one to the other.

Clara was torn. "I want to do both," she said.

Jay laughed. "You need to think about it," he said.

He came up to her room and she made coffee. They sat side by side on her narrow bed and they talked with an ease she had not experienced with anyone since the fracturing of her friendship with Ruby. With Felix everything had been tentative and awkward. With Jay it seemed effortless and exciting. They talked about politics and discovered that they shared a sense of urgency and a belief that direct action had to be at the heart of what they did. When she explained about her 'Story of Self' work, helping young people to speak out about climate change, he was fascinated, wanting to know how she did it, whom she was recruiting, how she hoped to involve them. She told him about her family and he reciprocated but more reluctantly.

"I've got a bit of a past," he said. "Don't ask. I'll tell you one day." All he would say was that he'd grown up on the outskirts of London; that he hadn't done well at school; that he'd drifted between manual jobs, and finally two or three years ago, had fallen in by chance with a group of people at a festival who had introduced him to politics. He'd been helping to erect the perimeter fence and had begun to talk with a group from Greenpeace who had arrived early to set up their stall.

"That was it," he said. "That was my moment. It's been my life ever since."

He worked as a roofer, often travelling away to jobs organised by an old friend in the South. That was why she'd not seen him since she'd been in Sheffield. The casual nature of his paid work meant that he could commit himself to organising and agitating for the Climate Action Network. He'd been crucial to Climate Camp and was central to the big action being planned.

Was it hard, Clara asked seriously, being amongst people who were so much more educated than he was? She thought, she told him, that he was smarter than most of them put together and Jay laughed his warm, captivating laugh.

"University of life, that's me," he said.

It was one in the morning when Clara finally, reluctantly, told him she had lectures the following day and that she needed some sleep. Jay turned to her and kissed her and she found herself responding in a way that was unfamiliar to her. It was Jay who broke the kiss. He looked directly into her eyes and she noticed again the tiny crows' feet at the corner of his own eyes and thought how kind they made him look.

"Can I see you again?" he said.

She nodded.

"Tomorrow?"

Ruby's advice about the importance of making a man wait didn't even enter her head. "Tomorrow would be great," she said. He left and she lay awake for a good half hour, comfortable in the darkness, thinking of nothing but Jay.

The next night he stayed in her tiny student room. Finally they slept, curled against each other in the narrow bed. She woke feeling guilty about Felix but Jay's comfortable, confident presence dispelled her doubts. He took her across the road to a coffee shop for breakfast.

"There's something you need to know about me Clara," he said, biting into a croissant.

She looked at him in concern but he smiled with the enchanting smile that softened all his features and she felt that whatever he was about to say couldn't matter one bit.

"I'm not really into exclusive relationships," he explained. "I don't like to be tied down. I like you. I really like you but I'm not making any promises."

"That's OK," she said brightly, though her voice was brittle, steeled for disappointment.

"I'm basically polyamorous," he said.

She looked puzzled.

"Do you know what polyamory is?"

"No," she admitted, thinking that the term sounded Latin and fearful it was an STD she somehow hadn't heard of.

"At lot of people in the movement are into it. It's partly a feminist thing – that's how I got introduced to it anyhow. It's the idea that conventional, exclusive, one-on-one relationships are oppressive, that monogamy is the relationship model of capitalism, and if that's what we're opposed to we should be opposed to monogamy too. We know that marriage doesn't work – look at anyone you know – so we have to find alternatives."

Clara thought instantly of her parents, miserable and quarrelling, locked together by money, mortgage and responsibilities. But she also knew that the only person she wanted to be with right now, was Jay. Anxiety suffused her face and she looked at him in confusion.

"Don't worry," he said. "It's not a competition. There's nobody else I'm interested in at the moment. I just want you to know that I consider myself free and that you should consider yourself free as well." He paused. "Felix for example."

Clara blushed. "I'm not...we're not...it's nothing serious..." She stumbled on her words.

"It's cool," Jay said. "I don't need to know – unless you want me to."

"I guess I need to sort things out with Felix," Clara said. "Meeting you properly has made me realise that perhaps we're not right together."

Jay shrugged. "Up to you," he said. "Don't do anything hasty. Felix is a good bloke. He's a mate."

Clara's whole being was at that moment fixed on the man sitting opposite her, from her curiosity about his background and her delight in his lean, confident physique, to the way she could relax in the warmth of his affectionate gaze. At the same time it felt vertiginous. She was scared. She had never allowed herself to feel so totally, inextricably, breathlessly caught up in another person. And she felt guilty and slightly anxious about Felix. He had been kind to her. He had introduced her to this life and to his friends. He was a good person - which was maybe the problem. Perhaps, an oddly logical voice in her head said, polyamory wasn't such a crazy idea. It would allow her to remain friends with Felix. It would keep her feet on the ground with Jay. Clara looked across at him boldly.

"I'd like to see you again," she said.

"I'd like to see you," he replied.

"I said I'd see Felix this evening. Saturday?"

"Saturday would suit me just fine."

She left for her classes with her heart singing.

Esther

Esther sat waiting for Thomas Fortune. The year had turned. The days were shorter and she could feel melancholy pressing at the edge of consciousness. It had been autumn when Reuben had returned her letters, autumn when Gordon had left and autumn when Gordon had died. Phrases from the past pushed at awareness: 'Ye shall be sorrowful but your sorrow shall be turned into joy.' It was a long time since those words had felt comforting but Esther still experienced a shadow of hope as they drifted into her mind. She told herself that October was also the month of Jane's birthday and that one day, some day, this work with Thomas Fortune would come to an end.

The doorbell rang with Thomas's long and insistent ring. It felt to Esther as if he was announcing his importance but she reflected that perhaps he was just afraid that she would not hear him. Their supervision sessions had begun to follow a familiar pattern. Thomas would describe a patient, sometimes in a flurry of technical terms and sometimes in a babble of popular clichés. She would struggle to get a clear picture of the person's difficulties and history. The more questions she asked the clearer it became that he had failed to move beyond the most superficial appreciation of the person in front of him.

"How many siblings did you say?" she had asked once.

"Two, no three, maybe three," Thomas had replied.

"Which?" she had asked. "And where did she come in the birth order?" He hadn't known and he had blustered that he thought it wasn't relevant, it was the transference manifestations that told you what you wanted to know.

"And what were they?" Esther had asked, fully aware that the sweetness of her tone only partially concealed the barb in her question. She knew that he would not be able to make a coherent reply.

Gradually, Thomas's limitations or his laziness with each patient were revealed. Time after time Esther felt that the only person who really mattered was Thomas himself. Whenever a question threatened his pride, he would blanch briefly and then become bullish and assertive, lecturing her on an obscure theoretical point or dismissing the patient with contempt. She was troubled by the responsibility she felt, troubled by her inability to push beyond his defensiveness and concerned above all about the fate of the unknown Nicole.

Esther looked through the list of patients he had given her. There were still several that they had not discussed at all. She dreaded the now familiar pattern of his faulty exposition, her struggle to make sense, the exposure of his failings and the need to both confront and support him. She opened the door. Thomas was as neat as ever, charcoal grey suit, pale blue open-necked shirt, carefully manicured hands and well-shone shoes. But there were dark rings beneath his eyes and the muscles of his face were slack. He sat down heavily in the chair and opened the conversation.

"You'll be pleased to hear," he said "That I am no longer seeing Nicole." The words were carefully chosen for their neutrality but there was a tremor in his voice. He looked straight at her, challenging her to interrogate him further.

Esther wondered what had happened and asked cautiously, "How do you feel about that?"

"It's probably for the best."

"Do you imagine there will be any further implications?"

"Only that my wife is no longer speaking to me."

She made a small gesture with her right hand, inviting him to say more but he ignored it.

"What about Nicole?" Esther asked. "Is she happy to end things?" She could sense the anger rising in him.

"Yes," he said abruptly.

Esther felt sorry for him. He had been unable to distinguish love from transference, indulged in a reckless affair, destroyed his marriage and possibly damaged his career. It sounded as if it was Nicole who had ended the relationship and that Thomas found this too humiliating to discuss. She tried once more, directly this time.

"Would you like to talk more about it?"

"I'm here for supervision."

"Of course," she said. "And when you feel ready to discuss it in terms of your clinical practice, I'll be happy to do so." She paused and gave him a genuine smile of relief. "I am glad about your decision, Thomas. I think it's the right one." Perhaps next week they could return to the damage he had done to Nicole and what needed to be done about it.

They talked about another patient but all through the weary conversation Esther felt the presence of other preoccupations. Five minutes before the end of the session Thomas changed the subject abruptly, opening his briefcase and passing an A4 sheet with a screen-grab across the room to her.

"What do you know about APPA?" he asked.

She took the sheet. It showed the home-page of a website. The letters stood for Association for the Prevention of Psych-Abuse. Thomas's right shoe was tapping in tiny involuntary movements.

'Have you been hurt by someone who was supposed to be helping you?' asked the banner headline. 'Psychiatrists, psychologists, psychotherapists and counsellors are meant to be there for you,' continued the text below 'but sometimes they're not. We are a network of current and former patients and we speak out for those who have been abused - sexually, financially or emotionally - by unscrupulous practitioners, or harmed by faulty drug regimes, or forced to accept treatments they didn't want.' There was a column on the right hand side headed 'Julie's Story'. 'I thought my therapist was a hero,' began the text. 'Read more' it continued below a photo of a dark-haired woman. Below this was a list of previous blog posts. 'My Lithium Hell', 'News from the Inside', 'How to Come off Citalepram'.

Esther gave him a questioning look. Was Nicole involved with these people? Was he afraid that she might become involved with them? "I haven't heard of them," she said.

"I'm thinking of doing a column on them," Thomas said. "I trained with the chap who advises them. I thought I could get him to give me the low-down. John Williamson – do you know him?"

"No, I don't."

"Good chap. Consultant psychiatrist in York."

Thomas left. Esther was mystified. Why would Thomas, who could so easily find himself accused of abusing a patient, draw attention to himself by contacting an organisation dedicated to exposing just that kind of malpractice? It wasn't till the evening, when a memory of Edgar Allan Poe's story *The Purloined Letter* pushed into consciousness, that it clicked. It was the old trick of hiding yourself in a place so obvious that no-one would expect to find you there: Thomas, posing as champion of the abused was the equivalent of the stolen letter which sat, undisguised, in the letter-rack. It was a risky strategy, leaving Thomas vulnerable to any modern-day Auguste Dupin keen to discover him. Esther wondered if she should have insisted that he told her what had happened with Nicole. It was clear that he still didn't trust her. He would almost certainly have refused.

Thomas

Thomas sat on the train smarting at Esther Dunn's questions. He felt exposed by his admission that his wife was no longer speaking to him and he certainly did not want to tell her about his conversation with Gail. "Really?" Gail had said coldly, when he told her he was intending to move back home. "I don't know about that," she had continued when he suggested they should try to make another go of it together. There was a new hardness in her voice. "I don't think so, Thomas" she had said. "I've decided a divorce would suit me rather well."

He tried to push the supervision session behind him, took out his laptop and wrote an email to John Williamson.

'Dear John, It was a pleasant surprise to bump into you in London the other week. Are you likely to be in town again soon? I was hoping to pick your brains about APPA, as I'm thinking of featuring them in my column. All the best, Thomas.'

He pressed send and settled back in his seat, feeling a little more comfortable. If Nicole had spoken to John Williamson, this would nail him. Face to face, he could easily make him see that anything Nicole had said about an affair was nonsense. He imagined himself leaning confidentially across the table of a quiet restaurant. "Very difficult piece of work," he would say. "Erotic transference unfortunately – very tricky. I think we resolved it but I'm not convinced that she didn't still hope, somewhere deep down, that we could have had a relationship beyond the consulting room." And John would agree. Perhaps he would acknowledge that in sending Nicole he had sent a poisoned chalice. Thomas's fantasy wound comfortably on with John explaining that he'd chosen Thomas as someone he was confident could cope with Nicole's borderline tendencies. The conversation would segue into a theoretical discussion of complex cases and the whole mess would be comfortably consigned to history. Without Esther Dunn knowing anything more about it.

It was a full week before John Williamson replied and when it came, the reply was brief: 'Not likely to be in London till the New Year. Best to contact APPA direct. J.' Thomas was unsure what to make of it, swinging between paranoia – "He knows, he doesn't want to meet, he's planning to expose me" – and contempt: "Arrogant prick, thinks he's too grand for a cup of coffee."

He wrote a Sunday column anyway, not bothering to contact the Association for the Prevention of Psych-Abuse, but including their contact details at the end of the article. *It's Hard to Talk when Love Gets in the Way* described the confusion that could arise for both patient and therapist when the boundaries of the relationship became muddled. Thomas felt he had struck a good balance between condemning abuse and explaining the power of an erotic transference but the online comments which appeared were fewer and less complimentary than usual. One simply said 'This is S*** from beginning to end. Abuse is abuse is abuse.' Another was from John Williamson, politely pointing out that there were more up-to-date statistics than the ones he had carelessly googled. A third was a long story from a woman describing how her therapist had seduced her and a fourth was from APPA, repeating more temperately the message of the first. He had carefully replied to each online comment but the balance still didn't feel right and he felt more vulnerable than ever.

He hesitated and then quickly created a new email address, choosing a name that sounded both individual and common. The words of the fictional Rosa Thompson came easily to his fingers. 'Thirty years ago' she wrote 'I fell in love with my therapist. I fantasised about him, made flirtatious comments every time we met and longed for the day when he would reveal his true feelings. He disappointed me, of course, insisting on interpreting everything in terms of my neglectful childhood. At the time this infuriated me and if someone had suggested to me that I could accuse my therapist of abuse I might have welcomed the opportunity to take revenge. Fortunately those were different times. I worked through my difficulties, completed my therapy and eventually made a very happy marriage. Thank you Thomas, for a really important article.' He pressed 'send' and settled back in his seat, feeling a little more comfortable.

Clara

As Jay re-entered the Climate Action Network, Clara could see how central he was. His connections in the building trade meant he could easily borrow essential equipment or acquire it cheaply. Ladders, ropes and bolt cutters appeared magically on request. He organised transport. He had an opinion on everything and he was listened to. "Ask Jay," people would say whenever a practical problem arose.

Sometimes he clashed with Stefan, another veteran of the road protests. Where Jay was impulsive, Stefan was a strategist. "In another life," Felix had said in the days when they were still talking, "Stefan would have been an army officer or a guerrilla leader." If you were in an affinity group with him you could be sure that it would be effective and that even if you were arrested there would have been no violence and your legal rights would be respected. If Clara wanted to be involved in an action, Felix had said, then Stefan was the person to speak to. Stefan would make sure she was OK. Clara had bristled, feeling patronised once more. And now everything with Felix had come to a painful end.

She had met him, as arranged. It was awkward. Felix had bought cinema tickets and she had sat through the film, unable to concentrate, uncomfortably holding his hand. Afterwards, she had persuaded him into a quiet bar rather than returning to his flat. The words which she had been rehearsing all day and which had sounded so reasonable fell like stones on Felix's hurt and angry face.

"I saw Jay the other day," she began.

"I heard he's back in town," Felix replied without interest, looking at the rain which was beginning to streak the window. "We should finish this and get back."

"There's something I need to talk to you about," she said, sipping her drink more slowly.

"What? Can't we talk when we get back?"

"There's something happening between me and Jay," she said and then before he could reply she made her speech about polyamory, how it was the best of all worlds, how it meant they could all explore what they meant to each other, how she felt too young to be tied down, how she really liked him but she liked Jay too, how important it was to question the soft institutions that supported the status quo. The words were exactly as she had rehearsed them but spoken across the table to the real flesh-and-blood Felix, they sounded hollow and dishonest. His face had crumpled, first in puzzlement, then in hurt and finally in anger.

He had interrupted her: "No Clara. No, No and No. Polyamory sucks. It's an excuse for people like Jay to play around."

"I don't agree," she had said. "If we really want to challenge capitalism we have to challenge all its institutions."

"That's bollocks. Love isn't an institution. Loyalty isn't an institution. Honesty and caring for people aren't institutions."

"They are when they're wrapped up in the conventions of capitalism," she had replied weakly, surprised at his vehemence.

"You're just repeating the garbage he told you to get you into bed with him." He had paused and then demanded: "Have you slept with him?"

She had stared at the table and refused to say, tears pricking at her eyes.

"You'll find out," Felix said bitterly. "You'll get hurt. He's got form. He says this to every woman he meets. It's because he can't make a commitment. He has to leave himself a get-out. Listen Clara. Jay's a mate of mine. I know he's an attractive bloke. I can see why you like him. But he isn't right for you. Even if you don't want me, steer clear of Jay."

Clara had wiped her eyes with a paper napkin. "I'll decide who's right for me," she had said stiffly.

They had sat in silence for a while. Then Felix had said: "I guess that's it then," and Clara had nodded miserably. He had walked her back to the student residences and they had parted with a brief, unhappy embrace.

A week later there was an argument about the plans for Copenhagen. Jay proposed joining the Danish anarchists in an occupation of the conference centre itself. Stefan cited the ferocity of the Danish police and the need to consolidate new support with a less risky, more inclusive action. Gradually the argument went Stefan's way and this decided Clara. If Copenhagen was going to be a tame experience she was no longer much interested and she asked Jay to find her a place on the late November action.

Jay, wounded by the meeting, was pleased. "Leave it with me," he said.

Two days later Clara found herself sitting in the back room of a small terraced house with six other people, all slightly older than herself. One was a woman who had discovered she was pregnant and was no longer confident about taking part. She had come to say goodbye and Clara would be replacing her. Amongst the others it was a dark-haired, assertive woman called Helen who drew Clara's attention. She reminded her a little of Ruby. She had a similar liveliness and warmth and she was a natural organiser. Helen explained that they would be one of four groups who would stop the train which ran from the coal depot to the power station. While other groups closed down the open-cast mine and occupied the power station, they would halt the train which transported the coal. As Clara listened carefully to the arrangements she wondered wistfully if she and Helen might become friends. She left the meeting with a feeling of deep satisfaction. She was finally in. She was finally doing what she believed was right.

Thomas

Three weeks later Thomas was sitting in the dentist's waiting room. His column on abuse and the erotic transference was behind him. He had followed it with more upbeat offerings on procrastination, self-awareness and hypocrisy which had all attracted an enthusiastic online response. He had added a minor member of the aristocracy and a well-known actor to his case-load and he was booked for a private dinner with a Junior Minister whom he was confident would become a useful friend. He was becoming resigned to the ending of his marriage. Gail's new-found hardness had persisted and his efforts at reconciliation had been flatly rejected.

"I don't think so," she had said again. "I think I'm better off without you."

When he had demanded to know who had turned her against him, he discovered to his chagrin that there was nobody. She had, she said, worked it out for herself and was surprised that it had taken her so long. She was impervious to his suggestion that they should consider the children, saying vaguely that she was sure they wouldn't mind. And she was impervious to his ultimatum that the house would have to be sold. She didn't mind that either. Everything was now in the hands of lawyers.

He glanced at the expensive wristwatch which she had bought, at his suggestion, for his last birthday. He was due to teach in an hour. He paid a lot of money for private dentistry and he didn't like to be kept waiting. The receptionist brought him a cup of coffee. Mr Brunswick would be about a quarter of an hour. There had been an emergency. Thomas grunted ungraciously and flipped through the pile of magazines on the table in front of him. They were clean and recently purchased. Copies of Country Life and Vogue were interleaved with celebrity life-style magazines, presumably because – however much they protested publicly - Mr Brunswick's celebrity clientele liked to see themselves reflected in the popular press.

Thomas picked up the topmost one, thinking that perhaps he ought to understand more about popular culture. There was probably an article he could write, some neat piece of theorising about the fantasies of the millions who bought this dross. A beaming couple he didn't recognise graced the cover beneath a headline foretelling 'Married bliss for Angie and Mark.' Grouped round this picture were tasters for the stories inside. 'Selina – my voyage to recovery' 'Love-rat Ryan caught in the act.' He flicked idly through the pages, trying to get a feel for the emotions that were being played to. Envy? Schadenfreude? The thrill of identifying with others' misdemeanours? *Affairs by Proxy: Thrills and Regression in the Popular Press.* That would do.

Pleased with his title, Thomas turned the page and there to his astonishment were his own face and that of Nicole staring out at him from the background of a centre-fold shot of 'Love-Rat Ryan' and a pretty blonde woman: the couple whom Nicole had remarked on in the restaurant and whom they had followed onto the street as they left. The focus of the picture was the celebrity couple, ducking their heads away from the camera but he and Nicole were both clearly recognisable behind them. Thomas remembered now how Nicole had run across to the photographer to find out which magazine he was from so she could follow the story later. Reading through the text he saw that she had done more than ask which paper he worked for. 'Is it all over for Ryan and Estella?' screamed the banner headline. 'New Dad Ryan O'Connor caught on camera leaving the newly refurbished Tarabella Restaurant, arm in arm with Sophie (X-Factor) Sampson,' proclaimed the text beneath the picture. And then, in the middle of the short paragraphs which comprised the story itself he read 'Fellow diner, model Nicole Morgenson (enjoying a quiet night out with celebrity shrink Thomas Fortune) told *Starstruck* 'They were billing and cooing like turtle doves – they definitely looked like they were in love.'

His thoughts tumbled over each other in panic. Why had she said she was a model when she hadn't modelled in years? Why had she revealed his name when she knew how important discretion was for him? What else had she said? She'd lied. She'd betrayed him. She'd exposed him.

He could feel a constriction in his chest and became aware of a woman opposite, looking at him. There was an uncontrollable tremor in his right leg and his foot was tapping the floor in a regular, agitated motion. He forced himself to breathe calmly, brought the tremor under control and finished the short article. There was no more mention of himself or Nicole. Slowly he began to rationalise. Who read this trash anyway? Would anyone who mattered have seen it? Would anyone believe it if they did? Even supposing anyone had seen it, no-one apart from John Williamson and Esther Dunn knew that Nicole Morgenson was his patient. If anyone was to ask, he would say – what? She was just a friend? A friend of his daughter? A relative? No. It was nobody's business whom he dined with. He would not offer an explanation. Why should he justify himself?

But it felt intolerable to sit for another minute in this tasteful waiting room with its pile of distasteful magazines. He surreptitiously slid the offending magazine into his briefcase, got up and walked across to the receptionist's desk. "Could you tell Mr Brunswick that I couldn't wait any longer?" he asked. "I'll email about another appointment."

By the time he walked into the Foundation's headquarters in Merton Square for his teaching session, he had recovered his equilibrium. Despite its location in East London, the Georgian terrace and the plane trees in the square opposite had a sense of weight which pleased him. He felt a comfortable ownership of the polished brass plate and the legend 'Foundation for Pluralistic Psychotherapy' each time he crossed the threshold. He was on the third of his lectures on the History of Psychoanalysis and would follow this with a study group on Elements of the Therapeutic Relationship. He was a popular teacher and feedback from the trainees was consistently good. He had just made himself a cup of coffee and settled into one of the easy chairs in the staff room when Melissa Augustine, the Director, put her head round the door.

"I thought I saw you come in, Thomas. Do you have a moment?"

"For you Melissa, any time," he said expansively, indicating the seat opposite him.

"I'd prefer to talk in my office if you don't mind."

She was an imposing woman in her late fifties. Many people were afraid of her but Thomas had found that a mix of gravitas and flattery would usually charm her into agreement. On this occasion however he got up and followed her without comment to her office.

"Something has come to my notice," she said, once they were both seated, "that I thought I ought to alert you to."

"Not more budgetary problems I hope?" He was used to Melissa consulting him on administrative issues. Although he was no longer part of the Foundation's ruling council, he liked to maintain his influence and was expert at making himself seem subtly indispensable.

"Nothing of that sort, no. It's more delicate."

He opened his hands in a concerned gesture. She sighed and spoke again.

"I really don't know how to put this Thomas but there are some unpleasant rumours circulating amongst the trainees. I overheard a conversation in the kitchen yesterday and it wasn't the first unfortunately. It's an accusation that you might have had a sexual involvement with a patient."

His stomach somersaulted but he managed to keep his poise, raising his eyebrows in what he hoped was an expression of shock.

"I put a stop to the conversation instantly of course and I hope we won't have any repetition but I thought you ought to know."

"Absolutely." He frowned and put his fingers together in a gesture of serious thought, as if trying to fathom what on earth the accusation could be about, or what on earth should be done about it.

"I wanted to reassure you that we have every confidence in you and absolutely no reason to think that there is any substance in what is being said," she continued. "On the contrary, it's a source of embarrassment for us that such a rumour should be circulating here."

"Thank you Melissa, thank you," he said. He intensified his serious frown. "Is it possible to tell me which trainees have been talking in this way?" he asked.

"I don't think it would help, Thomas," she replied. "I don't think it will happen again."

She would be right about the second statement, Thomas reflected. Most of them were terrified of her. But why did she have to be so damned prissy about who it was she'd caught? He tried to conceal his irritation. "Of course," he said. "I quite understand."

"In fact, I was wondering," she continued "whether you had any idea about where these rumours might have come from, how they might have originated?"

He opened his hands in a gesture of world-weary stoicism. "As we know," he said "envy is a very powerful emotion." He ran through the groups of trainees in his mind's eye, checking off one or two who had occasionally challenged his authority.

She nodded sagely, reflecting his mood.

"Add that to the human propensity for projection of one's own weaknesses and fears onto those we otherwise admire, stir in a small portion of malice, and I think you will find we have the perfect recipe for rumours such as this." What information did they have? How the hell had they had acquired it?

"Indeed, indeed," she said.

"All we can do, I think, is stay alert. Make sure that our trainees are receiving adequate therapy for their own neuroses, make sure our supervision is up to scratch, make sure our monitoring procedures are properly applied." He would find out who they were. He would finish them. He could feel the anger rising through his throat. They could kiss goodbye to their careers.

"Absolutely, absolutely."

Thomas risked a final pitch. "We should perhaps be enquiring more deeply into the practise of those who make these allegations. Are they the ones who have overstepped some boundary? Have they in fact committed the acts they accuse others of?"

Melissa Augustine hesitated. He had gone too far. He relaxed his face muscles and smiled. "I become too passionate about these issues, don't I?" he said, meeting her eyes, inviting her complicity. She responded instantly.

"We wouldn't have you any other way, Thomas," she said warmly.

He'd got it right, just the right degree of intimacy, just the right suggestion of flirtation. He could wrap this up for now. "Maybe just some additional seminars," he said. "Put more emphasis on our coverage of boundary issues."

"I think that's an excellent idea," she said. "Thank you so much Thomas for making this so easy for me. I do appreciate it."

"It's my pleasure." Thomas stood up, terminating the interview. "Let me know if you want any help organising those extra sessions."

"I will, I will," she said. As he turned to go she added "And I'm so looking forward to hearing your keynote at the conference next week. I'm so glad they asked you to do it."

Thomas's paper for the international conference *Working with Intimacy in an Age of Uncertainty* was prepared, sitting in his briefcase in fact. He smiled at her with the air of a man who could afford to drop some small favours to those positioned beneath him. "We must have lunch some time," he said. "Catch up properly."

Sitting in the staff room he opened his lap top, logged into the Foundation's website and entered his password for the confidential information held on trainees, scrutinising it for any clues about who might have spoken to John Williamson, Esther Dunn or even Nicole herself. He found what he was looking for quickly enough. Esther Dunn was listed as the personal therapist of a second year trainee, Brenda Burton. Not an obvious candidate for gossip. One of the anxious, do-gooding, Mumsy brigade but, he told himself, you shouldn't underestimate the malevolence that lurked behind those comforting exteriors. If Esther Dunn had opened her mouth he would finish her too.

Clara

Clara found a seat near the back of the bar, checked the time and laid her phone on the table. It was quiet. The lunch time rush had not yet arrived. She had been surprised to hear from George but not surprised that he had given her no notice of his arrival and no indication of why he was in Sheffield. Clara was due to meet Jay and it was not convenient. She had no wish to see her feckless brother. Five minutes later George appeared at the door, looked vaguely around the bar and fumbled his way across to her.

"Hey, Clar, am I glad to see you. Bit of a muddle. Need a bit of help." He slumped into the seat opposite her. He hadn't shaved. His pupils were slightly dilated and his skin was a pasty yellow.

"What's up?" she said, trying to conceal her distaste. "Why are you here?"

"Get me a drink, would you and I'll explain. I would get you one, I meant to get you one but things have gone a bit tits up." Clara hesitated. "A beer, just get me a beer."

She went to the bar, fetched a half of bitter for him and some mineral water for herself and returned. He swallowed it, almost in one.

"So?" she said.

"I've been in Manchester," George said. "I'm back in touch with Mikey. I'm writing songs again."

"Well, that's good."

"Yeah, except they still don't want me back in the band. They got me to go all the way up there and Mum paid the train fare for me and then Mikey says they just want the songs, not me. And that really pissed me off 'cos it was my songs that got them where they were. And so then, I had a bit of a heavy night of it, and the cock-up is I've lost my return ticket and I only had enough money to get a single to come across and see you."

Clara looked at him, the familiar rage rising from her stomach.

"Listen," he said beginning to sing quietly. He still had a beautiful voice and the melody was unusual, its falling notes whispering a melancholy refrain. "'In all your blue fragility/ rests my culpability/and so I weep, earth, I weep'. You see, Clar, I've been listening to you – I care too. You think I'm just a drunken dickhead but I think about stuff too." The hurt in his ravaged features was momentarily genuine.

"You've always written beautiful songs George," she said. "But maybe you need to go back into rehab first."

"That's what Dad says," he replied gloomily. "He's got some place in America he says would fix me up proper but Mum just cries when he talks about it."

The bar was beginning to fill up and Jay appeared, through the crush of people. He walked purposively across to their table and kissed Clara affectionately on the cheek, taking a curious sideways look at George. She introduced them.

"Drink, anyone?" asked Jay.

"You could get me a beer," George said quickly, before Clara could intervene.

"Clara?"

She shook her head. "I've got a seminar to get to shortly." Jay went over to the bar.

"Is he a new one?" George asked. "Did you give up on the geeky chap?"

"None of your business," Clara said shortly. She took out her purse. "Listen George, I can give you enough for the bus, but that's all. OK?"

George pouted. "You're selfish, Clara. You're not very sisterly, y'know. I've come all this way to see you and you're really not being very nice."

"Do you want it or not?"

"You've got your student loan and you've got all that money you earned in the summer and you know how hard it is for me, having to ask Mum for money all the time."

Clara held out the notes. "Yes or no?"

George took the money and pushed it into his pocket. Jay returned with two pints of beer and began to chat affably, allowing George to riff on his favourite topics – the egotism of lead guitarists, the perfidy of agents and his own song writing. Clara relaxed. Jay was so genuinely interested in other people it was no hardship to him to pass half an hour with someone like her brother. She resolved to try to imitate him more, to refuse to let people get under her skin. She looked up at the old-fashioned station clock above the bar and noticed that it was ten minutes to one.

She stood up abruptly. "I'm late. I've got a seminar." She swallowed the remains of her mineral water, grabbed her bag and kissed Jay appreciatively. She gave George a quick hug. "Go carefully," she said to him. "And love to Mum and Dad."

"And you, sis." He waved an arm expansively as she vanished through the double doors, and turned back to Jay. "You known my sister long?"

"A few months."

"You take care of her then. She's a good one, my sister." George had the slightly exaggerated speech of the perpetual drunk. "I'd get you a drink," he continued "only the reason is, I'm a bit embarrassed for cash at present. That's why I had to come and see Clar."

"Don't worry mate. I've got to go and I'm driving."

"Right, right." George sucked again at the last dregs in his glass.

"I can get you another one though, if you want."

George's face lit up. "Yeah? Well I won't say no. It'd set me up for the effing bus."

Jay went to the bar and when he came back George was holding a mobile phone in his hand.

"This yours mate?" Jay put the drink down and shook his head. "Then it must be Clara's. It was on the table here. She must have left it behind."

"I'll take it. I'm seeing her later." Jay put out his hand for it.

"Whoa, hold on, hold on. How do I know you'll give it to her? How do I know you aren't going to sell it? She's my sister, you know. I gotta look after her. It's a valuable phone." He stumbled over the word 'valuable' and Jay realised that he had probably been drinking since he got up that morning. George was playing with the phone, tossing it provocatively from hand to hand.

"Come to think of it, I could sell it myself. I could get a few quid. Which would serve the little bitch right."

"It wouldn't do you much good. You don't know her passwords."

"Now that's where you're wrong, Mr Smart Arse. Clara only ever uses our birthdays – we're all the fourth of the month except for her – July's me, January's our Mum and February's our Dad." He fiddled again with the phone and it sprang into life. "Look at that. She hasn't got any protection on it at all – you just turn it on and away you go."

Jay reached across and tried to take it from him.

"No you don't." George had the belligerent expression of the cornered drunk. Half of the new pint had disappeared already. Jay sat back in his seat and considered.

"Reckon I could get ten quid, twenty quid for this," George said. "It's a nice piece of kit. What do you think?"

"I think you should give it to me so I can give it back to Clara and that you should go and get your bus."

"Make me."

Jay looked at him. He could knock him to the ground without difficulty but the bar was now crowded with lunchtime customers and he couldn't afford a scene. He didn't want the police to be called. He reached slowly into his back pocket for his wallet. "I'll give you a fiver for it," he said.

George laughed derisorily. "You gotta be joking. Twenty and you can have it."

Jay opened his wallet, showing it to George. "Ten quid. That's all I've got."

"You've got some change, haven't you? Ten quid and all your change."

Jay found four one pound coins and placed them on the table, alongside the two five pound notes. George quickly reached towards the money but Jay had slapped his own hand over it before George could grab it. "The phone first." George slowly released the phone, shoved the money in his pocket, swallowed the last of his beer and headed rapidly for the door, just turning to wave: "Cheers, mate. Enjoy my tight-arsed sister."

The phone started to ring. It was Clara, speaking from someone else's phone and panicking.

"Yes, yes, I've got it," he said. "I'll drop it in later. But this is serious Clara. You've got no protection on your phone and your dozy brother knows all your passwords."

Later that evening, Jay sat in Clara's compact student room, fiddling with her phone and then fiddling with her computer. She leant her head comfortably against him.

"So here's where you enter the new password. You need a combination of letters and numbers and other symbols. And you need a different one for every account."

"But how will I ever remember them all?"

"Fix the laptop first, so no-one else can get into it if you leave it lying around."

Clara looked at him helplessly.

"You need a system. So, for example, think of a couple of people you know well..."

"Like you and Ruby?"

"Don't tell me – but yes. Then take the first two letters of each of their names, decide that two letters are lower-case and two are upper-case and pick a symbol – doesn't matter what."

"So – lower-case ja, upper-case RU, ampersand - "

"Don't tell me, Clara. It's important that you're the only person who knows this. But yes, that would do. That's the bit you have to remember. Then for each account you add a birthday to that. And all you write down is a person's name. Put it in a notebook somewhere."

"So in my notebook I'd write 'laptop – Mum'? But what I'd enter online would be jaRU&0401?"

"Exactly. So anyone finding your list is none the wiser – only you know what it means. But stop telling me."

"I think I'd like you to know," she said.

Clara had discovered a deep pleasure in relying on Jay. Throughout adolescence she had depended on Ruby to introduce her to the ordinary matters of adult life – everything from how to cope with her periods to how to fill out her university application had been done with Ruby's guidance. Her father had believed that young people should be left to make their own mistakes while her mother was clearly as adrift as Clara was herself on anything beyond the intricacies of the County Archive where she worked. Gail Fortune's litany of "Oh dear" and "I don't know" had quickly taught Clara that it was pointless to seek her mother's advice on even the most commonplace of problems. Without Ruby, Clara panicked in every new situation, covering her anxiety with chilly reserve or a false and fragile assertion of competence. Jay's easy willingness to explain brought her welcome relief. She flourished in the warmth of his regard, asking questions, admitting her ignorance and becoming genuinely more confident. It was novel to her to be cared for without criticism. She snuggled against his shoulder.

"You're hopeless," he said, kissing her, "absolutely hopeless."

Esther

As October slid damply into November, Esther found herself increasingly anxious. She was worried about Felix. He was monosyllabically cheerful in his phone calls, saying that everything was "Fine, fine" until she probed a little and he would become combative: "Don't ask me – I'll only have to tell you lies." When she protested that she was genuinely interested, Felix would shift his stance and accuse her sarcastically of interference: "I'm an adult Mum. Remember? I've performed that unusual trick called growing up."

Esther read the papers. The government released a map showing the world in 2060 – parts of Africa uninhabitable, deserts stretching across Southern Europe, major cities vanishing beneath a rising sea. Felix and Jane would be old people then and their grandchildren the age they were now, struggling to make a future in a wrecked world. The rain pattered on the skylight windows and she felt unbearably sad. There were pessimistic reports about the intentions of China and the United States. The Prime Minister warned that the world was on the brink of a catastrophic future and an activist travelling to Copenhagen had already been turned back by the police under terrorism laws. She knew that sooner or later there would be an action and that Felix would be involved. But something else was wrong. Esther phoned Jane.

"Is it that girl?" she asked.

"Of course," Jane replied. "She's ditched him for someone else – someone in the same circle. But he's well shot of her. Much too young, hopelessly neurotic, totally unsuitable.'

Shot of her or not, Esther knew that her son would not, as Jane advised, forget about Clara Fortune. His affections, once engaged, were constant. Her heart ached for him and she cursed the Fortune family.

Thomas was causing her concern of a quite different kind. Over the last few weeks he had made a complete volte-face. From insisting on the reality of his feelings for Nicole he had switched seamlessly to describing himself as the victim of an erotic transference, tangled in the unfortunate web of Nicole's sexual fantasies. He also now presented himself as an expert on the subject. He had written a popularising and rather poor explanation of it in his Sunday column and when he spoke to Esther on the matter, he patronised her, quoting a multiplicity of authors as if she had not read them. His own behaviour was completely forgotten. His passionate attachment, his careless disregard for therapeutic boundaries and his sexual involvement with Nicole seemed no longer to exist in his mind. She could not decide whether he believed the story he now spun or whether it was a consciously constructed lie. And she could not decide which was worse – to be so completely self-deceiving or so utterly contemptuous of the truth.

She lit the fire in the sitting room that looked out over the garden and stood peering into the dark, rain-drenched garden. The restlessness would not leave her. She flicked through programmes on TV, made herself supper and then sat, motionless in the armchair, wishing for it to be time for bed, time to end the day and its difficulties.

Nestled between two volumes of a dictionary on the bottom shelf was an old pamphlet. Esther had not looked at it for a long time, though she knew perfectly well it was there. She pulled it out. '*The Story of Esther*' proclaimed the title in strong, black letters. It was the only thing she had taken with her from her childhood home, the day her sister Ruth had helped her escape. The pamphlet's explanation of the Biblical story ended with a short prayer which Esther had repeated every night until the day she had left: 'Lord make me as faithful and obedient as thy servant Esther that I may truly serve Thy purpose. Amen.'

She missed her family still. Her long-dead father, her mother, her sister and her brothers, even her angry, elder brother Reuben. On nights like this she could not stop her mind from playing 'what-if?' What if I had never gone to university? Never met Gordon? Kept my faith? Married within the Community? I would not have disgraced my mother. I would not have broken my father's heart. Reuben would not have become a tyrant. Gordon would still be alive. I have blighted the lives of so many people. I have been neither faithful nor obedient.

She rang her friend Meena and Meena came round. Meena made chai, a sweet, comforting mixture of warm milk, tea and spices. They sat side by side on the sofa and once they were settled, Meena said "I could hear from your voice that all is not well." She stroked Esther's arm. She was a small, neat woman with a heart-shaped face and a small, red bindi on her forehead, attached neatly between her eyes.

"I'm not good at the moment," Esther said.

"Is it the old trouble?"

"The old trouble and new ones."

Meena had known Esther since their eldest children were babies and their friendship had deepened as they discovered that they shared a sense of being outsiders. Meena and her husband straddled a sometimes awkward line between the Gujarati community and the English friends they had made through work and their children, while Esther struggled to explain the peculiarities of her background and felt that she constantly misunderstood the most commonplace customs of her contemporaries. How often should you phone your friends? When were you supposed to take a gift? What was the correct way to address your child's teacher? They had laughed together over their mistakes and embarrassments and been delighted at the enduring friendship that had developed between their second children, Felix and Anusha.

Sometimes Esther envied Meena's wide network of siblings, cousins, aunties and uncles, the rounds of religious festivals, elaborate weddings and family celebrations. Sometimes Meena envied Esther's privacy, her self-sufficiency and independence. Meena had become used to Esther's autumn descents into misery. Some years Esther seemed to escape: the mood would hardly touch her. In others it would overwhelm her.

Meena picked up the pamphlet that lay on the floor. The cover showed a picture of the biblical Esther being dressed by servants in preparation for her first meeting with King Asahueras. Esther knew the picture intimately, from the beautiful, silent face, to the individual pearls which hung around her crown, to the camel sculpted on the side of the pot holding the rose tree at her side. It had played a central role in her childish dreams of marriage.

"You've been looking at this again?"

"Sometimes I can't help myself. I time-travel. I rewrite the story. "

"You've been playing 'What if?'"

"That's why I rang you."

Meena replaced the pamphlet between the dictionaries. "You should dream of the future, not the past."

"I don't seem able to see the future. I don't know what I'm for any more. When the children were young, it was obvious. I was there to look after them, to work for them, to love them. But now...What's the point of me?"

Meena reminded her of her children's love, of the friends who cared, of the work she was respected for but it made no difference. "Something has upset you," Meena said, "Something particular."

Esther told her about Felix. They had both wondered, once, whether Felix and Anusha would transform their childhood companionship into a romance but they hadn't. When they were five years old Anusha had declared repeatedly, "When I'm grown up I'm going to marry Felix," but the childhood friendship had stayed just that – a friendship. They sparred like siblings.

"He's like Anusha," Meena said. "Anusha thinks all men should instantly understand her as well as Felix does. She makes no allowances so they find her difficult and then they break her heart. I think Felix does the same."

"So what do we do?"

Meena laughed: "You want me to arrange marriages for them?"

Esther smiled, imagining strong-willed Anusha's response.

Meena shook her head. "We do nothing. We wait for them to find out."

Esther sipped the dregs of her chai. Her mood had not lifted, despite the smile.

"It's something else, something more," Meena persisted.

Eventually Esther told Meena guardedly about Thomas Fortune, being careful not to mention his name or any details that might identify him. Meena asked the same question that Tisch had done.

"Is he a bad man? Or a foolish one?"

"I thought he was foolish," she said. "I thought he wanted my help to recover from a stupid mistake. But now I'm not sure. He's arrogant and he hides things. I can't reach him and so I look at everything else I do and think it's useless too. It infects the rest of my work."

The logs on the fire sputtered and the flames threw shadows across the dark floor. Gradually the words spilled out of her.

"It's like I'm nothing but an observer. I watch other people's lives go by – my children, my friends, my patients. I observe their lives but I can't do anything, even if they wanted me to. I just sit there, cataloguing people's misery, witnessing their grief. I'm like the conservationists who log the decline of species after species, another one endangered, another on the Red List, another extinct, but they can't stop it, they can't do anything."

Meena placed an arm round her friend's shoulders. "You're a good person, Esther," she said. "I know you help people. You don't deserve this. You tell this man it's time to pack his bags."

The rain dripped on, bending the branches of the trees with its weight, soaking the grass and running in noisy rivers from the gutters and pipes. Eventually Meena took up her umbrella and stepped back into the black night.

"I'll ring you," she said.

"Thank you."

Esther watched her tiny figure bent against the wind till she reached the corner of the street. 'Be strong and of a good courage' said the voice as she put out the lights and climbed the stairs. She wondered wryly whether it was the strength of Joshua to fight battles or the strength of the early church to face martyrdom that was more likely to come to her. She slept without dreaming.

Clara

After a couple of nights of sleeping crammed into Clara's single bed, Jay had said laughing:

"Clara – you have to move, you have to get a place that will fit a double bed."

"But I like being up close with you," she had said, picking up his jokey mood and snuggling into his shoulder.

"And I like being up close with you," he had said, "but not so close that your elbows puncture my rib cage."

She had said: "Don't you have a place we can go to?"

"I'd prefer to stay at yours. I reckon you're going to have to find another place if we're going to carry on seeing each other."

She had looked at him to see if he was serious and was alarmed to see that he was.

"But I can't..." she had stammered. "I'm paid up till the end of term and I have a contract for the whole year."

He had shrugged, as if it was her problem and pulled on his work boots. "I'm not very domestic," he said. "Think about it. I've got to go to work."

Terrified that she had annoyed him, she spent the morning scouring the small ads, calculating the cost of breaking her contract, paying a deposit and a month's rent in advance and realising that she couldn't possibly afford it.

He met her the following evening after her affinity group meeting and walked back towards the centre of town with her. She was very quiet.

"What's up?"

"I can't afford it."

"Afford what?"

"To rent somewhere else."

"Why would you want to do that?"

"Because you said...because we need...because my bed's so small."

And he had laughed. "My bad mood," he said. "You shouldn't take me seriously."

"I spent the whole morning looking at the small ads, working out my money..."

He stopped beneath a lamppost and drew her towards him. He stroked her hair, damp in the night air, and kissed her softly on the lips.

"Clara – you are so sweet. I don't deserve you," he said. "I'm an old grouch with my bad moods."

"So we could stay at your place?"

"Yeah. Not tonight. It's a mess. But yeah."

Jay's moods disconcerted her. He could be unpredictably withdrawn or abruptly terse. When he was due to travel away on a job he would frequently be distracted and irritable. When he came back he would be briefly distant. It would take a little while for him to return to the man she knew and loved, the kind, attentive, dependable Jay. Her increasing reliance on him made his volatile shifts hard to bear.

It was a couple of weeks before Jay took her to his place. He lived off the London Road, quite a way out of town. The one-bedroom flat stood in an anonymous block behind a row of takeaways, a betting shop and a shabby launderette.

"I thought you'd have lived in a shared house," she said, thinking of the people in her affinity group, with their cheerful, messy kitchens, anarchist posters and communal meals.

"Bit of a loner, me. I get grumpy. Need my own space."

The flat was sparsely furnished and strangely anonymous.

"I thought you said your place was a mess," she teased.

"I cleared up. For you."

The sheets on the bed showed the fold-lines from their packaging and the box from the new duvet was pushed behind the bathroom door.

"You've bought new bedding."

"The old stuff wasn't fit for a dog," he said. "All in honour of you Clara. I run the risk of becoming domesticated."

She poked around in the bathroom, opened the wardrobe doors and looked in the kitchen cabinets and the fridge. For the most part they were empty. His clothes spilled out from a holdall on the bedroom floor and his jacket hung on the back of the door. There was some milk in the fridge, tea and coffee in one of the cupboards. A bottle of wine and a vegetarian ready-meal stood on the kitchen counter.

"You don't have any books," she said, running a finger along a set of empty shelves.

"I travel light."

"What do you like to read?"

"I'm not much of a reader really – I never got into all that."

"But you must have read the climate change stuff – you've read George Monbiot, Mark Lynas, all the important people?"

"I reckon there's only three things you need to know about climate change: – it's real, it's caused by us and it's very, very dangerous."

Clara looked at him, puzzled. The words were taken from one of her talks. He laughed. "I listen to you, Clara. You're my education. You and all the other people in the movement. I don't need books."

She was flattered but disappointed too. "I think you'd like them if you tried," she said.

"At the end of a long day, I'd rather be with you than with a book," he said, moving across to kiss her.

In the kitchen Clara helped him prepare the supper, shaking the bagged salad onto the two plates he took from the cupboard. "Shall I make some salad dressing?" she asked.

"I'm not sure I've got any garlic or vinegar."

The truth was there wasn't much of anything in the kitchen. It was puzzlingly ill-equipped. Clara looked along the worktop – cornflakes, cooking oil, sugar, salt and pepper seemed to be the sum of it. Face down, at the end were two photographs. She turned them over. They were school portraits, a girl of about ten with her dark hair caught in bunches, and a boy of maybe seven with a crew cut and a missing front tooth. She held them up to him questioningly.

"My sister's kids," he said, putting the ready-meal into the microwave. "My nephew and niece, Jasmine and Connor.

"I didn't know you had a sister."

"Lots of things you don't know."

"You should put them up properly. They're nice."

"I think I'll put them away. I don't want to lose them." Jay's voice was suddenly tight and proprietorial. Clara felt she shouldn't have commented on the pictures, shouldn't even have looked at them. He went through to the bedroom and stuffed the pictures in his holdall. Disconcerted, she picked up the wine bottle and wrestled with the corkscrew. He came back into the room and took the bottle from her, gently brushing her hands as he did so.

"Male privilege," he said, expertly popping out the cork and filling a glass. One of his mercurial mood changes had restored his crinkly-eyed smile. His deft, confident movements enchanted her and she smiled at him, relieved. They sat down on opposite sides of the small table and he raised his glass. "To us."

"To us," she echoed.

They ate in silence for a while. Clara would have liked to talk but Jay seemed content just to eat. She stole glances across the table at him. He tore chunks of bread from the loaf, wiping them enthusiastically round his plate and then sliced into the ripe camembert, spreading it onto the bread and piling salad on top.

"You eat like a bird," he said, looking at the way she carefully separated out each item of salad before placing it carefully in her mouth.

It was what Ruby's mother used to say, a remark that had always made her feel both criticised and cared for. He spread a chunk of bread with camembert and passed it across to her. "Eat," he said. "Eat properly."

She nibbled at the edge of the bread unsure how to reply but Jay was speaking again, changing the subject.

"There's things I ought to tell you Clara."

She looked at him questioningly, anxious about what he might say next.

"I think you've worked out that I don't like talking about myself."

"That's fine. You don't have to tell me things you don't want to."

It wasn't true. Clara was hurt that her long explanations about her family, her brother, her old friends and her new ones were not reciprocated. She wanted to know about his parents, where he came from, what he'd done before he came to Sheffield but her questions typically drew one word answers in response. Occasionally there would be a story about his workmates, a hint of a past spent working on building sites abroad or an allusion to a family he was estranged from. She was learning to wait but he was difficult to read and every time she mis-stepped she was terrified that she would lose him for good.

"Some things it's only fair that you know," Jay said. "You've worked out I've not been in this flat very long."

She nodded.

"And the reason is to do with Paula. You know Paula?"

Clara did know Paula. She was an older woman, a single parent in her mid-thirties, on the fringes of the movement, restricted in what she could do by family responsibilities. She was vociferous and opinionated when she did make it to a meeting and Clara had found her intimidating. She was puzzled that Jay should have been attracted to someone so old and so forceful.

"I used to have a scene with her. It's over, been over for a time but I was still lodging there till recently. She needed the money and it was convenient for me with all my working away. That's the reason I haven't got a lot of stuff here. I haven't been here long."

"How long were you with Paula?" she asked.

"Couple of years."

"And is it really over?" She couldn't stop herself from asking.

"That's what I said." His tone told her to stop but she pushed on.

"Were you still seeing her while we've been together?"

"None of your business."

"But you told me, you told me there wasn't anyone else."

"There isn't – at the moment. But I explained. I'm not into monogamy. Don't start thinking this is an exclusive relationship."

"But that doesn't mean I shouldn't know, does it? Surely we should be honest with each other. Isn't polyamory about being honest, being open?"

"I've been honest with you Clara. I've been open. I told you right at the start what I'm like. No illusions."

"But don't we have to agree what polyamory means for us?"

"I know what it means. You know what it means. I'm free to see other people. You're free to see other people. End of story."

"But I thought..." What had she thought? She had no idea. Jay had told her, right from the start, that he was polyamorous and it had felt exciting. It had made her feel as if she was in the vanguard of a new way of doing everything – not just politics but relationships and social life too. Despite his capricious moods, Clara had felt secure in Jay's care and regard. She texted him or spoke to him almost every day and she had felt proud of their relationship and contemptuous of those stuck in the dull routines of convention. But now she felt the chill of his disdain, the terror of having displeased him and the spectre of abandonment.

Her confusion must have shown on her face. Jay softened as quickly as he had flared up, leaned across and stroked her cheek, gently pushing her hair back behind her ear. "Let's just enjoy what we've got shall we?"

His touch brought the tears to her eyes. Forcing them back she nodded and said, "You're the best thing that's ever happened to me, Jay."

He didn't reciprocate but said, "We're OK then?" Her fingers were shredding a piece of bread and she was staring at the pattern on the plastic-topped table. He took her hand away from the bread and spread the remainder with cheese. "Eat."

She looked up at him and he repeated "Eat. You're too thin."

Clara moved the bread slowly to her lips. The sharp crust felt like knives in her throat but she chewed obediently, pushing her feelings down with the food.

After a few moments Jay repeated: "We're OK then?" and she managed to reply, "Yes. We're OK. It's just that I thought we ought to be talking about it."

"My Dad used to say 'Don't ask questions you don't want to hear the answers to,' and I reckon he was right. Laying it all out on the table just makes people upset and jealous. Look at you now. You're upset. I'm irritated. And there's no need."

She drank in the reference to his Dad, longing to ask him more about his family. Realising it would only bring more irritation she simply said "I'm sorry."

"You're a lovely person Clara," he said. "You're beautiful and you're smart and one day you'll find someone much better than me. I like to think I'm trustworthy. I like to think I'm sincere. But you need to remember – I don't do commitment. I'm not that kind of guy."

"OK," she said. "OK."

She sipped at her mineral water, he drank another glass of wine, and they left for that evening's meeting.

Esther

When Thomas Fortune entered her consulting room the following morning Esther felt she was ready for him but she was not prepared for his opening speech.

"I have something very serious to talk to you about Esther."

The expression on his face was a new one and she could not quite pin down the tone: a headmaster sorrowfully expelling a pupil? An employer raising the inevitability of redundancy? Was Thomas about to tell her he was quitting? She opened her hands in an invitation to continue.

"There are rumours circulating about me amongst the trainees at the Foundation – rumours of my having had an affair with a patient – and I've come to the distressing conclusion that the only possible source of these rumours is yourself."

Esther's stomach flipped, her mind racing over what she had said to Tisch three weeks ago and what she had said to Meena the night before. Meena she quickly dismissed: she had not mentioned Thomas' name, it was only twelve hours ago and Meena had no connections in the psychotherapy world. Tisch? No. Tisch hated gossip. She stiffened in her seat and said, "Thomas, that's absurd. What on earth do you mean?"

"There are only two people who know about my difficulties with Nicole – Nicole herself and you. Nicole has no connections to the Foundation, quite apart from the fact that she would have no interest and no motive in circulating rumours about me. That leaves you – and Brenda Burton your training patient."

"You imagine I would talk to one of my patients about you?"

He spread his hands sententiously. "Esther, I have to say that I am surprised – and shocked too. But I have come to learn that people are not always what they seem and that sometimes those who set themselves up as the most trustworthy are those one should be most wary of."

Thomas might have been talking about himself. Outrage gave her strength. She looked straight at him and said: "Thomas, I have said nothing about you anywhere that could have led to trainees at the Foundation gossiping about you. You came to me because confidentiality was extremely important to you, because you were anxious about your reputation, because you knew that you had made a mistake that could have terrible repercussions on your career if it became publicly known. I have respected that confidentiality."

A flicker of doubt crossed his face and she finished, "I am not the source of this rumour."

He was silent. Esther allowed a good thirty seconds to elapse and then continued. "If you wish, we can discuss where this rumour might have come from and what you might do about it. But if not – if you are not prepared to trust my professional discretion, if you are not prepared to discuss your work openly and realistically with me – then we should agree to go our separate ways."

Thomas's face weakened. She realised he had not thought this through. He had turned up, full of indignation but had not imagined where his accusation might take him. He had not thought beyond the drama of his self-righteous opening lines. This was not the old bravura Thomas, the man who never put a political foot wrong. This was a man on the run. She glimpsed again the troubled child, the uncertain teenager, the gauche student. She softened her face a fraction but she did not relent.

"Well?"

He was suddenly awkward, his eyes were on the floor, then on the bookshelves, anywhere but on her.

"I...I agree that it's possible that there could be some other explanation," he said finally without meeting her eyes.

"Shall we talk about that possibility?"

He seemed to acquiesce and she said, with a sudden flash of intuition, "Tell me why you were so interested in the Association for the Prevention of Psych-Abuse."

Thomas flannelled briefly, asserting his right to an interest in the topic, claiming that they represented an interesting development in the field and then collapsed.

"My old colleague, John Williamson, the man I trained with and who's their special advisor is the man who referred Nicole to me. I'd completely forgotten that was how she came to me. And I'd also forgotten that he was some kind of distant cousin of hers. But I don't think he could be behind this rumour. He's not that kind of chap – terribly upright. "

"Might she have spoken to him?"

"I know she saw him. She told me she'd run into him at a family party. But she didn't know him well. She wouldn't have talked to him about something as intimate as this."

"Might he have told her about APPA?"

"I can't think why."

Esther took her laptop from the desk and found the APPA website. "When you spoke to me about APPA before, I took a look at their website and there was something that I noticed."

She passed the machine to him. Under the heading 'Get Involved' were two short paragraphs of text. After an invitation to survivors to volunteer with the organisation and make it their own, it read 'We also welcome professionals who can use their expertise to offer advocacy, support and counselling to people recovering from Psych-Abuse. Placements may be available to those in training.'

Thomas passed the machine back to her and quickly took out his own, demanding "How do I connect to your Wi-Fi?"

She told him, watching as he rapidly pressed the keys and waited impatiently for the machine to connect. There was a viciousness in his voice when he spoke again.

"I've got it. Nailed it. The little bitch." He had logged into the private part of the training organisation's website and was scanning the list of trainees and their placements.

"Joanna Macready," he said, looking at Esther in triumph. "I should have suspected. Placement with APPA, started last January. Uppity, gossipy attention-seeker. I never liked her." He paused and snapped the laptop shut. "Well, she's out. She's finished."

"Thomas..." Esther began.

"I know, I know. I can't confront her directly. But she's broken confidentiality. She's betrayed the trust of a client. That's a cardinal sin as far as I'm concerned. And there are other ways to fail someone. She won't last."

He was excited. His cheeks were flushed and there were beads of sweat above his upper lip.

"Thomas," Esther managed to say in the brief pause which followed. "I understand that you're angry but I think we need to think about this more rationally."

"I've never been more rational in my life. I won't have this. I won't be dragged through the dirt by some wannabee therapist who believes every juvenile fantasy she's spun by every disturbed patient who waltzes through the door."

Esther found her eyes focusing on the cushions on the couch. The room felt fragmented by his anger and their usually soft colours appeared to her as shards of brittle light, reflected in the winter sun.

"Thomas, it looks like Nicole has made contact with APPA, whether through her cousin John or independently and we need to think about the consequences of that. It's possible that they'll encourage her to make a complaint and I think you may need to be prepared for that."

"There are no grounds for complaint. An eroticised transference is no ground for complaint."

"When you first came to see me, you were considering leaving your wife and embarking on a permanent relationship with Nicole."

"Yes, yes. I was right about leaving my wife, wrong about setting up with Nicole. I understand that now. I'd let myself get embroiled with her fantasies. I'm past that. It was temporary."

"But you also told me that there had been repeated physical contact and some sexual contact."

"The physical contact was justifiable therapeutically. I stand by that. I absolutely stand by that."

"And the sexual contact?"

"It was a mistake, a stupid mistake. But she initiated it. She wanted it. It was consensual."

In Esther's more generous moments she viewed Thomas as a man who was the victim of his own ignorance, someone whose fallibility could be, if not excused, at least understood and who might with help recover from the errors he had stumbled into. But as he spoke now, she could feel the power of the man, how convincing his self-deception was, how easy it could be to accept his fiction of persecution.

"I don't think that is how a complaints panel would see it," she said.

Her words riled him as she knew they would and he began again.

"Sometimes Esther, I feel that you are not behind me, that you fail to understand just how pernicious an eroticised transference can be, what jeopardy it places a therapist in. The domination of this profession by women means that men's difficulties in this area are not properly addressed, in the literature, in supervision or in a bloody complaints panel, should it ever end up there. It's something that needs addressing and which I'm going to be writing about but in the meantime I'd appreciate it if you could keep your prejudices to yourself."

Thomas had run himself to a stop. There was no point in trying to rebut the self-deception, the arrogance or the misogyny. Esther said instead:

"I'm sorry that what I said upset you. What I meant was that you need to consider the possibility that Nicole might bring a complaint against you."

He was silent.

"Have you spoken to her recently?"

He muttered a 'No'.

"If she was thinking of bringing a complaint, there's a lot that can be done short of that, through mediation, through apology, through some kind of acknowledgment of mistakes made..."

"Nicole would never want to bring a complaint against me," Thomas said, recovering his voice. "You're absolutely wrong about that. Wrong. Wrong. Wrong. I know that she would never do that. But perhaps I should contact her..."

"It might be better done through a third party," she said. "And I also think you should contact your insurers."

He looked at her in surprise.

"Your professional indemnity insurance," she said. "Most policies require you to alert them to anything that might lead to a claim. I think it might be wise to speak to them."

Thomas was silent for a moment and then acquiesced. "No harm in giving them a heads-up, I suppose."

As Esther waited for the click of the door, the words that echoed in her head were those of Jeremiah. 'The arrogance of thy heart hath deceived thee. I will bring thee down from thence, saith the Lord.' She realised that she was afraid for him, that she feared that it was beyond her power to stop him and that she was simply a witness to the inexorable progress of his self-destruction.

Felix

Felix joined the queue waiting outside the town hall. He was disconcerted to see Clara and Jay standing a few places in front of him. He hung back, squeezing himself into the shadow of the building. Clara was talking animatedly to other people in the queue, explaining the techniques of the 'Story of Self, Us and Now' and the talks and workshops she did. Jay had his arm proprietorially on her shoulders. Felix looked at them bitterly. He had enabled her presence here. He had introduced her to the groups she was now part of, opening the door to the people who were now her friends. Jay, turning his head slightly, spotted him.

"Felix," he called "How are you mate?"

Felix gave a curt nod of acknowledgment. Clara turned also and gave a confident wave before turning back to the people she was talking to. Felix, humiliated, refused to meet their eyes.

The queue began to move and they entered the large, Victorian meeting room. A rare appearance by the Secretary of State for Climate Change, who represented one of the local constituencies, had drawn a large crowd. One group of activists had established themselves in the front rows, another clustered at the back with banners and placards.

As the Copenhagen negotiations approached, opinion in the press was increasingly gloomy. The United States was unwilling to build on existing frameworks. The Chinese were unlikely to agree to verification procedures. The African nations had withdrawn from a preliminary meeting in Barcelona because the commitments by developed nations were inadequate. Conversations amongst activists swung between hope, fear and rage.

Felix could not quite describe the feeling in his gut. It reminded him of the last time he had seen his father, two weeks before his death. Gordon's new wife had been away at her parents with the baby twins. Gordon had opened a bottle of whisky and they had watched the video of ET. By the time the film had ended Gordon was incapable of making supper. Jane had put the pizza into the oven and they had gone to bed leaving their father crying quietly into his whisky. Dropping them off at their mother's house the next morning he had hugged Felix with an uncomfortable intensity. "You're what makes life worthwhile," he had said. "Never forget I love you."

Felix moved deliberately away from Clara and Jay, finding himself a seat on the other side of the hall. Stefan flopped into the seat beside him: "OK mate?"

"OK."

They chatted about football and matters that were already public knowledge, careful not to mention the coming action.

"Your Clara's doing really well, isn't she? She's got three coachloads of students signed up for the London demonstration and at least a dozen willing to come to Copenhagen."

"Sore point."

"Why's that?"

Felix gestured towards Jay. "We're no longer together."

"Sorry mate. I hadn't picked that up."

"Doesn't matter."

The minor speakers were arranging themselves on the platform. As the hum of expectant conversation increased and the Chair rose to announce the start of the evening, the group of activists at the back began a low chant "Don't be a fossil fool, no more fossil fuels" which, as the Minister made his appearance, rose to a loud crescendo accompanied by foot-stamping and cat-calls. The Minister quickly took the mike from the surprised Chair. Felix was surprised to see how much presence he had. He quickly quietened the interruption, addressing the demonstrators directly: "Thank you. Thank you. I hope that there aren't any fossil fools here and that in a few years' time there won't be any to be found anywhere on the planet."

The meeting settled itself, the Chair made his introduction, the minor speakers gave their three minute pitches and the Minister once more took the microphone. His speech moved rapidly through the suffering of people affected by floods in Bangladesh and in his own constituency, his pride at the 2008 Climate Change Act, a list of the government's achievements and their plans for a low-carbon transition. As he argued in favour of clean coal technology, claiming it would return jobs to the Yorkshire coal fields, chants of "Fossil fool, fossil fool" erupted from the back of the hall and security guards moved in to disperse the demonstrators. Finally he talked about Copenhagen. He acknowledged that the talks were at risk but he was upbeat.

"We know that change doesn't happen because politicians will it to happen. It happens because people demand that it happens. It will happen at Copenhagen because the optimists and idealists and innovators who are here tonight have been working to make it happen. Because you have been exercising the pressure, convincing the waverers, standing up to the deniers."

He praised, he flattered, he encouraged.

"Together, we are the people who can safeguard the world for future generations. We are the idealists. We are the optimists. We are the future."

The audience rewarded him with thunderous applause and the questions followed rapidly. A climate change denier made a long rambling statement that was quickly dismissed. Stefan challenged him about so-called clean coal. Helen accused him of being in thrall to neo-liberal ideology. As time began to run out it was Clara's eagerly waving hand that caught the Minister's eye. "What is it," she asked "in the run-up to Copenhagen, that we should be doing to ensure that there is a successful outcome?"

"I need you to keep up the pressure," the Minister replied. "Hold my feet closer to the fire."

The meeting closed. The Minister was whisked away and the crowds made their way slowly out of the hall.

"Coming for a drink?" asked Stefan.

The two men crossed the road together. In the pub they edged their way towards seats in the back corner and Stefan went to the bar. Felix watched as other activists came in. Owen and Sophie from his affinity group joined them. Clara, Jay and a group of young people who were presumably students settled themselves a couple of tables away. Felix pretended not to have seen Jay's cheery wave.

"What do you reckon?" Owen asked. "Can he pull it off?" He was addressing himself, as they all did, to Stefan.

"As far as Copenhagen goes, he wants a deal – that's genuine - and he'll do what he can to get one."

"And coal? All that crap about clean technologies?"

"He'll do what the elite want. Helen put her finger on it. The G8 come up with a massive investment programme for carbon capture and he has to join in. His heart may be in the right place but he's trapped by the fossil fuel lobbies, by the big money, by assumptions he's scarcely aware of."

"So what we're about to do is very, very important," Sophie grinned.

Stefan raised his hands in a gesture of caution: "Careful." Turning back to Owen he asked "Are you still rooting for Wigan Athletic?"

Owen laughed. "No option where I'm from."

The noise in the bar increased and their conversation shifted – to Sophie's involvement in the postal worker's dispute, the new nature reserve that Stefan's job made him responsible for and the public housing project that Felix hoped his firm would design to Level Six of the Code for Sustainable Homes. Occasionally Felix would catch Clara's clear Southern tones over the hubbub. He thought bitterly how confident she sounded, how the naïve, tentative girl he had met in the summer had transformed herself into a respected authority who could sit at the centre of his friends – people he had introduced her to and now felt estranged from. He sipped his beer morosely, trying to listen to Owen explain his planned PhD. A lull in the next table's conversation carried Clara's voice clearly across the bar.

"When he said 'I need you to hold my feet closer to the fire' he was talking directly to us as activists. What he meant was that he needs the pressure from direct action – not just demonstrations or pathetic little personal carbon reduction plans but real disruption."

Somebody with a quieter voice had obviously asked her what she meant because she continued. "We need to be occupying and disrupting the big polluters. What I mean is the kind of thing we're planning for..."

Her next words were drowned by a burst of laughter from an intervening table but Felix and Stefan's eyes met in alarm. Stefan, stuck in the corner, gave Felix a shove: "Stop her. Shut her up." Felix, stumbling to his feet, made his way blindly across the crowded pub. Unable to catch Clara's attention he grabbed her roughly by the shoulder, hissing "Shut up. Shut the fuck up" in her ear. Clara turned and wrenched her body away, meeting his eyes with fury. Jay was instantly on his feet and the two men stood glaring at each other.

"Don't speak to Clara like that." Jay spat the words like bullets across the table.

Felix's hand dropped to his side and then went automatically to his glasses, nervously removing and replacing them. Jay continued to stare at him, forcing his gaze to return to meet him.

"I just meant...it's important..." said Felix.

"I don't care what you meant." Jay gave a jerk of his head. "Sit down and finish your drink. I can deal with this."

Felix turned, went back to his table and slumped silently into his seat.

"What happened?" asked Stefan. "Is it OK?"

"It's fine," Felix said curtly. "Jay's on to it. But I need to go." He pulled on his coat and shoving his hands into his pockets left the pub.

Checking his phone he saw a missed call and a text from his sister Jane. "Thinking of Dad. Thinking of you," it said. He walked back to the flat he shared with Owen, made a cup of coffee and shut himself in his bedroom. He sat in silence, hunched up on the bed for a while and then slowly scrolled through to Jane's number. She answered immediately.

"I thought you weren't going to call."

"Sorry. I was at a meeting."

"I rang Mum and she's fine but I think she'd like you to ring."

Jane liked to memorialise their father's death. As a teenager she would mark the anniversary by placing a candle in front of his photograph, dimming the lights and sitting in silence for quarter of an hour. Their mother, finding this mawkish, had tried to discourage her and Felix, who would have preferred to forget that his father had ever existed, had been relieved to see that it was disapproved of. But Jane had said it helped her and their mother had given way, sitting quietly with Jane while Felix had fidgeted in the background. As he grew older he had contrived always to be absent on the anniversary.

"Did you light a candle?" he asked.

"I did. It's been twelve years."

"So he's been out of my life longer than he was in it."

Jane ignored this. "I was remembering that holiday when he took us camping."

"The one where he had the motorbike and the sidecar?" Felix was drawn in, despite himself.

"Yes. He'd got the camping equipment on the pillion and us in the sidecar and he left most of our clothes behind because there wasn't room."

"That was because he'd got a crate of beer round our feet."

Jane laughed. "Come on, it was a couple of bottles."

"How old were we?"

"I was nine. You were six. We camped in a field in Gloucestershire, somewhere near the Forest of Dean."

"I remember the woods."

He remembered his father helping them make a tree house in the woods beyond the campsite. He remembered sitting up there, alone amongst the green summer leaves, examining the insects that crawled along the bark, listening to the chatter and calls of songbirds that he couldn't identify. His father had given him a notebook and some pencils and he had drawn the creatures he found, crude but accurate observations of insect life. His father had taught him to draw. His father had shown him how to build. His father had taken him into nature. His father had begun all this.

"What else?"

Felix buried the memory of the treehouse and said, "I remember him letting us ride on the motorbike round the field. He'd hold me in front of him and you'd cling on behind."

"He did. He did."

He could hear Jane smiling in remembered delight. Perhaps this was enough. "Tell me how you are," he said. "How's school? How's Adam?"

She seemed content to let the conversation move on but she probed in response. How was he? Had he seen Clara? Was he talking to anyone about what had happened? Was he sleeping properly? He resisted and then told her what had happened that evening. When he put the phone down he realised to his surprise that he felt a little better.

Thomas

Thomas arrived at the final day of the conference fashionably late. He had not attended the first day, explaining that his commitments to patients and the demands of Mental Health Week - an extended edition of his radio show and an appearance on the 'Today' programme - would not allow it. He entered the morning coffee session with a reassuring smile for the anxious organiser and a gracious acknowledgment for the IT technician who hurried to set up his presentation.

A patient who was the son of a diplomat had once described to Thomas how the ambassador would always arrive forty-five minutes late at any reception, circulate clockwise and then leave. Thomas had thought it good advice. Declining a cup of coffee he now began to work his way around the room. His technique was always the same. Extending his right hand, he would place his left casually on the other person's shoulder. His warm smile and his memory for names and small details would briefly capture each one. An enquiry after a family member, a compliment on a recent publication or the remembrance of a previous encounter was all it took to make each person feel special. He would hold each hand for a fraction longer than was expected before releasing it with a final squeeze and moving on.

The room formed into the awkward semblance of a queue as he made his way around it. Ten seconds for trainees - "Louise, so glad you're able to be here"; a fraction longer for the ranks of acquaintances whom he allowed a short reply before breaking eye contact and releasing the hand that he held. With his enemies his smiling put-downs were necessarily abrupt: "Edgar, so sorry to see they rejected your paper." This gave him a full minute for a genuine exchange with the half dozen people who might be useful: the source of future invitations, well-paying patients or possibly the academic post he was hoping would materialise in the next twelve months.

Half-way round the room he was aware once more of the technician at his elbow. He needed to be miked up. They needed to check the light levels for the filming. Thomas smiled generously at the man. "Thirty seconds," he said, moving across to speak briefly with the president of the Institute and a visiting professor from Harvard. In the conference hall his presentation was loaded and the first slide up on the screen. The technician threaded the mike up beneath his jacket, clipping it neatly to the lapel.

Thomas flicked expertly through his slides. He had added two paragraphs which made it clear where he stood on the question of the erotic transference and had found a striking picture of a beautiful young woman and a good-looking older man to accompany them. His slides were never a dull written summary but an eclectic mix of eye-catching images that would fix what he said in the minds of his audience. He was beginning to feel comfortable. He would speak for forty-five minutes, take questions for half an hour and then be treated to a very nice lunch at the top table before the conference dispersed.

The raked seats in the auditorium were filling up nicely. At last, the Chair stood up, tapped a teaspoon against a glass and called for silence. Some stragglers, still in their outdoor coats, crept in and found seats in the less populated side aisles. The room settled down. The Chair's introduction was fulsome. They were delighted to have been able to secure Thomas Fortune as their keynote speaker. No-one had done more than he had in recent years to raise the profile of the profession. No-one had been quicker to grasp the challenges of the new millennium. He offered a rare contribution of theoretical rigour and popular appeal. He was known to the public as the compassionate face of psychotherapy and to colleagues as a courageous exemplar of theoretical innovation. "I need say no more," she concluded and sat down, smiling enthusiastically at Thomas.

Thomas rose to warm, expectant applause which he quietened with a skilful gesture as he moved to the lectern. He let his eyes pass across the room, drawing each person into his inclusive gaze.

"We are told," he said "that we live in an age of uncertainty but I want to suggest to you that alongside the confusions of identity, the instability of the ego, the crises of the self, that the unconscious is, as it ever was, the most certain part of us. It remains determined and ruthless and it is in our most intimate relationships that this paradox plays out most acutely." He clicked on the first slide – a reproduction of Fuseli's 'Nightmare'. He had them. He could feel their eager anticipation as he moved from slide to slide.

He was about five minutes in when he caught a movement in his peripheral vision. Someone in the left-hand aisle had stood up. There was movement on the right-hand side as well. Four people, dressed in capacious outdoor coats, were making their way down the steps towards the low dais on which he stood. The Chair looked towards him with surprise. Thomas looked briefly at the four women – he could see now that they were women - advancing towards him and said jokily, gesturing towards the back of the room "The exit and the toilets are that way". They ignored him and stepped up onto the dais, ranging themselves in front of the table, placing themselves between him and the audience and obscuring the audience's view of the screen. Three of them produced placards from beneath their coats, waved them briefly towards Thomas and the Chair and then held them up towards the audience. The first said in capital letters 'END', the second 'THERAPIST' and the third 'ABUSE'. At the bottom of each one was the logo of APPA, the Association for the Prevention of Psych Abuse. The fourth woman picked up the roving microphone that lay ready on the table for the question and answer session and begin to speak, loudly and clearly.

"We are here to make our voices heard. We are here to ask a profession that claims to be able to listen, to listen properly. We are here to speak truths to a profession that prefers to ignore, disavow and belittle its victims. "

Thomas stepped forward, trying to move in front of them, faltered, stepped back, tried to speak, saying "I think...if you would wait..." but as he did so the women began to stamp their feet shouting a chorus of "End therapist abuse. End therapist abuse," until he retreated. The Chair stood up and attempted the same manoeuvre with the same result. The woman spoke on.

Psychotherapy was a relationship of unequal power, she said. It provided an arena for the abuse of the vulnerable by misogynist, sexist men. Its culture was arrogant and complacent. Its complaint systems were not fit for purpose.

She gave examples of vulnerable people whose so-called treatment had compounded their difficulties. She gave examples of the way that flattery, deceit and 'gas-lighting' were used to confuse and disorientate victims. The abuse was not just sexual, it was emotional and financial too. Statistics suggested that there would be at least thirty people amongst those present who would be guilty of such abuse.

The audience were turning to each other, disconcerted. The Chair was signalling in an ineffective dumb show to a member of staff at the back. Someone shouted "Get off!" After what seemed an eternity to Thomas, two uniformed security staff appeared, stepping uncertainly towards the demonstrators. The woman held up a hand, ordering them to stop and they waited.

"I have almost finished," she said. "We will not take up much more of your time. We are from APPA. We work to support those who have been abused. We help them to recover from the treatments that have damaged them. We help them to bring claims against those who have abused them. And we work to make the public, the profession and policy makers aware of the true nature of these professions. We are appearing at a lot of events during Mental Health Week, invited and uninvited." She turned to Thomas and the Chair and finished: "You will all be hearing more from us."

Then she led her co-demonstrators in a dignified retreat, up the steps between the raked seats and out through the swing doors, followed by the two security men. The auditorium broke into a hubbub of confused chatter. One man shouted, "Bring them back. We should engage with them. We need to discuss this." He was rapidly shouted down by others demanding that Thomas should resume his presentation and as the Chair rose to her feet and once more tapped a teaspoon against the side of the glass the noise began to subside.

The Chair apologised for what she termed a 'surprising interruption' and invited Thomas to continue. He was rattled. He had lost his momentum but he attempted to rise to the situation.

"I know that everyone here," he said "takes the question of patient abuse very seriously and I hope you will join with me in applauding the courage of those who try to call us to account, however uncomfortable that may be for the profession."

There were small murmurs of approval from the audience. He smiled in acknowledgment and continued, "But our task today is not with that question but with another, equally urgent one – the relationship of our troubled times to the human need for intimacy."

He clicked on the next slide and continued with his presentation but the heart had gone out of him and out of the audience too. Their attention was no longer his. They wanted to talk about the interruption, to be scandalised, to gossip and to blame. And they had begun to think about lunch, the last bits of networking they needed to complete and their trains and flights home. He limped to the end and was rewarded with polite applause. The question and answer session was muted but as the company moved out towards the dining hall, the buzz of conversation increased in volume. Over lunch there was only one subject which people wanted to talk about: who were the demonstrators? Why had this conference been targeted? And who - if the statistics were correct - were the thirty people guilty of abusing their patients?

"Do you know anything about this outfit?" asked the Chair who was sitting next to Thomas.

"Very little." The food tasted like ash in his mouth. "I'm familiar with their website. I thought they were just a small charity who provided support for people who'd been abused. I'd no idea they got up to this sort of thing."

A woman sitting opposite joined in: "Maybe we need to be challenged. Maybe they're right. There's a good piece in today's Guardian."

"Is it really such a problem?" queried the Chair.

"Isolated incidents I think," said Thomas. "I wouldn't trust a group like this. It's very easy to take advantage of vulnerable people who've not been able to make the best use of therapy, misinterpret what's happened, build on unresolved transference issues and disappointments."

To Thomas's relief the conversation moved on. The lunch which had felt interminable finally drew to a close. He refused coffee, explaining that he was doing an extended slot on the radio station for Mental Health week, and left. Passing a newsagent's by the tube station he picked up a copy of the Guardian. By the time he reached his stop he had not found the article the woman referred to and had begun to hope that she was mistaken. His producer's cheery greeting restored him a little and he entered the studio with a slight bounce in his step. They hadn't been targeting him personally after all. It would all die down. He really had nothing to worry about.

Unlike his regular slot which was pre-recorded, this was a live phone-in and the challenge of responding spontaneously excited him. The sense of the invisible, receptive audience both comforted and stimulated him. He took two calls in quick succession, one from a woman whose mother was showing signs of dementia and one from a student whose best friend was obsessed by exercise. "I hope that's some help, Gloria" he concluded and was gratified by the way she replied, "Thank you so much Thomas." The anxieties of the morning began to drift away.

"And now we go to Sally from Dagenham who has a question about anti-depressants," said the presenter. "Go ahead Sally."

The caller's voice came through clearly. "Actually Dickie my question's about therapist abuse, specifically about therapists who use their position to pursue sexual relationships with patients. I want to ask Thomas why he and so many other therapists think it's OK to behave like this, to tolerate this and when it does come to light, to blame the victims and refuse to take responsibility for their actions."

The presenter cut in: "That's not the question we were expecting Sally, so let's find out if Thomas is able to respond." He was looking anxiously at Thomas whose face had become quite white. Thomas nodded and found to his surprise that he was stuttering in reply.

"It...it's a very important question," he stammered and then to his relief and the presenter's he found his familiar, smooth voice. "This is a distressing and difficult subject, so thank you to Sally for raising it. It's a rare an occurrence however, and always taken seriously if a complaint is received."

The caller broke in. "That's not my experience or the experience of others I've spoken to..." but the presenter cut her off saying, "Hold on Sally, let Thomas finish his answer and we'll come back to you."

Thomas continued, hardly aware of what he was saying, desperately filling the space with platitudes about responsibility, training and complaints systems. He paused to gather a final thought but the presenter cut in: "Thank you Thomas. We'll be back after the break and the traffic news with more of your questions. You're listening to Dickie Emerald and I'm 'Talking with Tom', London's favourite agony uncle."

The producer came over the headphones, apologising and promising that the next questions would be on depression, anxiety and mid-life crises as planned. Thomas managed to smile professionally and say, "No problem, no problem," but his concentration was destroyed. He stumbled through the last questions, left the studio and sat on the tube in a haze of anxiety, rattling across town to his small flat, his consulting room and the remaining patients of the day.

It was gone eight 'o' clock when he finally opened the newspaper again. This time he found the article, in a back section that dealt with social issues. The full page piece featured the work of APPA and there tucked between the story of its founder, the arguments and the statistics, were three personal testimonies. 'Confusion, self-doubt and guilt are common reactions amongst those who have been abused by their therapists' he read. And then:

'Nicole Morgenson described how initially she had believed she was in love with her therapist and how he had encouraged her affection, finally seducing her in his consulting room. 'He was a lovely man,' she said 'And in some ways I still have feelings for him – that's what makes it so difficult to come to terms with the fact that what I suffered was actually abuse. He was taking advantage of his position and my vulnerability. It wasn't till I ended the therapy and talked with a family member about what had happened that I began to understand it. I couldn't have got through this without APPA.'

Thomas put down the paper and sat staring at the white plastered wall. Esther had been right, the bloody woman had been right. John Williamson had put Nicole in touch with APPA and these lies were the result. It wouldn't take much for someone to connect this with the article in *Starstruck*. He could be identified, labelled, destroyed. He moved to the window and stared down at the street below. There were a few people standing at the doors of the corner pub, smoking. A taxi cruised past with its light up. A group of young women clattered by in high heels, laughing and joking. They reminded him of Nicole.

Thomas had, as Esther had suggested, contacted his insurers but he had not spoken with Nicole. The idea of apologising to her, negotiating with her, pleading with her not to damage him, all these were anathema to him. He could not imagine how such a phone call could commence, let alone conclude. He preferred to think of her as he had at the start of their last evening together, when she had been so tantalisingly, so nearly within his grasp, her slender body and astonishing legs folding into the front seat of his car, her lips opening in a sweet, welcoming smile. He did not want to hear her harsh, Essex tones and the trivialities of her conversation. In his heart he still clung to a dream of her transformation, where her flat vowels were rounded, her stupid giggle eliminated and her irrelevant chatter elevated to intellectual debate. He still imagined her from time to time standing in a conference hall in a small black dress and impossible heels, her perfectly manicured hand resting lightly on his arm, explaining the neuroscience of animal behaviour to his colleagues. She would smile that soft delectable smile and say, "It was Thomas of course who started me on all this".

He poured a large glass of whisky and reflected that apologies and pleas for understanding were not the only options. He reached for his phone. Nicole picked up just before the answer service cut in.

"Thomas?" Her voice was surprised, puzzled.

"Nicole. I thought I should give you a ring. I've been wondering how you've been getting along."

"I'm OK thanks Thomas." She sounded wary. For a couple of minutes they exchanged the platitudes of strangers - how are you?/Are you well?/How's work?/ - until he said abruptly, "I saw the piece in today's Guardian."

Nicole laughed an embarrassed laugh, "Oh that. I didn't know if they'd publish it. I was in it, was I?" Thomas could hear the lie.

"Yes. I was..." he hesitated, searching for the right tone and settling on an appeal to her residual attachment. "I was surprised to see that this was how you saw our relationship. I was upset that you hadn't told me this yourself."

It misfired. Nicole was silent for a moment and then said "Actually Thomas, I'm not supposed to talk to you."

Angered, he mis-stepped again. "Who says you can't talk to me?"

"I'm just not supposed...when I went to APPA they said...it's supposed to be best if I don't..." He had frightened her. He had forgotten how easy it was to send her into retreat. Thomas changed tack, just as he had so many times in the consulting room. If he could shift her attention onto himself, make her realise how he was affected by what she said, he could usually draw her back into contact.

"It's all right Nicole. It's just that I was upset that you hadn't spoken to me about this. I thought we understood each other. I thought we trusted each other."

"I'm sorry Thomas. It's been quite confusing recently."

If he trod carefully, perhaps he could detach her, unhook her from this notion of abuse, restore himself as therapist not lover.

"I understand," he said gently.

His questioning became careful and concerned, his responses empathic and personal and Nicole began slowly to talk about her muddled feelings. Thomas talked about the strength of fantasy. He talked about the oddity of memory. He filled in the gaps in her tentative answers respectfully and sensitively. He talked about the legacy of her childhood with its mixed messages, neglectful parents and deceitful adults. He talked about how often she had trusted prematurely and been disappointed. He reminded her that the therapeutic relationship was unlike anything else. It was both intimate and professional. It was a place for risks and mistakes. Nicole began to follow him, echoing him, agreeing with him. Thomas could feel her relaxing into his attention, becoming malleable.

"It is nice to talk to you again Thomas," she said.

Glancing at the clock on the wall he noticed that they had been talking for a full ten minutes.

"Would it help you to come and see me again?" he asked.

"For therapy you mean?"

"I feel responsible for your confusion," he said. "I feel there are things we didn't work through properly and I'd be happy to try to put that right." One session, one session with her in the room, would put paid to all this.

"I don't know." The banal, delaying phrase was familiar. These were the words Nicole habitually used when she was about to concede and agree.

"One of the things about therapy," he said "is that you get to know someone very well. You come to care for the people who consult you."

Nicole was silent. She was so almost there. One more moment and she would agree. As he held his breath, searching for the right words, a dog began barking in the background.

"Oh - it's Oscar," she said. "Just a minute."

The phone was put down and he could hear Nicole opening and closing doors, soothing the dog and then the sound of her footsteps returning.

"Sorry about that," she said. "The kitchen door had swung closed on him. He's OK now."

"So," Thomas said, struggling to recapture the mood "what do you think?"

"About Oscar? Oscar's OK."

He laughed, trying to make his voice affectionate, "About coming to see me."

"I don't know Thomas." Her tone had changed. She was slipping away from him. The next thing would be an edge of defiance, an incoherent attempt at opposition and a collapse into the shaking, disturbed child who sheltered beneath the blanket on the couch.

Thomas stopped pushing. "Nicole," he said in his warmest tones "I just want you to know that I'm concerned for you and that the offer is there."

"Truly?" Nicole's voice was tentative. It was the old question from the consulting room, the old demand for reassurance, full of the longing to be special. He grabbed it.

"Truly," he said firmly. "We spent a long time working together. That matters to me. You matter to me. I feel responsible for you and for your experience of our work. I'd be sorry if you came to remember therapy by a few foolish mistakes from the final weeks. I'd be sorry if you lost the real value of the therapy, the part that endures."

"I do appreciate what you've done for me Thomas," she said. "I'd never want you to think that I don't appreciate it."

Thomas waited but she was silent now. He allowed himself a familiar interjection. "So ...?" he said.

"Can I sleep on it?" she asked.

"Of course," he said slowly, disappointment coursing through him. He pushed the disappointment away and finding his most understanding tones said, "Sleep on it. Let me know. I'll call you in a few days anyway, just to check."

"Thank you for ringing, Thomas," she said.

"That's OK."

She was ready to put the phone down. Panicking, he made one last advance.

"Before you go Nicole, I just wondered if you'd talked to anyone else about this?"

"Not a soul," she said. "Lots of journalists have been phoning APPA. It's been mental apparently. But I said I didn't want to talk to them and the people at APPA thought that was best too."

"Do be careful," he said. "You're very vulnerable to people with an agenda, people who may want to use you for their own purposes."

"They've been very nice to me."

"Of course, of course. People always are when they want something."

"What do you mean?"

"The press are looking for sensation. And APPA - they're looking for – how shall I put it – they're looking for scalps – prominent people whom they can shame or destroy as a means of promoting their agenda."

"Oh Thomas, I wouldn't want to do that." She was upset again. "You've done so much to help me. I'd never do anything that would harm you personally. I only did that interview on condition that I didn't have to say who I was talking about. I wouldn't make a complaint, or anything like that."

He made one last pitch. "Listen Nicole, I don't want you to worry about this. I don't want you to feel bad about it. I phoned because I wanted to make sure that you were all right. I know how difficult these things can be for someone as sensitive and vulnerable as you are. I just wanted to make sure that you knew that you could always come back to see me, that I'm always ready to talk with you, that nothing has changed in my sense of professional responsibility for you."

"Thank you Thomas," she said. He could hear the confusion in her voice and he pressed on.

"Just be very careful who you speak to," he said. "Not everyone has your best interests at heart."

Nicole was silent for a moment and then said, "I need to go and walk the dogs. Thank you for phoning, Thomas."

He had lost her. He put down the phone and kicked the sofa again and again and again.

Esther

"You've got post," called Esther's departing patient, stepping over the envelopes in the narrow hallway.

Esther waited for the click of the closing door, went out into the passageway and picked up the usual bundle of junk mail and bank statements. Slipped between them was a folded and stapled piece of paper which looked as if it had been torn from a school exercise book. It was addressed in neat, black letters written in a careful, round hand and there was a first class stamp in the top right hand corner. She knew instantly who it was from and made a cup of tea to quiet her racing heart. Carefully prising out the staples she opened the letter and read.

'Dear Esther,
Mother is much worse. It is Alzheimers and Parkinsons now as well and she can't be at home with us anymore because she isn't safe. They say it may not be long now. She is in the Greenacres Home on Bury Lane. We take it in turns to sit with her. Thursday is my day. If you come in the afternoon, it will be safe for you to see her. You are still in my prayers.
With love from Ruth.'

Esther knew exactly what it had cost her sister to write this letter. Ruth had never married and when their father had died, twenty years ago now, Ruth and their mother had moved into Reuben's house. Reuben was prosperous by then, married and flourishing within the community and he had taken over what little independent life Ruth might have had. She worked part-time in his business, cared for their mother, helped her sister-in-law run the household and looked after her nephews and nieces. Each week would be the same round of Sunday assembly, evening prayer meetings, Bible readings and housework. There would be little free time and little privacy and over it all was the lowering presence of Reuben, harsh, short-tempered and fanatical, interpreting the Bible to his own convenience: - guilt, obedience and judgment. Reuben would control her money, as their father had before him, handing out small sums on request for whatever he considered necessary. It was impossible for Ruth to pick up the phone without being overheard, and almost as hard for her to purchase writing paper and stamps.

About every five years one of these letters from Ruth arrived. They were short but they contained snippets of family information which Ruth had decided Esther should know: Philip is married, Aunt Elizabeth is with the Lord now, David's wife is blessed with another baby. At the end of each one she wrote 'I hope you will come back to us one day. Do not write back or try to phone or Reuben will stop me.'

It cheered Esther that this remnant of the sister she had known remained. The little girl who had wept in terror at her father's sermons, had always been stout in her condemnation of the characters in the Bible whom she did not like. The things which she had objected to were idiosyncratic. "I think the servant with one talent was right because he kept the money safe. I think Joshua gave people headaches with the trumpets. Mary wasn't good at sharing."

Gradually their father's repeated explanations and their mother's slaps had taught Ruth to keep her opinions to herself but the stubbornness remained. Esther could imagine Ruth, quietly deciding that she would write and taking the paper from one of the children's exercise books while cleaning their rooms. She would have sat up in bed with the purloined paper, concealing it in her Bible till she could find the stapler to seal it, the stamp to send it and a moment when she could pass the post-box unobserved. The stamp was an old one, filched perhaps from Reuben's office. The colour was wrong for 2009.

Esther read through the short letter again and opened her laptop. She scrolled quickly through the train times. If she left early on Thursday morning she could be there by two o' clock. She picked up her diary, scanned the appointments and spent her lunch break making phone calls and sending texts and emails, varying her message slightly according to the anxieties of each person she would disappoint. By seven o' clock she had accommodated almost everyone, squeezing them into Wednesday, Friday or the following Monday. The only person she could not find a space for was Thomas Fortune. He was urgent in his demand that they should meet that week but was irritatingly unavailable, emailing back that both Wednesday and Friday were impossible. He could manage Saturday afternoon, he wrote, as he would be seeing his wife to discuss the divorce. Esther tapped her fingers on the table, looking again at the crammed list of appointments and the oasis of her weekend. 'Regret Saturday not possible,' she replied and then added 'If you care to phone me at our usual appointment time I will be on a train. I may be able to speak to you then about anything urgent. Otherwise I will look forward to seeing you at our usual time next week.' She pressed 'Send' and immediately regretted the offer of the phone call.

Esther walked the half mile to the station in a damp, grey dawn. Somewhere in the shuttered compartments of her mind she had known it would be like this. She had known that there would be no joyful reunion with her mother. But in other more lively imaginings, she had introduced her mother daily to Jane and to Felix: 'She has a tooth,' 'He can say Dada', 'She got all her exams'.

The two realities had existed side by side. In one Esther had grieved the loss of her family, slowly accepting the reality of her transgression against everything she had grown up with and everything they believed. In the other, she chatted in imagination to her mother and sometimes to Ruth, telling them the acceptable stories of her life, sharing the small joys and setbacks, never the tragedies or sadness. 'Jane has had her ears pierced', 'I am going to Navratri with my friend Meena,' 'Felix is in the football team.' Her mother rarely replied in these fantasies, she was simply a nodding, comforting presence, agreeing in imagination to behaviour she would never have countenanced in reality.

"We idealise those we have lost," Tisch had said to her, towards the end of her therapy. Esther had agreed but it had not stemmed her imagination and she had preserved the secret space where her mother lived on.

Now, the collision of the two realities brought the grief flooding back and she crossed the station forecourt with a tightness in her chest, closing her eyes briefly in a futile attempt to banish the images of the past. She pushed her ticket into the machine, thinking that her mother had never done this, never travelled anywhere except for the

Assembly's Saturday rambles on the moors and their summer camps at Morecambe Bay or Mablethorpe. Those had been good times: crowds of children milling across the sands, chasing each other in pointless games or organised into races and sports teams. They had sat round camp fires, playing clapping games, drinking cocoa, singing hymns. Her parents had relaxed too. She had lain in the clear night air beside her father while he pointed out the constellations which God had set in the sky. Her mother had laughed as she chopped vegetables with the other women, freed from her own cruel timetables by the organisation of others. And she had come across her parents once, sitting in the dunes, holding hands, absorbed in their own conversation. She had crept quietly away, comforted by their tenderness.

Later, in imagination, Esther had taken her parents with her, on her own holidays with the children, showing them the life they led, its ordinariness, its joy, its freedom from the anxiety of a punitive God. 'We camp too. We look at the stars. We see the beauty and magnificence of creation,' she had pleaded to the ghostly figures and in imagination her parents had nodded, quietly agreeing that it was true that you could have love without God.

Esther brought her hand up to the side of her head with a sharp, hard slap and then looked round anxiously to see if anyone had observed her. The streaming crowds were all preoccupied with their own business, struggling with ticket machines, scanning departure boards and rushing head-down for stairs and subways. No-one had seen her. The blow had worked however. It had brought her back to the raw November air, the clatter and scream of the early morning trains and the reality of now. Esther bought a newspaper and made her way to the correct platform.

Felix

Felix felt the van stop and heard, rather than saw, the back doors being wrenched open. Crushed in the back with eleven other people it had been an uncomfortable journey. Six of them tumbled out onto a cold, misty, grass verge, pulling rucksacks onto their backs. The sun had not yet risen but they could see the orange lights of the processing works on the distant side of what looked like a pitch-black, rutted ploughed field. Stark against the gradually lightening sky they could see the shapes of the machinery – enormous excavators, as tall as houses - that stripped out the coal from the surface of the destroyed land, gradually working deeper and deeper below the surface.

Jay was shouting: "Run! Go on! Run! Run!"

Felix heard the slam of the van's doors behind them and the roar of the engine as Jay sped round the site to drop the second group by the main gates. They ducked through the strands of barbed wire which were all that separated the site from the country lane and began stumbling across the wrecked land of the open-cast mine. The powdery black surface was wet from the constant spraying that was supposed to control the dust. Water stood stagnant in deep pools and ruts which could catch your ankle in the dark and send you face downwards into the black.

Their progress was impeded not just by the ungiving terrain but by the fact that three of them were dressed in polar bear suits and one as a yellow canary. It took them half an hour to cross the five hundred metres that separated the country lane from the excavator that was their object. The D-locks and arm-tubes were heavy on their backs and they toiled across the land mostly in silence, looking round to wait for each other and communicating in nods and gestures of agreement about the route to take.

Standing beneath the enormous bulk of the excavator Felix began to feel the familiar exhilaration of an action. They climbed quickly to the top. There was a surprising amount of space on the roof of the huge machine. They dumped the polar bear heads by the railings and set up the tents they would retreat into to make it harder to remove them. Then they unfurled the banners, hanging them down the sides of the excavator: 'Don't be a fossil fool', 'Green jobs for all' and 'Keep it in the ground'. They turned on the cheap phones bought specially for the action. The signal was poor but they managed to connect with the other groups on the site. Eight people were locked on at the gates, eight were attached to the washery, six were on another excavator that they were just beginning to make out as the sky lightened in the East. Felix climbed down and took photos, transmitting them one by one to the media group who were waiting at the gate. It was six 'o' clock. The first workers would not arrive for an hour. They poured coffee from their thermos flasks and waited.

It was half past seven before anyone appeared. Two security staff stood beneath the digger looking up at them.

"What's all this about?" asked one.

"You'd better come down," said the other.

Felix read their brief, prepared statement. "This is a protest about climate change. Mining coal and burning coal are crimes against humanity and crimes against the rest of the natural world. We are occupying this site to prevent emissions of carbon dioxide and to draw attention to the harm already done. This is a peaceful occupation. We wish you no harm."

The security guards did not seem impressed. One of them pulled out his radio. "We've got what looks like" – he stared up at their grubby polar bear suits – "three rabbits on this one. Yeah...yeah...that's in addition to the clowns on the North side. Oh – and something in yellow," he added as Sophie in her canary costume emerged from behind Felix. "Winnie the Pooh, maybe."

He waited, listening to instructions from the other end. "OK, OK, I'll tell them."

"The police are on their way," he said. "I'd suggest you come down and piss off while you still can." They walked back towards their Landrover and drove off.

It was another half hour before the police turned up, two local officers in uniform who walked around the digger, as if evaluating the climb to the top. They stood beneath it and called up.

"Come on lads, you've made your point, come down." They seemed nonplussed and a little uncertain as Felix read the statement again. Then the more junior one said: "Give us a break chaps. I've got better things to do than watch you lot all day" and the older one got back on his radio.

An hour later a more senior officer appeared and introduced himself by name. "I'm Inspector Edward Evans. We recognise your desire for peaceful protest and wish to facilitate it but your current actions constitute aggravated trespass and we will arrest you if you fail to co-operate."

Felix read the statement once more, adding, "It is our intention to keep this facility closed until the end of the working day."

The Inspector tried again: "I can see you're all educated people. If you get a criminal record you won't be able to become a lawyer, a teacher - anything you want to do. I'm sure that's not what you want. I'm sure that's not what your Mums and Dads want."

Felix repeated that they were not coming down and that they had nothing more to say. The Inspector had one last try. "If you come down now, we will escort you off the site and release you. If you don't, you take the consequences. We've called for back-up and they are not pussycats. It will not be a tea-party."

"No comment," called Felix and the group echoed him with a shout: "NO COMMENT."

The Inspector withdrew, leaving the two junior officers sitting in their vehicle as reluctant and bored guards.

Sophie brought them together in a circle. "Let's check in," she said. "How's everyone doing? Anyone cold? Hungry?"

She went round the group, inviting each to say in turn how they felt. Their spirits were good.

They checked the points on the digger where they would lock on, ate sandwiches and settled in for what would probably be a long, dull day. Confused text messages were coming through from the group tasked with stopping the train and Felix thought anxiously about Clara, cursing Jay for involving her in the most risky and difficult part of the action, then cursing himself for caring about her. He looked out across the distorted landscape. There wasn't a blade of grass for miles. There was no birdsong. It looked like the photographs of a First World War battlefield. He took out his notebook and began to sketch. The strange landscape yielded easily to his pencil and he settled quietly into the absorption of childhood.

It was two 'o' clock before the promised reinforcements arrived. The first indication was a cherry picker bumping awkwardly across the rutted landscape. It was followed by a convoy of eight or ten police vehicles – unmarked cars, police vans and more 4x4s. Officers wearing black ski-caps and bullet-proof vests spilled out of them, some making a great show of unpacking their equipment – cameras, climbing gear, ropes, electrical cutting gear – others simply milling around. There were at least twenty, dark-dressed purposeful looking men but for a long time nothing happened apart from the constant crackle of the police radios and the occasional whine of machinery as an officer tested the cutting gear. The mood around them had changed and the group locked on. A light drizzle began to wet their hair, condensing on their woollen hats and dampening their skin. Felix looked at Owen, who had never taken part in an action before. He was a slight, pale young man. The rain was obscuring his glasses and he was beginning to shiver. Amber, veteran of many previous actions, shuffled across to him, as much as the arm locks would allow, in a gesture of solidarity.

"It's OK," Felix said. "They're doing this to intimidate us. Hold your nerve."

Sophie texted the media group, sending a photograph of the assembled police. A message came back. 'Same at the washery and front gate. We're holding out.'

The rain became more persistent and two of the officers came up on the cherry picker, one filming, the other apparently to negotiate. He was terse and sharp.

"I'm going to say this once," he said. "This is the deal. You come down now. We escort you to the front gate where the Press are waiting. You get to tell your story. You go home." He paused. "Or my men come up and they bring you down. It won't be fun. They're not careful people. Any injuries you sustain will be caused by you resisting arrest."

Felix repeated their agreed statement, adding "The Press already have our story and you should know that we are filming you."

The officer went back down.

"Hold out?" asked Sophie. "Hold out," said Amber, echoed rapidly by Jess and Louis.

"Hold out for a time," said Felix more cautiously. "It'll be dark soon and we'll have stopped a day's work. The press coverage is there and there's no point in having a barney over the last half hour."

"I'd go for that," said Owen. His voice was shaky and the others looked at him with more concern.

"See how long we can stall them for?" asked Amber.

They agreed.

When the officer came back up, he had an iPad in his hand and he began pointing at them individually, checking back from time to time to the information on his screen. "Sophie Linklater, postal worker. Owen Mulstratton, final year chemistry student. Felix Dunn, nice job at the Angus Balfour Architectural Practice – shame to lose that. Amber Radford, in breach of your bail conditions I think."

He had all their names. He knew what they did. Felix heard the hiss of Sophie's astonished outbreath and Louis' muttered "Shit. The shits. The fucking, fucking shits."

"We already have all your friends," the officer said. "Time to call it a day."

Carefully keeping all expression from his face, Felix repeated: "This is a peaceful occupation. It is our intention to keep this facility closed until the end of the working day."

"We don't really care about that. My men will be up in in seconds, the moment I give them the signal." He focused his eyes on Owen. "You've final exams in May, haven't you? Hoping to study for a PhD, aren't you? We will make very sure that you are not available for those exams unless you come down now."

Owen's colour was not good. Felix looked straight at the officer. "Give us five minutes," he said.

"No more than five," the officer said and lowered his platform slightly.

"How do they know my name? How do they know what I do?" asked Owen.

"Let's talk about that later. We need to decide whether or when we're coming down."

"Can they really make sure I'm in prison for my finals?"

"They're not talking about prison – this is only aggravated trespass – what they mean is that they'll make sure the court hearing happens during your exams."

"And can they?"

"Probably not. It would come up long before then. They're just threatening."

The light was fading fast. The sky was covered by a mass of dark grey cloud and there was not a hint of sun in the sky. The drizzle had changed to a steady downpour. Sophie tried to shake the drips off her yellow canary suit: "This is shite. It's gone three 'o' clock and I'm getting wet."

"We unlock?"

"I don't particularly fancy being thrown off this thing by those goons."

Felix looked at them. The polar bear suits looked increasingly bedraggled and absurd. The temperature was falling and the rain showed no sign of letting up. The sense of anti-climax was a familiar one. You planned for months, researching every detail of the site, its workers, their timetable, the access. You wrote slogans, created banners, organised transport. You built the group, trained the new members, planned publicity and press releases. And it was all done in the utmost secrecy, knowing that one small mistake could destroy everything. Then there was maybe twenty-four hours of pure exhilaration. The sense of finally doing something proportionate to the threat was intoxicating and you felt momentarily powerful. There was nothing but the demands of the moment, the thrill and triumph of a real engagement. And then it was over.

Felix looked at the pale, intense faces of his comrades. Over the last few months he had begun to feel that he knew them better than his own family but now that would fade away. He could see Owen retreating into the study that was his other passion, Sophie going back to crazy nights out and too many 'E's. He needed to concentrate on his Part Two course and Louis had promised his pregnant wife that there would be no more actions till after the baby was born. It had to end somehow. Slowly they agreed. They would unlock and come down. Felix leant over the edge of the machine. "We're coming down."

"You come down one by one. You will be searched for any offensive weapons and anything which we consider to be one will be confiscated. You will each state your name and address clearly to the officer filming. We will be arresting Ms Radford for breach of her bail conditions. My officers will drive the rest of you clear of the site and you will be released without charge."

They unlocked themselves.

"I'm leaving this crap here," said Amber unzipping herself from the dirty white suit. "I don't fancy appearing before the magistrates as a polar bear."

"Do you want one of us to come with you?" Felix asked.

"No, it's fine." Amber already had a long list of minor convictions – obstruction, aggravated trespass, breach of the peace – and she seemed to be doing community service almost constantly for one offence or another. She would be OK.

They abandoned the D-locks, arm-locks and polar-bear suits on top of the digger, adjusted one of the banners that had become tangled and climbed carefully down onto the crunch of the coal waste. Amber was led away by the local police. Felix and Owen were pushed into the back of one of the big 4x4s, Louis, Jess and Sophie into another.

"See you tomorrow," Amber shouted.

The police encampment was packing up. The cherry picker was wobbling its way back across the desecrated land. Felix leant back in the warm vehicle and briefly closed his eyes, opening them again as they bumped off the site at the main entrance. All that was left of the action there were the banners on the gate. Felix pulled his rucksack onto his knees in anticipation of the vehicle stopping but it drove on. Ten minutes later they were still driving. Felix leaned forward.

"Where are we going?" he asked. "Where are you going to drop us?"

"Shut up and sit back," was the only reply.

The vehicle was climbing and Felix could see the red tail lights of the car in front. Everything else was black. They were somewhere in the countryside, driving along a twisting, minor road.

"I'm supposed to ring home tonight," Owen said.

"Sit tight. This is just a wind-up. They'll drop us soon."

It was another quarter of an hour before the vehicle in front slowed down and pulled into a layby. Louis, Sophie and Jess were being bundled out onto the road.

"Out," said the officer and Felix and Owen stumbled onto the tarmac too.

As the vehicles pulled away, the officer leant out of the window and shouted "Have a nice walk," before they sped away over the brow of the hill and into the distance. The wind whipped round them and the rain pelted their faces. They were somewhere high up, far out in the countryside, staring into darkness. Sophie was still wearing her yellow canary suit, hopping from foot to foot and shouting at the retreating tail lights.

"Bastards. Bastards. Bastards."

"Don't you want to get out of that canary outfit?" Felix said to her.

"It was a bit tight," she replied "So I put it on without my jeans. And I don't seem to have them with me anymore."

Felix offered her his waterproof over-trousers and she accepted, stuffing the coal-spattered yellow costume into her rucksack.

They checked their mobile phones. No-one had any signal.

"What do we do?" asked Owen.

"Walk till we find some sign of where we are and where we can pick up some signal. Then phone Jay. Hopefully he can come and get us."

"Which way?"

"The way they've gone, I reckon. They'll be heading the fastest way they can back to civilisation."

They set off down the exposed moorland road and Owen returned anxiously to the question of how the police had so much information about them.

"They knew my name, they knew my course, they knew what I'm intending to do next."

"Face-recognition software," said Louis. "They'll have images of us from other demonstrations and they'll be matching it with other publicly available information – Facebook, stuff like that."

"But this is the first thing I've done," said Owen. "I've never been somewhere the police have been filming before."

"And it's hard to see why they'd spend all those resources creating files on us."

"Maybe they're more stupid or we're more dangerous than we think," joked Felix. He was too tired to think about it, fed up with the conspiracy theories that lurked beneath the surface of every activist discussion.

They spotted lights below them and ten minutes later a bend in the road brought them into a small hamlet.

"Who looks most like a respectable walker lost on the moors?" Sophie said. "It's definitely not me."

Felix knocked on the door of the cottage and returned to the group a few minutes later.

"Nice bloke," he said. "If we carry on down into the valley there's a small railway station in about four miles. He's given me the time-table and if we hurry we might be able to pick up a train. He says it's difficult to get taxis to come out this far. He'd have offered to drive us but his wife's ill."

The rain had begun to lighten and they stepped out, trying Jay every few minutes without success. By the time they eventually got through to him they were on the train.

"Leave it man," said Felix when he offered to come to the connecting station. "We'll be quicker by train." Jay was the last person he wanted to see at present and it was midnight before they emerged, exhausted, from Sheffield station.

Esther

Thomas's phone call came on the dot of ten 'o' clock. The connection was poor. It was difficult to catch every word but Esther could hear the tension in his voice.

"I've got a difficult decision to take. Some things have happened that you may not be aware of."

She listened with disquiet as Thomas described how the conference he was speaking at had been invaded by a demonstration from APPA, how they had ambushed him on his radio programme and how Nicole had featured in a Guardian article about abuse in the mental health professions.

"I've spoken to Nicole," he said. "She's not going to make a complaint but I'm not sure I can stop her talking. She's easily flattered, easily influenced."

"I think you need to consider the possibility that she has been damaged by what happened in the therapy with you," Esther said.

It was the wrong thing to say. It brought a torrent of self-justification – he'd worked hard, he'd been sincere, he'd gone the extra mile, Nicole was borderline, she was deceitful, she was impossible. It ended with him saying, as the train entered a tunnel, "I sometimes wonder whose side you're actually on, Esther."

By the time she re-made the connection, Thomas had calmed a little and the reception had improved.

"That's not what I wanted to talk about though. I had a phone call on Monday from a journalist asking me for a comment on the Morton case."

Dominic Morton was a psychiatrist who had been struck off after it emerged that he had started a sexual relationship with a vulnerable patient. When the relationship broke up and the patient had tried to make a complaint, Morton had threatened her and she had attempted suicide. The publicity had encouraged other complainants to come forward and the results of the subsequent enquiry, damning of Morton himself but also of the profession, had just been published.

"I thought it was the usual stuff - my media profile means I'm often asked to comment about mental health issues - and it was, except that at the end she sprung something else on me. She asked me if I'd like to comment on allegations being made that I was guilty of something similar myself - that I'd also abused a patient by starting a sexual relationship."

"What did you say?"

"I told her there was absolutely no truth in the allegation and asked her where she'd got her information from. She gave me the usual crap about not being able to reveal her sources. But they've published it of course. Yesterday's *Telegraph*. Did you see it?"

Esther had not.

"I'll read it to you. There's a load of stuff about Morton and then this. 'Critics are claiming that the Morton case is just the tip of an iceberg and that much-loved celebrity therapist Thomas Fortune is one of several facing allegations. Fortune told the *Telegraph* that 'There is absolutely no foundation to these rumours'. Joy Lasenby of the Association for the Prevention of Psych-Abuse said 'Abuse of this kind is endemic'.'"

Esther found herself strangely detached. "These things often blow over don't they?" she said. "When the press find something else to focus on?"

"This isn't going to blow over. APPA have decided that I'm someone to use to make their point. They don't care whether it's true. They're not interested in the complications of these cases. They don't care what damage they do to me, or to Nicole for that matter."

Recurrent images of her family, the noise of the train and the interrupted staccato of the call robbed Esther of attention.

"Every other journo in London has picked it up," Thomas continued. "The phone's been ringing constantly since the *Telegraph* piece. I give the same denial. I explain that patient confidentiality means that I can't elaborate. I repeat that there's no substance to the claims. But this morning there were two of them outside the house, door-stepping my patients. It'll make my work impossible if this goes on."

This was certainly true. "Can't the police do something?" she asked.

"They say no offence has been committed."

"It sounds like you've done what you can." Esther said, struggling to hear against the competition of station announcements.

"Absolutely not. I have to stop them. Sooner or later one of them will find their way to Nicole and God knows what she'll say if she's confronted by a journalist. If I don't find a way to get my story out there first, I'm finished. The truth doesn't matter to these people."

"I don't see what you could say though..."

"One of the people who rang is a journo I know from way back. She's offered to do a profile of me - something where I can talk about myself, my work, make my ethical position clear, present myself as I really am. The drawback is she's now with one of the tabloids."

Esther was suddenly more engaged. She had no illusions about what the tabloids might do to Thomas.

"Thomas," she said, "would that be wise?"

"If I can keep control of the interview then yes – it could do me a lot of good, make it clear that I'm still the person the public think I am. I don't have a lot of options and this may be my best chance to put the record straight."

The ticket inspector distracted her and she fumbled in her bag. "Couldn't this wait until next week, when we have a chance to talk properly?"

"That's not how the media works." Thomas was patronising now. "I have to take a decision."

"I'm afraid this could make matters worse," she said, extracting the ticket from her wallet.

The phone crackled as they entered a deep cutting. Another tunnel broke the call. As the train emerged into daylight Esther tried repeatedly to reconnect but all she got was his answerphone. She put the phone on the table in front of her and stared out of the window. Her gut told her that an appeal to the public via the pages of a tabloid newspaper was likely to misfire. Her head told her that Thomas Fortune would do whatever he thought best and that her opinions would be feathers on the wind.

Clara

Clara lay with the rest of her small group at the side of the single track line, hidden amongst the scrubby bushes of an embankment, shivering in the cold morning air and waiting for the correct train to pass. The track was used only for coal traffic to the power station and ran through isolated farmland and scrub, crossed only by a few minor roads. A climbing rope lay curled in front of her. Her hand was on the cold metal of a shovel and she could feel the weight of the two D-locks in the small rucksack on her back. A van with additional equipment was parked discreetly, just off the road on the edge of a small wood. After ten minutes lying motionless on the damp ground, Clara flexed her toes and felt cramp grip her calf. Her face contorted suddenly with the pain, as she suppressed the urge to cry out.

"What is it?" hissed Helen.

"Cramp."

Helen reached across and began expertly massaging the muscle back to life. She was carrying a small hand-held camera and would be transmitting live footage of the action to the media group. Like Anusha she was a few years older than Clara but her seriousness was lightened by a sarcastic sense of humour and a bold indifference to authority.

"Not long now," she whispered.

Two of the others were already beside the line, dressed in the orange safety jackets of Network Rail, ready to fix a red flag across the track and halt the train the moment it was clear that it would be running to the expected time. Clara turned onto her back and gazed up into the bare branches of hawthorn and wild damson silhouetted against the grey expanse of sky. A tiny black insect dropped from a branch into the leaf litter beside her. Two birds wheeled and circled high above.

They could hear the train long before they could see it. As its rhythmic clanking and grinding became louder Clara could feel her heart beating faster through the white boiler suit which she, like everyone else, was wearing to protect against the coal dust and make them stand out in the photographs. The locomotive was already slowing as it passed them. The heavy wagons juddered to a stop in front of them, their wheels screeching on the damp rails.

"Now," called Helen and a dozen of them instantly broke cover, swarming rapidly towards the wagons. Two of the experienced climbers threw the hooks and secured the ropes. In seconds, they were quickly assisting the rest of the group onto the huge trucks. Clara's hands slipped on the cold metal and she bruised her thumb as she scrambled up to stand precariously beside the others on the heaps of shining black coal, looking out across the flat, agricultural land and the river snaking its way towards the sea. It was a moment of pure exhilaration.

The track maintenance impersonators walked nonchalantly towards the stationary cab and explained to the puzzled driver that there were demonstrators on the track, further down the line, adding as the first group scrambled onto the wagons, "Looks like they've arrived here as well."

They read a prepared statement to the man. "We wish you no harm. This is a peaceful protest about climate change. You are free to call your superiors..." The driver retreated to his cab, radioing urgently for advice.

Minutes later another group had run ropes securing the locomotive to the girders of the bridge over the river where it had stopped. They hung banners from the side of the wagons: 'Leave it in the ground' and 'No more fossil fuels'. Helen started to film and they began shovelling the coal out of the wagons. Signal was good and Helen was rapidly transmitting footage to the media group who in turn reported back that the local and national press were on their way. The sole journalist whom they had trusted with advance news of the action climbed up onto the wagons beside them, asking questions, taking notes on an IPad and then retreating to make his own phone calls.

It was half an hour before the police arrived, a lone patrol car with two bewildered local officers who quickly retreated to their radios. Clara found the shovel hard to use and discovered that it was quicker – and more satisfying – to rapidly throw the lumps of coal one by one out of the wagon. She felt joyously alive.

"Speak to camera for me," called Helen.

Clara paused, coal in hand and turned. She removed her protective mask and held the black rock up to the camera. "My name is Clara Fortune. I am nineteen years old. My world, and your world, is being destroyed by the reckless mining and burning of fossil fuels. I am here to protest about this. I am here to stop this. I am here to make sure there is a future for me, for you, for nature, for everyone."

"What about legality?" prompted Helen.

"We are here to achieve justice for nature, justice for our generation, justice for all those who will have to live with the climate crimes of the elites who make the law. We are here from necessity. We are here through urgency. For anyone who knows, for anyone who understands, for anyone who cares about what climate change will do there is no other option."

"Brilliant," Helen said and scrambled across to film on the next wagon.

They shovelled and chucked coal till their arms ached and the coal dust made them cough through their protective masks. By eleven 'o' clock there were some very satisfying piles of coal scattered along the track and they stopped briefly to open their thermoses and unwrap their sandwiches.

What shocked and surprised them all was the speed at which the police reinforcements arrived. As Clara took the first sips of hot, sweet liquid a shout went up from the lookouts perched on top of the locomotive. Clara stood up, slipping in the heaps of coal. In the distance she could see a line of vehicles speeding along the twisting lane between the flat fields. She watched as the convoy stopped on the road fifty yards away, hindered from getting any closer by a padlocked gate and stared in astonishment as a group of burly men grabbed bolt cutters and flung the gate to one side. They pulled into the field below the embankment. Vanload after vanload of solid, black-uniformed men in stab-proof vests spilled out into the field and began to unload cutting equipment and climbing gear. It was only an hour and a half after the train had shuddered to a halt.

"How did they get here so quickly?" Clara asked.

"Don't know," Helen replied.

"They were supposed to go to the mine first."

"Keep shovelling. We need to keep this going as long as we can."

There was a standoff. Some futile negotiations were followed by a police retreat as they continued to empty the contents of the wagons onto the track and the police appeared to be waiting for further instructions. Press photographers appeared, calling up from the track below. Clara's arms had begun to ache. The dust from the coal was penetrating her mask and she had begun to cough uncontrollably. She retreated temporarily to the top of the locomotive with a bottle of water, watching as two more police vehicles arrived and a more obviously senior officer emerged.

Shortly afterwards a shout went up from the lookouts. "They're coming in. They're coming in. Lock on. Everyone lock on." Clara scrambled back to join her affinity group, pulling her D-locks from her rucksack. The police had ascended the embankment and were running towards them down the track, a line on each side of the stationary train. They were on the wagons in seconds.

The man who was standing over Clara was swarthy and dark-eyed. His skin smelt of aftershave and his breath of toast. He placed his face close to hers. "There's two ways of doing this," he said. "You can unlock yourself and I take you down. That's the easy way. Or I use the metal cutters and I can't guarantee what will happen." One of her locks was attached to a chain that ran through her sleeves and the other was round her neck. Both were then attached to the structure of the wagon. She began to cough again, the metal of the D-lock sliding against her neck. "If you move while I'm using the cutters" the officer said "I can't guarantee your safety."

On the other side of the truck Clara could see that Helen and the two people on either side of her had refused to relinquish their keys. Her cough became uncontrollable then, racking her body, pressing it against the hard, lumps of coal. The officer moved his face back a few millimetres and said "We've no ambulances here, you know. And it's a long way to A and E."

"Stop threatening her," Helen had shouted. And then, as Clara had continued to cough, had said to her "Unlock yourself Clara. It's fine to unlock. You'll just be a little ahead of us."

Esther

Esther changed at Leeds, staring up in confusion at the departure boards. Everything was simultaneously familiar and strange. The smoke-blackened brick, the soaring metal arches and the dusty grey platforms had hardly altered but the layout was quite changed and everything was overlaid with the modern paraphernalia of retail outlets, automated ticket machines and flashing neon. She found herself a seat on the connecting train and retreated into the corner. The last time she had sat on this train was twenty years ago and she had been with Gordon, travelling to her father's burial, their marriage only just intact. "You must wear a suit," she had said and irked he had asked why, as if he did not know. But he had come, repeatedly taking her hand in an awkward gesture of comfort. He had suggested, even then, that this might be the moment for reconciliation with her family and his incomprehension had made her feel even more alone. "They won't speak to me," she had said. "I no longer exist for them. I'm worse than dead."

The news had reached her in the same way in a note from Ruth, written that time on a piece of card, cut from a cereal packet and sent like a postcard so that anyone who cared to could have read what she wrote. 'Father has had a stroke,' Ruth had written, 'and is with the Lord. The funeral is on Friday. They will not let you into the service but the burial is at the public cemetery, 2 pm.' Scrawled up the side, she had added 'I am sorry to tell you like this.' And 'You are always in my prayers.'

Their father had not been old, sixty-two or sixty-three. As a child her parents had appeared monolithic to her, united in severity, constant in criticism and unanimous in discipline and punishment. It was only as an adult that she had understood that the punishment came at her mother's insistence and that her father was a gentle man who was as frightened of his wife as he was of damnation and perhaps did not properly distinguish between the two.

Esther and Gordon had stood, a short distance off, and watched as her family and members of the community gathered around the graveside and the coffin was lowered into the ground. A few people looked across at them curiously, perhaps not recognising her. But her brothers and their wives, and her mother hunched on Reuben's arm, had not let their gaze rest on her for a second. Ruth had looked round nervously and briefly made a gesture that might have been an acknowledgment or might just have been a move to push the hair from her eyes. It had been brave of her to write at all.

When they had all left, Esther had stood with Gordon beside the heaped earth. "Leave me for a moment," she had said. She had spoken to her father then, accusing him of cowardice and betrayal. "You abandoned me," she whispered to the mute soil. "I always kept a place in my heart for you. All you had to do was speak. All you had to do was pick up a pen." Then, overwhelmed by sadness and guilt, she had spoken to him in the same way she had spoken to God as a child, when she had imitated the archaic phrases of the Bible in her prayers. "Dear Father, forgive me for the shadow that I cast on your life. Look with mercy and love upon me, as I do upon you."

Gordon, hovering anxiously nearby had returned and quietly taken her elbow, standing silently beside her as she stared at the damp earth and the flattened grass. "Enough?" he had asked at last.

"Enough," she had replied.

They had collected the children from Meena. Felix had run shouting from the back of her house, "Mummy, Mummy, Mummy!" and "Daddy, Daddy, Daddy!" winding his arms round her legs and then jumping at Gordon till he picked him up and he curled his warm little body into Gordon's arms, resting his head against Gordon's shoulder and peeking out at her in quiet satisfaction. Esther had felt life and joy rush back into her. Jane had proprietorially taken her hand, turned to Meena and said gravely, "Thank you for having us Meena," and Meena had laughed and kissed them all and Esther had walked the hundred yards home in a tentative glow of renewed hope.

Now she bought flowers at the station and stepped into a taxi. The care home was on the outskirts of town, in new-built suburban streets that she did not recognise. She took the taxi-driver's card, turned off her phone, and went through the institutional, glass doors into an anonymous reception area of potted plants with a low table and a couple of chairs. There was a corridor in front of her, corridors branching off to left and right and signs with pointing hands reading 'Dining Room', 'Resident's Lounge' and 'Office'. She turned into the corridor marked 'Office', aware of her beating heart and the feeling that she was trespassing. At the end of it was a woman vacuuming, mechanically pushing her machine along a carpet which to Esther's eye seemed already clean. The woman looked up and paused the machine.

"I've come to visit Mrs Mackie," Esther said.

"Mrs Mackie?" the woman replied. "She is on the nursing floor." Her accent was East European. "Come."

Esther followed her to a lift and they travelled up to more corridors with doors like hotel rooms. The woman counted her way along them, "Twenty three, twenty four, twenty five...this one I think." She knocked, peered round the door and said in the falsely cheerful tones of people who work in institutions, "You have a visitor Mrs Mackie." She stood back to allow Esther to enter and closed the door behind her.

Ruth jumped up from a chair beside the bed.

"Esther, you came." Ruth stepped forward uncertainly. Esther instantly recognised her sister's shy face and stubborn brown eyes but little else about the woman in front of her was familiar. Ruth had been a lively, nervous teenager. She had not been conventionally pretty but had been beautiful in the way that all young people are beautiful when they carry the hope of youth. Esther remembered a slim, energetic girl with almond shaped eyes who laughed as much as she prayed and whose obedience was tempered with occasional quiet rebellions. "I won't wash your shirts," she had once said to their father, "unless you undo the buttons before you put them in the laundry." Surprisingly, this had made him laugh and he had complied.

The woman who stepped towards Esther was plump and ungainly however. Her lips had an anxious tremor. Her clothes were drab, a pale pink jumper rucked over a grey skirt of indeterminate shape which hovered half-way between her knees and a pair of lumpy, unpolished lace-up shoes. Her hair was flecked with grey and drawn back into an ugly bun and she smiled cautiously at Esther through a pair of thick-rimmed glasses.

"Esther, I'm so glad you came."

Esther took her sister's hands between her own, noticing Ruth's rough-cut nails and worn skin between her own smooth fingers and delicately polished nails. She kissed Ruth on the cheek and Ruth, stepping back a pace to look at her properly said, "Oh, you do look nice. You always looked nice. And you smell lovely."

Esther, embarrassed now by the faint musky perfume she had dabbed behind her ears that morning and her carefully chosen, dark cashmere coat and bright silk scarf, tried hard to meet her sister's eyes. "It's good to see you Ruth. It's so good to see you," she said. "Thank you for writing."

Ruth drew her across the room, ushering Esther into the bedside chair. Their mother lay, propped up on pillows, her eyes closed, her hands motionless on the covers. Her hair was white and thinner than Esther remembered. The perpetual frown on her forehead had relaxed but the firm set of the lips remained.

"Mother sleeps a lot now," Ruth said. "Everything is tiring to her. It's difficult for her to speak and she doesn't always know us. She remembers Reuben but sometimes she calls him Father and we don't know if she means Father or Grandfather. She asks for Father all the time."

Esther nodded, taking one of her mother's bony hands in her own. The skin was paper thin, marked with the dark spots of age.

"And you?" Esther asked, "Does she know you?"

"Sometimes. I take her out in the wheelchair still. She likes that."

"How long has she been here?"

"Six months now. We couldn't manage at night. She was getting up and wandering into the street. She can't do that now because she's so shaky but Reuben said it was better here. She sometimes says things she doesn't mean."

Esther looked at her, puzzled and Ruth said "Curse words. Swear words. The doctor says it's the illness speaking, not Mother but Reuben doesn't like the children to hear her like that. We pray for her. Reuben says the Lord will know it's the illness."

Ruth crouched at the other side of the bed and gently shook their mother's shoulder, speaking quietly into her ear. "Mother, it's Esther. Esther has come to see you."

The old lady slowly opened her eyes and smiled at Ruth. Ruth gestured towards Esther and the old lady turned her head. She looked blankly at Esther.

Esther smiled at her, willing the empty eyes to meet her own. "I'm Esther, Mother."

Their mother opened her lips a little, as if wishing to speak. Eventually the words came out, stuttered with difficulty, "Give...me...some...water." Ruth propped her forward slightly and held the glass to her lips. She drank clumsily and sank back on the pillows. Ruth dabbed at her chin with a tissue.

Esther tried again. "I wanted so much to see you Mother," but the old lady stared through her, the hand on the covers shaking now with a regular small tremor.

"She's sometimes much better than this," said Ruth. "Sometimes we manage to talk. I think she's tired. I took her out this morning, just for some fresh air and it tires her."

They sat in silence for a moment. Esther was aware that Ruth had stood up and was shifting nervously from one foot to the other and cocking her head as if listening to sounds that Esther could not hear.

"I'm going to go downstairs," Ruth said. She picked up the flowers. "I'm going to put these in the Resident's Lounge. It wouldn't do for Reuben to see them – he'd ask who brought them."

"I'm sorry," Esther said. "I should have thought."

"I'm afraid Reuben might come. We never know when he's going to drop in. If he's got a gap between meetings or isn't needed in the office he comes and sits with her for half an hour. If I stand in reception I can see his car pull in and I can get up here to tell you before he arrives. It'll cause terrible trouble if he sees you."

Ruth was twisting her hands together in apology. She was afraid. Fantasies of rescue passed briefly through Esther's mind: she was dragging Ruth into the taxi with her, buying her well-fitting clothes, introducing her to Jane and to Felix who were being loving and kind to their lost aunt. She looked at her sister's anxious face.

"I'm sorry," she repeated. "I won't stay long."

"Just sit with her for a bit. Or read to her. She likes to hear the Psalms still." Ruth's hand was on the doorknob and she had slipped out with the flowers before Esther could say anything further.

Esther took her mother's hand again, stroking the pale skin. "I've wanted to see you so badly, Mother," she said. "I wanted to tell you about my life, about Jane and Felix, about what happened to Gordon, about my work and my friends. I wanted to know about you and my brothers and their wives and their children." She paused. "I'm so sorry about what happened."

The old lady's eyes had closed again. It was impossible to say whether she was asleep or whether she had just retreated into a more comfortable absence. Esther spoke again, "I never stopped loving you Mother. I never stopped loving Father. It's just that your life was impossible for me."

There was still no response and Esther felt a brief wave of anger. Her mother would never give way, never compromise, never relent. She had punished her then and it felt as if she was punishing her now. Her mother opened her eyes and seemed to look at her. Was there a flicker of a smile? Was it recognition? Or was she seeing just another member of staff or some unconnected figure from the past? Or was it, as with babies, an illusion caused by wind? The eyes closed again and Esther looked at the blue-veined eyelids, the wispy hair and the shallow but steady breathing.

"I want you to know," Esther said more forcefully to the sleeping face. "I want you to hear what happened to me."

She began to speak, recounting in an even tone the story of her life since she had left home. She told her about the excitement of meeting Gordon, of her elation at life, of the thrill and delight of freedom. She spoke about how she had felt when Reuben had returned her letters, how grief and depression had overwhelmed her, how she had slowly recovered through therapy but how the scars remained. She told how the children had been born, how Gordon could not cope with the restrictions of domestic life, how he had left, how he had died, how she had remade her life once again. She spoke about how she had felt standing in the cemetery excluded from her father's funeral, how courageous she thought Ruth was to defy them and ask her to visit, even now when perhaps it was all too late.

It was different from the imagined conversations that had peppered the last thirty five years. Esther spoke the truth this time. She told her mother that she had been cruel. She told her that she had been wrong. She told her that she had been cowardly. "Sometimes," she said "I have hated you."

Her mother lay there, perhaps sleeping, perhaps with her eyes closed against her, perhaps simply confused by the sound of her voice, rising with anger, falling in sorrow. Esther stopped. Travelling up on the train she had not imagined what she would say. She had not intended to say any of this.

"I hope you have heard me," she finished. "I hope you have heard what you have missed and know what I have missed. I have missed you, Mother. I have tried to live well without your love but I could have lived better with it. I did not want this."

She looked at the slight form beneath the bedclothes, the lined face and wrinkled skin, the tremor in the hands. She knelt down beside the bed, reaching an arm across the shrunken body in an awkward embrace, stroking the thin white hair, placing her face next to her mother's and smelling the powdery talc on her skin. Her mother shifted slightly and Esther sat up again, willing her mother's eyes to open but they stayed closed.

Esther picked up the Bible which lay on the bedside table. It fell open at Deuteronomy and she began to read the familiar words with which Reuben would threaten and storm in his market-place sermons: 'Cursed shalt thou be in the city, and cursed shalt thou be in the field. Cursed shall be thy basket and thy store. Cursed shall be the fruit of thy body, and the fruit of thy land, the increase of thy kine, and the flocks of thy sheep. Cursed shalt thou be when thou comest in, and cursed shalt thou be when thou goest out.'

Her mother stirred slightly and Esther stopped. She turned to Psalms, flicking through the pages and began to read again, aloud this time, from Psalm 121. "I will lift up mine eyes unto the hills from whence cometh my help." It had been one of her mother's favourites. She would stand in the garden, looking out towards the moors, repeating the first two lines as she hung out the washing. Esther carried on, arriving more calmly at the final verses. "The Lord shall preserve thee from all evil: he shall preserve thy soul. The Lord shall preserve thy going out and thy coming in from this time forth, and even for evermore."

Her mother's eyes remained closed but her lips were moving, struggling to form the words and she managed to enunciate with sudden clarity the one word, "Amen."

Esther looked at her, wondering if her mother would speak again but the effort had exhausted her and she lay back on the pillows silently, her breathing subsiding, her chest returning to its gentle rise and fall. Esther closed the Bible.

"Amen, Mother," she said. "So be it."

She kissed the papery cheeks, gave the wasted hand a last squeeze and left the room, quietly closing the door behind her.

She found Ruth in the reception area, moving nervously from foot to foot, her eyes focused on the car park. They sat down in the chairs beside the potted plant.

"I brought you something," Esther said, reaching into her bag and bringing out a pad of notepaper, some envelopes and a book of stamps. "Will you take them?"

Ruth hesitated. "I'll take the stamps," she said. "I've no real call for the other except to write to you and if Reuben finds them he'll ask where they came from. But I will write. When Mother passes, I'll let you know." She slipped the stamps into the pocket of her skirt. "Did she speak to you at all?"

Esther shook her head.

"I don't think it will be long," Ruth said. "I think she's ready."

"It seemed that way to me," Esther said.

"I've got something for you as well," Ruth said, reaching into a plastic carrier bag at her feet. She put two photographs on the table. One was from their childhood, all seven of them on a windswept beach at Mablethorpe. Reuben looked about twelve years old and stood in the centre, feet planted firmly in the sand, arms crossed across his chest, scowling seriously at the camera. Esther stood on his left, her two long plaits reaching below her shoulders and her thin summer skirt blowing against her legs. Next to her, four year old Ruth's podgy little hands gripped her on one side and their mother on the other. On Reuben's other side Philip and David, six and seven years old, were grinning as if they had been told to behave themselves. Finally their father, in a white open-necked shirt and a pair of khaki shorts had drawn himself up into a tense, military pose and was staring determinedly straight at the camera. The picture had been scanned onto a page of A4.

"Where did you...how did you....?" Esther asked.

"Jerome – Reuben's youngest – borrowed the album for a school project about family history and they scanned some of the pictures. This one was..." Ruth hesitated. "It was in the waste bin. Reuben wouldn't let him use it."

"Because I'm in it?"

"Yes."

Esther had known it would be so. Had he thrown out all the other pictures of her? Had he cut her physically from the group pictures? "Show me the other one," she said.

"We had a celebration for Mother's eightieth," Ruth said shyly, placing the colour picture on the table. It showed the entire family. Reuben the patriarch, standing behind their mother's chair and around him his wife, their brothers and their wives and a bevy of children from toddlers to teenagers. Ruth was off to one side, holding the hands of two little girls who were straining to leave the picture.

"I've written everyone's names on the back," Ruth said "in case you don't recognise them all."

"Thank you Ruth, thank you," Esther said, leaning across and kissing her sister's weathered cheeks.

Seeing this picture, all fantasies of rescue vanished. Ruth was welded to the family, dependent on her brother for a home, without skills, without knowledge, without resources. There had always been women like this in the community. Those who didn't marry became skivvies to their relations, scurrying to make themselves useful, fearful of causing offence, disappearing seamlessly into the background of other peoples' lives. It would be like uprooting a tree.

"I brought you other things too," Esther said. She took out lip balm, and a small jar of sweetly scented hand cream. "Can you take these?"

Ruth hesitated but opened the hand cream and smelt it. "It smells lovely," she said. "It smells like you." She hesitated again and then handed the little jars back. "I can't," she said. "I'll smell different and someone will ask questions. Reuben will find out."

"Take the lip balm," Esther said, opening the tiny round tin. "Look – it hardly smells at all." She rubbed some gently onto her sister's cracked lips and eventually Ruth took the tin and slipped it into her carrier bag. Her eyes kept travelling to the window and the car park.

"I should get back to Mother," she said. "I don't want Reuben to find me down here."

She was afraid of him still, as they had all been afraid of him then. As if reading Esther's thoughts she added, "Reuben is a good man."

"Are you happy Ruth?" Esther asked, taking her sister's hands again.

Ruth's face closed. "The Lord didn't put us on this earth to be happy," she replied. "I thank the Lord for everything he has given me."

"Of course."

They sat in silence for a few moments and then Esther stood up. "I'll go now, Ruth," she said. "Thank you for letting me come."

"I'll pray for you," Ruth said.

They embraced and Esther stepped out through the glass doors. She turned once as she crossed the car park but Ruth had already vanished, hurrying back upstairs to their mother. Esther found a quiet side street where she could call a taxi without attracting attention. The light was fading and by the time she was on the local train it was dark outside. The smell of the diesel engine and the violent swing as the carriage rattled across points made her nauseous. Changing trains in Leeds she felt assaulted by the clamour of the station and in the hum of the fast train she withdrew thankfully into the anonymity of a window seat and silence. The rain drove against the train windows. Her mind was empty and her feelings numb, except for a phrase from St. John's gospel repeating in her head: 'It is finished.' It felt sacrilegious.

Late that evening as she sat staring into the fire and the glowing caverns of collapsing logs her phone pinged. It was a text from Felix. 'Safe home. See press. Don't worry,' it said enigmatically. She googled images of the opencast mine and the ambushed coal train and was glad she had not known earlier.

Clara

Clara drew her knees up to her chin and stared at the white tiled wall in front of her. There was no window, the light above her head was harsh and she had begun to lose track of time. Her phone, rucksack, shoelaces and belt had all been taken from her and there was nothing to do but sit, think and wait. Her left hand was bruised from climbing into the wagon. The exhilaration of the day had vanished and from time to time a burst of terror would overwhelm her. The custody officers had joked amongst themselves about the charges that would be brought against them.

Transgression

"You'll be going down for a very long time," one had said
as he showed her into the cell. "You can get a life sentence
for pissing about with the railways. That's right isn't it, Ed?"
he had called to the colleague who was pushing Helen into
the next cell.

"Correct," the colleague had replied. "Malicious Damage
Act 1861 – don't expect to see your family for a very long
time."

"Don't listen to them Clara," Helen had shouted before
the doors banged shut on both of them.

The solicitor had arrived but twenty-seven of them had
been arrested and he was shuffling between this custody
suite and one on the other side of town. It would be a time
before they could all be questioned, processed and bail
arranged. When they had asked if she wanted to let anyone
know where she was, she had given them Jay's number.

"Not your parents?" the officer had asked. "Are you sure
you're over eighteen?" and Clara had angrily repeated her
date of birth.

She counted the tiles on the wall in front of her, seven
across and seven down like a Connect 4 grid. She examined
the residual ink on her fingers from the prints they had
taken. She listened to the gradually quietening noises of the
custody suite, a door slammed here, receding footsteps
there. And she ran over the day's events repetitively
wondering what she could have done differently, why the
police had arrived so promptly, whether what had happened
could be construed as a success. She was ashamed of her
decision to unlock herself and was fearful that she had let
the others down. Eventually she drifted into fantasies of
herself in court, making speeches from the dock to a grizzled
judge and jury who broke into spontaneous applause. At
some point she must have pulled the blanket over herself
and fallen asleep because she was woken by a woman police
officer entering the cell with a lukewarm cup of tea and two
pieces of toast.

It was half-past ten the following morning before she found herself standing alone, outside the police station, in an unfamiliar part of town. Her shoes, her bag and her belt had been returned to her. They were each being released individually, as they were processed and there was no sign of anyone she knew. The charge was not the simple one of aggravated trespass which they had expected but that of obstructing an engine on the railway. It carried a much more serious sentence and would need to be heard at the Crown court.

She scanned the streets for Jay. Buffeted by passers-by, she slowly realised that he would have no idea when to expect her. She fumbled in her bag for her phone but all she was carrying was the cheap replacement that she had used for the action and it did not work. In the moments before the police had stormed the wagons she had disposed of its battery and sim card beneath the coal. Her breathing would not settle and overcome with dizziness she crossed the road and sat down on the low wall outside a church.

"You all right love?" asked an elderly woman with a shopping trolley. Clara nodded but the woman waited and said, "You look like you need to get home. Where've you to get to?"

The woman gave her directions to the right bus stop and Clara sat with her head leaning against the cold glass of the bus window, bumping her way back towards more familiar streets and the student room that was no bigger than the police cell where she had spent the night. She had missed that morning's lectures. She needed a shower. And more than anything else she wanted to see Jay.

It was four 'o' clock before he responded to any of her calls and texts.

"I'm at work Clara," he said curtly. "I'll be with you at seven."

Tears sprang to her eyes. She told herself that he didn't mean to be abrupt, criticised herself for expecting him to be available when he was working, reminded herself that it was dangerous to be distracted by phone calls on a building site and tried to settle to the essay that needed to be handed in that week. Texts came in from the other members of her affinity group and Helen called, warm and encouraging: "You did great. We did great. It'll be days before they get the line clear and the press coverage is fantastic." But it was Jay that she wanted and she was helpless in her dependence.

When he arrived he was carrying a bunch of flowers, an enormous smile and a bear hug that swung her off her feet.

"How's my favourite activist?"

His presence transformed her and her confidence rushed back. She chattered happily to him as they walked to the debriefing meeting that was taking place in a draughty church hall across town.

The room was full and the mood was high. Video of the train action was being transmitted onto a screen at one end of the room, the media coverage onto a screen at the other. Clara could see herself, clearly identifiable in the video and in a couple of the press photographs.

"Have you told your parents?" Jay asked.

"No." It had not occurred to Clara since she had angrily told the custody officer that they were not her preferred contact, that they might have seen some of the press coverage. "I'll call them after the meeting."

They broke into their affinity groups and trawled over the action, checking how each person was feeling, reliving the high points, puzzling over the difficulties and failures. Stefan, who was helping to facilitate, joined Clara's group. The same questions came up again and again. How had the police collected so much personal information? Why had they gone to the ambush first and not the mine as expected? Why had they only arrested the people on the train? Why were they bringing such draconian charges?

It was Stefan, slightly aloof from the action itself, who teased out the rational explanations and quietened the paranoia. He thought the police might have been monitoring phone movements, perhaps spotting an unusual cluster near the railway line. And once the ambush group had been arrested the custody suites would have been almost full. "They needed to leave some space for real criminals," he joked.

"That doesn't explain why the SWAT team arrived so quickly," objected Helen. "They came from London - and they wouldn't have been called until at least 7.30, when they found the first groups at the mine."

"The campaign against coal isn't a secret and they may have been on alert because it's the run-up to Copenhagen. If they were ready to go it's only a couple of hours up the motorway and they'd have diverted to the ambush, the moment they knew you were on the line."

Clara thought he was complacent. She didn't trust him.

As the meeting broke up and they left the hall Clara noticed Felix and Stefan poring over the laptop that had been used to show the press coverage. They were looking at a news feed.

"Anyone know anything about this?" Stefan said, turning to no-one in particular. Seeing Clara approach, Felix stepped away from the laptop, pretending to busy himself with cables and leads that needed to be tidied up. Clara peered briefly at the headline which read 'Leaked emails seized on by sceptics.'

"What's it about?" Jay asked her.

"Something about some leaked emails at a climate research unit. I need to phone my Mum." She had been worrying all through the meeting that her parents might have seen the press coverage. She flicked through her phone and pressed 'Home'. It was her mother who picked up and she sounded flustered.

"Oh, Clara, what a time to call."

"I'm sorry Mum I didn't realise 9.30 was late for you."

"It's not that it's late. It's everything else that's going on."

"I just wanted to give you a bit of a heads up about stuff you might have seen in the press..."

Her mother interrupted "Don't talk to me about the press. I've had them on the doorstep all day, ringing the doorbell, talking to the neighbours, climbing up the tree to peer through the window, half a dozen of them..."

Clara was astonished. "But that's extraordinary. Why were they looking for me at yours?"

"Don't be silly Clara. Why would they be looking for you? It's your Dad they're after."

"But..." In the background Clara could hear her mother's mobile ringing.

"That'll be your Dad. I've got to go. Talk to your brother." Her mother put the phone down with a clatter and Clara could briefly hear her berating her father on the mobile till she moved out of range. She was about to cut the call when George came on the line. Gradually she got the story out of him.

"Dad's been involved in some dodgy stuff with a patient and it looks like she's blabbed to one of the papers. So the rest of them have been round here all day looking for him. We couldn't get out the door without one of them jumping on us."

"What do you mean 'dodgy stuff'?"

"You know Clara, stuff the tabloids are interested in."

"I don't know. What do you mean?"

"Yes you do. He's been having an affair with a patient and apparently that's really off the scale. Off the effing Richter if you're a psycho-whatsit. Professional ethics and all that."

Clara struggled to take in what he was saying. The thought of her father involved in any kind of sexual relationship was repulsive but gradually the story became clear to her. Her mother would not be remotely concerned about her arrest because her father had somehow got himself all over another section of the media for something infinitely more interesting.

"Don't worry about it Clara. It'll blow over. I told Mum, it's Dad today, some soap star tomorrow."

Clara could see George puffing out his chest with protective male pride. It was almost sweet.

"Anyway," he continued "Why did you phone?" In George's world people only ever phoned when they wanted something. Feeling slightly deflated she told him about the action and the arrest.

"That's cool," he said. "Two members of the family with media profile. Really cool. But you know I'll be up there soon, when I sell my new songs, when I can get a new band together..."

She heard the click and hiss of a can of lager and realised that he was drinking. "George, will you tell Mum?"

"Yeah, yeah." He had lost interest.

"Tell her not to worry."

"I'll tell her."

Unsure whether he would or not, unsure what to think about the meeting, unsure what to think about the strange news from home, Clara snuggled against Jay's shoulder and they walked back to his flat.

WINTER 2009-2010

Esther

Esther sat at the kitchen table turning the pages of one newspaper while scanning the online stories of another. She was trying to establish the truth of Thomas Fortune's claim that he was 'all over the press' but her eyes were drawn to other stories. A harassed and elderly climate scientist, surrounded by a forest of microphones, struggled to finish a sentence. A waspish, balding journalist crowed triumphantly about scientific outrage. An overweight peer with dyed black hair whom she remembered from the expenses scandal accused the scientists of conspiracy. The press were calling it 'Climategate'. Leaked emails seemed to show that scientists had manipulated data to confirm their assumptions about global warming. She had spoken to Felix.

"If there's a conspiracy," he had said darkly "it's between the hackers and the oil companies who fund the denialist think-tanks. Follow the money."

"But it doesn't look good," she had said tentatively.

"Mum," he had said in the voice he reserved for moments when he thought she was being particularly stupid, "the facts of climate change are not altered by this. The world is warming. It's desperately dangerous. And they've chosen to release this crap two weeks before the most important climate negotiations of the decade. It's not a coincidence."

This was probably true.

"Anyway," he had said, "That's not why I'm phoning. I need to talk to you about Christmas."

He had called to explain that he would not be home until Christmas Eve and would have to leave again on Boxing Day. "I'm going to Copenhagen after all," he said.

Esther's feelings followed a familiar arc of anxiety before settling into silent disappointment. Felix's friend Stefan was part of a group who would be providing help to small states who could not afford to send enough diplomats and civil servants to represent them and he needed an extra person. At the previous year's talks Stefan and his team had covered meetings, taken notes, read and summarised the innumerable papers and run messages for the senior delegates of a small island state. Felix's firm would allow him to take the time off if he covered the break between Christmas and the New Year when no-one else wanted to come in. Esther could hear the elation and the urgency in Felix's voice.

"This is important Mum. I have to do this. And it's different from the other stuff. It's official. I'll have a delegate's pass. I'll be in the Bella Centre where the talks are taking place, not out shouting on the streets." He was trying to reassure her.

She had made one last attempt. "There are no trains on Boxing Day," she said.

"Stefan's going to pick me up," he said. "He's taking the car to his parents in London and he'll pick me up on his way back."

His phrase 'I have to do this' came back to her as she turned the pages of the newspaper. It was what she had said to Ruth on the day she had left, "I can't stay here. I have to do this." When you were young there were things you felt compelled to do whose consequences you could not imagine. The difference was, she thought, that the things which she had felt compelled to do were selfish and the things which Felix felt compelled to do were not.

She dragged her attention back to the coverage of the 'Psycho-Scandal' as one of the tabloids had begun to call it. There was little understanding in the press of the difference between the medically qualified psychiatrists and the less formally regulated psychotherapists and counsellors. Many of the articles were confused and confusing. Until Sunday the coverage had been limited. Most of it was concerned with the psychiatrist who had been struck off and Thomas's name was only mentioned in passing, along with a couple of other people whom APPA had clearly outed.

On Sunday however, the interview that Thomas had given to one of the tabloids had been published and in the days following a storm had broken. The interview was extremely damaging. Under the headline 'How they get away with it - celebrity therapist reveals the tricks of the trade' the journalist systematically destroyed Thomas's professionalism, his ethics, his appearance and his character. It was clear to Esther that Thomas had attempted to explain the complications of an erotic transference but what filled the pages, alongside an unflattering photograph of Thomas himself, was a portrait of a self-serving apologist for the worst kind of patient abuse. The journalist laid into 'the psychobabble of seduction', 'the shameless excuses of the predatory psych' and 'the delusions of a superannuated Don Juan'.

The story had been picked up with delight by every tabloid and Thomas's reputation and that of the profession was trashed across their columns. The quality press was more muted but one paper had clearly found its way to Nicole or at any rate to somebody representing her. 'Thomas Fortune much loved host of radio show 'Talking with Tom' is another of those being drawn into the scandal,' read the article. 'A former patient, who wishes to remain anonymous claims, "We had a short affair. He told me it was therapeutic and I believed him." Fortune denies the allegation and stated that patient confidentiality means that he is unable to comment.' This was, if anything, worse than the tabloid exposé which had at least contained no verifiable facts. Esther turned the pages to an editorial, calling for more regulation and contemptuously quoting the inadequate remarks of the Chair of the national association who had been wheeled out in a hopeless attempt to defend the profession. The irony was not lost on Esther. In other times it would have been Thomas performing this role and he would have done it effortlessly. His fall was spectacular, shaming and complete. Esther folded up the paper, closed her laptop and went through to her consulting room.

She watched Thomas get out of a taxi, putting up an umbrella to protect his expensive woollen coat as he stepped through the puddles to her front door. It felt as if it had been raining since September. "Warmer, wetter winters," Felix had told her "That's what to expect."

Thomas placed his coat carefully on the couch and seated himself in the chair opposite her. She noticed his gold cufflinks and the thin stripe in the subtle charcoal weave of his suit. The dove-grey socks matched the handkerchief in his top pocket and echoed the slightly darker shade of his shirt. His expression gave nothing away. She began before he did.

"I'm so sorry to see what has happened in the press Thomas. This must be making things very difficult for you."

He was silent for a moment and then said, "I have been traduced." The choice of words was strangely Shakespearean. "I knew that journalist at university. I trusted her. And there wasn't a hint - not a hint - during the interview that she was going to do this." A note of anguish had entered his voice.

"We need to discuss what to do," she said. "Some of your patients may have read this."

"My patients are the least of my worries."

She raised an eyebrow in surprise.

"I had a phone call from my editor this morning. They're dropping my column. And an email from my producer. They're suspending my radio slot – until further notice, whatever that means."

"I'm sorry to hear that," Esther said. She gave what she hoped was a sufficiently long pause before returning to the question of his patients. "I think we need to consider the effects of this publicity on any of your patients who may have read it."

He looked at her with a mixture of pity and contempt. "You don't get it, do you?" he said. "You really, really don't get it, do you Esther?"

She looked at him questioningly.

"This is my livelihood, my income. My column and my radio show – they're what pay the mortgage. They're what supports the family. Psychotherapy – I don't know how anyone can make a proper living from psychotherapy – psychotherapy's the icing on the cake." Catching her look, he shifted metaphor. "Well, the foundation perhaps, a building block."

"And it's what we're here to discuss."

He made a gesture of dismissal. "My patients are fine. They understand me. They support me. They know this is lies. My problem is how to deal with the fallout from the press coverage. Whether I can sue. Whether I can get an injunction. Whether I need to employ a publicist."

She raised an eyebrow again.

"It's the only language these people understand," he said. "I've got an appointment with a publicist this afternoon and I'm seeing my lawyer tomorrow morning."

There was something tragic about him. He did not seem to see where he was heading. "I think the lawyer may be a good idea," she said. "If there is some kind of investigation..."

"There's been no complaint."

"If your professional association decides on an enquiry..."

"There can't be an enquiry without a complaint. I've spoken to Nicole and she doesn't want to make a complaint."

"Thomas, the press have quoted her as saying that you had an affair and that you presented it as therapeutic."

"And it's lies." He was becoming angry. She pressed on, angered herself.

"Thomas, you told me yourself that you had some kind of sexual relationship with her."

"She's not going to make a complaint and there are no grounds for an enquiry. I've spoken to Melissa Augustine and the Foundation are backing me. I need a lawyer to tell me whether I can get an injunction and whether I can sue, not to defend me against some petty ethics tribunal."

She said nothing for several minutes. His smartly polished shoe was tapping on the bare boards of her consulting room. He was rattled but he was not going to concede. They limped to the end of the session, discussing one of his patients in a desultory way. As she got up, she put out her hand to shake his and held it for a brief second. "Think about what I said, Thomas. I'm very concerned for you, very concerned that a publicist and a court case might exacerbate matters. It might be that acknowledging your mistake and looking at the possibilities of apology and further training might settle things for you professionally."

He gave a curt nod and left.

Clara

Clara found herself restless, unable to settle to anything. Preparation for the court case was out of her hands, managed by the lawyers and the more experienced members of the group. They planned to argue a defence of necessity – that what they had done was necessary to prevent a greater evil – and she did not have the contacts to help assemble the expert witnesses required nor, she discovered, the logical mind that legal argument required. She had stepped back in frustration, anxious at the news that increasingly flooded the newspapers, envious of those who were going to Copenhagen and uncertain of how she could contribute now that the big action was over.

She was also beginning to panic at the prospect of the university vacation. She could not stay in her room beyond the official end of term. Jay had not responded to her tentative suggestions that she might stay with him once term had finished and she saw from Facebook that Ruby and her family would be spending Christmas in the Canaries. She spoke to her mother on the phone.

"I suppose I shall be here at Christmas," her mother said vaguely. "And I suppose George will. I don't know about your father. I don't know anything about your father these days. I imagine I'll cook a turkey."

Clara put the phone down and texted her mother "I'm a vegetarian. Remember?"

Jay was offhand about any Christmas plans. "I'll go to my sister's," he said "if I'm back from Copenhagen in time."

Helen was sympathetic but offered no alternative. "I'm away to Scotland to my family," she said.

Clara spoke briefly to her father who had become increasingly hard to contact, rarely picking up if she phoned. "Christmas?" he had said in surprise. "I've too much on to think about Christmas." And then, relenting slightly said "If you'd like me there, I suppose we could do one last Christmas as a family, before the house is sold."

This was the first time anyone had mentioned selling the house to her.

"Of course the house will be sold," her father had said, irritated at her surprise. "It'll be unaffordable after the divorce."

Clara felt stifled and panicky. Gradually the decision formed in her mind that she would go to Copenhagen after all, bail conditions or no. It would halve the time she had to spend at home and it would calm the restless, guilty feeling that she had not done all she could to influence the outcome.

"You can't," Jay said bluntly. "If you get stopped at the port they'll arrest you and breach of bail conditions is an imprisonable offence."

The conversation escalated rapidly into a row. He would not tell her what he would be doing in Copenhagen, would not say when he would be back in Sheffield and refused point blank when she suggested that they should travel together.

"If you're with me and you get stopped then that's both of us out of it. They'll arrest you and they'll make sure I miss the ferry."

"You're not on bail. There's no reason to stop you."

"Once passport control bring the police over they can keep you there for ever. If they don't find me on the stop list they'll just kick the back of the van and do me for defective lights."

"But that's not legal...

Jay looked at her pityingly, mocking her naivety.

"I'll walk through," she said. "You can drop me before the port. I'll go through as a foot passenger and meet you on board."

"Forget it Clara. Go home and see your family."

Clara lost all semblance of composure then and first accused him, then pleaded with him, then dissolved into helpless tears. He picked up his coat and left. She wrote a long text apologising but it was two days before she saw him again. He was kind but more distant than she remembered. She could not stop herself from asking "Are we OK? Do you still love me?"

Jay lifted her chin so that she looked directly into his warm eyes and the crinkly crows-foot lines. "I don't do love," he said. "You know that. But I do think you're beautiful and clever and lovely and I want to see you. OK?"

Clara had to make do with that. Jay promised that he would be back in Sheffield at the beginning of January and that she could stay at his flat for a couple of days if her student room was not available. She began to resign herself to the separation but the idea of four weeks at home was still anathema and she could not give up the idea of going to Copenhagen. She contacted the people she knew from the Youth Delegation. She scanned the online information about Klimaforum, the programme of alternative events that was taking place alongside the official conference. She checked how much money she had left in her bank account. Finally she sat cross-legged on her bed with the battered Connect 4 set in front of her. She sorted the counters into red and blue, closed her eyes and played a blind game against herself. "Four red and I go. Four blue and I don't." Opening her eyes she smiled. Four red counters sat in a satisfying diagonal across the frame. She bought her train and ferry tickets, handed in a final essay, packed her belongings into the storage cupboards at the end of the corridor and left.

Thomas

Thomas was on his way to the Foundation's headquarters on Merton Square. The weather had changed and the icy air threatened snow. The Georgian terrace and its familiar garden no longer gave him the same feeling of belonging. The bare branches of the plane trees silhouetted against the leaden sky seemed ominous rather than comforting. His meeting with the lawyer had been disappointing. No libel had been committed and he had no grounds to sue any of the offending papers. An injunction would be expensive to pursue and unlikely to succeed. His meeting with the publicist had been equally unsuccessful. "Unfortunately Mr Fortune," the man had said "I do not think you will be able to afford our fees. I suggest that you wait for this to blow over." He had left feeling humiliated.

It was true that in the passage of a week Thomas's name had largely disappeared from the press but the damage was done. His editor was not returning his phone calls and his radio producer was ignoring his emails. On the previous Sunday, the column which used to display a smiling portrait of himself had featured the headline 'Millennials under the Microscope' alongside a photo of a clinical psychologist who, the introduction stated, would be 'sharing insights from the latest research about you, your habits and your potential'. No explanation for his absence had been offered.

When he had received Melissa Augustine's summons to a meeting he had phoned Nicole again. He began to speak the moment he heard her tentative "Hello?" but she interrupted him.

"Thomas, I've been advised not to speak to you."

Thomas spoke rapidly. "I don't think you need take any notice of that Nicole but I won't keep you. I just wanted to let you know that the Foundation for Pluralist Psychotherapy may be holding an enquiry into the recent publicity and it's just possible that they may approach you for comment. If they do, I'd advise you to stay out of it.

These things can get very unpleasant and I wouldn't want you to be caught up in something that could be damaging to you."

"Thomas, I'm not supposed to talk to you."

"That's fine Nicole, that's fine. I'm phoning because I'm concerned, because I feel I still have a duty of care towards you. I don't want you to get hurt and I'm afraid that if you're pushed to make a statement, pushed to give testimony, then that is what will happen. My advice is to stay out of it. OK?"

Nicole had put the phone down without replying and he had been left feeling anxious that his call could be misinterpreted.

Melissa Augustine emerged from her office as he came up the steps and greeted him warmly, "Thomas, thank you so much for coming in. I always think these things are better done face to face."

She took him to one of the consulting rooms that was used for couple therapy. One of the three identical chairs was occupied by a neatly dressed, sharp-featured man of indeterminate age.

"You know Barry Fazackerly, don't you?" Melissa said.

Thomas did. He'd identified him a couple of years back as an annoyingly ambitious man and had deliberately diverted him to what he'd hoped was the dull backwater of the Ethics Panel.

"You'll remember that Barry's recently become Chair of the Ethics Panel," Melissa continued "so I'm very glad that he's been able to join us this afternoon."

Thomas leant across and shook hands.

"I wanted to start by saying how sorry we all are about the awful press coverage you've been suffering," Melissa said. "We can only imagine how disruptive and invasive that must have been. I also wanted to say personally that I have every confidence that your name will be cleared."

Barry Fazackerly said nothing and Melissa carried on.

"What we wanted to alert you to is that because of the press coverage and the constant enquiries from journalists that we've been receiving, the Foundation feels that the best way to clear the air is to hold an internal enquiry into the allegations that have been made against you. The Ethics Panel met last night and agreed that would be the best way forward."

Barry Fazackerly was nodding in thin-lipped agreement.

"I'm not aware there's been any complaint," Thomas said.

"No," said Melissa "there hasn't. It's just a question of clearing the air, making it public that we take these kinds of allegations seriously, drawing a line under the episode."

"But without a complaint there are no grounds for the Ethics Panel to be involved."

Barry Fazackerly came to life. "Not so," he said.

"Third party complaints aren't admissible," Thomas said firmly. He knew the Foundation's Code of Ethics. He had been responsible for drafting it.

"Under Clause Seven there are two possible avenues," Barry replied." Bringing the organisation into disrepute is one. The other is the provision for a member who is concerned about the competence of a colleague to practice to alert the Panel to their concerns and ask them to investigate."

"Neither of those apply," Thomas said. "That clause was only included to deal with gross breaches of professional conduct that can't be addressed in any other way. The Guidance Notes make that clear."

"In which case we disagree about the meaning of gross professional misconduct," Barry replied.

"This is a trumped up moral panic...Are you seriously telling me you'd rather believe the gutter press than support a colleague who's being dragged through the mud merely for doing his job responsibly, representing the profession to the best of his ability..." Thomas was aware that he was sounding shrill.

Melissa placed a hand on his arm. "Thomas listen, listen."

He could not calm himself. "And you of all people Melissa," he said. "You know me. You've worked with me."

Barry Fazackerly intervened again. "This was an Ethics Panel decision. It was democratically arrived at. The minutes will be available shortly."

"Please listen Thomas," Melissa said. Her voice was warm but there was an edge to it which he recognised from her dealings with trainees. "I'm sure that this will clear your name and set everything straight but you must realise that we can't treat you differently from anyone else just because we know and like and respect you."

Barry Fazackerly neither knew, nor liked nor respected him. Thomas cursed himself for failing to check the man's ambition. "This is envy, vengefulness, a petty attack with no substance..." he said and instantly regretted the words. He felt vertiginous, out of control.

Melissa ignored the remark. "It's in everyone's interests that this is dealt with as quickly as possible," she said. "We need to explain to you what will happen next, what the process is and what your rights are."

Thomas fell silent. There would be an Ethics Panel hearing in the New Year, as soon as it could be arranged. They had contacted the patient behind the allegation and she would be asked if she wished to make a statement. He could submit testimonials and statements in support of his position. He could be accompanied to the hearing by a representative, who could be a lawyer if he wished. There was a right of appeal to the national body.

Thomas didn't ask them how they knew who the patient was. It was humiliatingly clear to him that gossip, rumour and information from APPA had revealed it to anyone who wished to know.

"There's one more difficult thing," Melissa said finally, turning to Barry.

The man pretended to consult the notes that he held on his knee. "The Panel decided," he said, "that in the light of the seriousness of the allegations, you should be required to suspend your practice until this case is determined."

Thomas could not stop himself from blurting out, "But it's my livelihood, my income." Then collecting himself he changed tack. "My responsibilities to my patients make that impossible," he said firmly. "I can't do that. I can't abandon people in the middle of treatment."

Fazackerly stood up. "I'd advise you to comply with the Panel's instructions," he said. "The letter should be with you in the morning. Now, if you'd excuse me, I have patients to see." He left without shaking hands. Melissa steered Thomas into her office.

"I'm so, so sorry about this Thomas," she said.

He said nothing, merely nodded in acknowledgment.

"Christmas means that your patients will be expecting a break anyway," she said. "And I'd be very happy to help you arrange cover once the holiday is over. I know it's not ideal but the Panel were unanimous unfortunately. They felt they had to conform to what would happen in the public sector. And we really will try to expedite this."

In the public sector his salary would have continued to be paid. In the public sector he would have had a Trade Union to defend him.

Melissa Augustine drew the conversation to a close. "I hope you manage to have a lovely Christmas Thomas, despite all this."

Thomas pushed open the heavy front door and stepped out into Merton Square. Thin flakes of snow were just beginning to settle on the pavement. He felt utterly alone.

Esther

Esther scanned the news from Copenhagen, willing herself to understand it and willing – more for Felix's sake than for the world's – that the outcome would be good. If she had still been prayerful she would have prayed. Instead she turned the thermostat down, remembered to turn the lights out and tried to leave the car at home. She watched reporters muffled against the cold of the Danish winter, standing outside the dome of the Bella Conference Centre, talking about mitigation targets, parts per million and a leaked negotiating document that looked as if it might scupper the last vestiges of trust between the rich nations and the developing world. Occasionally the television showed images of the demonstrations – first the surging, chanting, singing crowds and then the hundreds of young people arrested, forced into stress positions on the freezing ground, their arms cuffed behind them. She tried to put the images out of her mind, willing Felix to text, willing him to be safe, willing for the conference to be over and for him to come home.

Esther gave her attention to her patients and prepared for Christmas. Her family had not marked the festival, considering it a pagan celebration. The mysteries of Santa Claus, Nativity plays and Christmas Dinner were hidden from her by the Assembly's belief that all were the work of the devil. Shortly after her marriage, a Christmas visit to Gordon's parents - a dull affair of sherry and stilted conversation - had convinced her that it had nothing to offer but embarrassment and gift packs of cheap toiletries. It was only when Jane and Felix were born that this had changed. Together with Meena she had discovered the pleasures of filling a stocking with small gifts that brought delight and wonder to the faces of four year olds. Together they had fallen in love with tinsel and fairy lights, negotiated the decorating of a Christmas tree and shed the obligatory tears at the Nativity play. "It's a celebration," Meena had said "It doesn't matter what it's for. Join in and enjoy yourself."

Gradually Christmas had become very special to Esther. After Gordon's death the quiet unity of the threesome who were now all the family she had, felt particularly precious. Esther was sadly aware that this was the last year that she could count on them all being together. Next year there would be Jane's in-laws and their competing expectations to contend with.

"Will you come as usual?" asked Meena on hearing that Felix would not be home until Christmas Eve. They habitually shared a celebratory meal that combined elements of a Hindu feast and a British roast dinner, one year at Esther's house, the next at Meena's. Both her children and Meena's clung to the rituals, the stories and the jokes that the years of intimacy between the two families had established.

"Of course," Esther said. "They wouldn't forgive me if we didn't come."

Ten days before Christmas the weather changed. Freezing arctic air swept across the country. Snow fell. Cars sat stranded or abandoned on motorways. Airports closed and ferries failed to run. Esther scattered salt on the doorstep, refilled her bird feeders and poured boiling water on the frozen garden pond.

The news from Copenhagen came in. There was no agreement. There was no treaty. The weak promises made came nowhere near the reductions needed and nothing was legally binding. Esther felt the same dull shock she had felt when Reuben had returned her letters and forbidden any further contact with her family. Something had ended. Something had broken which could not be recovered from.

Felix texted 'Stormbound in Ejsberg. Don't worry. Home soon.' And that was all. She felt numb, fearful at what this failure would do to Felix, ashamed at the world she had brought him into.

He arrived, as promised, on Christmas Eve. He had been travelling for three days. He was quieter than usual and he looked pale and exhausted. The spark of irritation that normally lay just beneath the surface had vanished and he did not respond to her enquiries about the conference.

"Let's just enjoy Christmas," was all he would say.

At Meena's house she watched him sprawled on the sofa with Anusha, leaning his head on her shoulder. Anusha stroked his hair in a quiet gesture of affection. Their usual banter was absent and Anusha herself seemed only half present, locked in silent solidarity with Felix's grief. It was left to Meena's husband Paresh to rescue the situation with his customary delight in cheating at Scrabble and a torrent of bad jokes from the Christmas crackers: "What do you call a donkey with three legs? A wonky!"

Anusha and Felix smiled weakly from the sofa and came across to watch the scrabble game. Anusha rearranged her father's letters. "Look Daddy, have 'boils' instead and you get the triple."

Late on Christmas night, after Jane had gone to bed, Felix took the new bottle of whisky and two glasses from the cupboard. "Want some?" The heavy glasses were engraved, one with a picture of a salmon, the other with an otter. Gordon had bought them, early in the marriage. "Which am I?" she had asked. "Otter or salmon?" "Neither," he had replied. "You're the river flowing round them." She looked at the delicate artist's fingers which Felix curled round the glass. They were his father's.

"I don't know why I thought there'd be an outcome," Felix said at last. "All these years we were saying 'Copenhagen, that's when it will get sorted out, that's what we're working towards, that's what we have to influence' but it was nonsense really. Power wins. Every time."

Slowly Felix told her about the long, disorientating days and nights in the stuffy atmosphere of the Bella Centre, the sharp-elbowed men in suits, the piles and piles of papers, of detail, of confusion. He spoke about the people from the small island state whom he had been working with. Their drinking water was already affected by salination. It wouldn't be long before their arable land was unusable. Two of the uninhabited islands in the archipelago had already disappeared beneath rising sea levels.

"They were good people," he said "but they had little expectation. They thought we were naïve."

He swirled the whisky in his glass and traced the indented outline of the otter with his finger.

"We went out for a meal with them on the Friday night. Everything that mattered to them had been deleted. They were leaving the following morning, not staying for the Plenary."

"The Plenary?"

"When the outcome would be announced. When the President of Denmark was supposed to bask in the glory of a solution."

But there had been no glory to bask in. The plenary had broken down in continued disagreement. The Accord that was salvaged from the two weeks of talks was toothless. It condemned the small island states to the waves. They might as well have signed their names in water one despairing delegate had said. The money promised to the developing countries would not even pay for the coffins of the dead children.

"They saved the banks," Felix said "but they won't save the biosphere."

They sat in a silence broken only by the ticking of a mantelshelf clock that had once belonged to Gordon's grandfather. When Esther spoke, the words came slowly. "Naivety allows you to have hope," she said. "I could only leave my family because I didn't know what the consequences would be. Innocence allows you to act."

Felix looked at her for the first time.

"And then it hurts," she finished. "It hurts terribly. It can feel as if the shock might kill you."

The silence continued, quiet, companionable, affectionate.

"I love you, Mum," he said and crossed from the armchair to sit beside her on the sofa. He picked up her hand and twined his fingers loosely in hers.

"What will you do now?" she asked.

"Don't know." He gave her a faint grin. "Are you hoping I might stop chaining myself to diggers?"

She smiled. "I think you'll do whatever you have to," she said. "I think you'll do whatever is right."

On the 26th, Stefan turned up as promised, apologising that he was afraid to stop long in case the engine would not start again in the cold. Felix left in a flurry of hasty farewells.

"I wondered," Jane said as they sat in the empty kitchen, "whether you might like to go to the spa again. And perhaps to the sales. And maybe have time to look at the designs for my bridesmaids' dresses?"

Dear, practical Jane. Esther worried sometimes that her sweet, competent daughter felt neglected. "You've never neglected me," Jane said. "It's just that Felix needs you more and accepts you less so he's always needed more time to get the same amount of love." For two days Esther lost herself with relief in massage oils, clothes and feminine conversation.

On the 28th post arrived. There was a letter in Ruth's familiar round handwriting, in an envelope this time and with a current stamp fixed firmly in the top corner. Esther knew immediately what it would say. She opened it slowly, read it and then passed it to Jane.

'Dear Esther,
Mother was received into the arms of our Lord on December 25th. Reuben was with her when she passed. The funeral is not until Jan 3rd because everywhere is shut and the ground is frozen too hard to dig. You may come to the Cemetery, 2.30 if you wish. Reuben knows I have written. I am praying for you and for your children.
Your loving sister, Ruth.'

"Would you like me to come with you?" Jane asked.
"I would like that very much," Esther replied.

Clara

Clara sat on a train, rattling northwards. The Christmas holiday was over. Her father had returned to London. Her mother had gone back to work. She felt as confused now as she had for the past three weeks. When she had walked successfully through passport control and onto the ferry for Denmark she had felt momentarily elated but the feeling had not lasted. Once on board she could not find Jay. As they left UK waters, she lost signal and as they approached the Scandinavian coast, texts and calls became prohibitively expensive. She wandered from one deck to another searching for him and spent an uncomfortable night propped at a cafeteria table because she could not afford a cabin. Finally, as the call came to disembark, she spotted him amongst the crowds moving towards the car deck.

"Clara!" he said in surprise.

And then he was swept away in the crush of people hurrying to retrieve their vehicles. Clara had stayed with a group of Danish campaigners, allocated randomly to their flat on the outskirts of Copenhagen by a flustered organiser, and tried to make contact with Jay. He was frustratingly elusive, billeted on the other side of the city and reluctant to share details of what he was doing. She was pole-axed by the cold, overwhelmed by the surging, chanting crowds of demonstrators and left breathless and terrified by the riot police. Wherever Jay was, he was not in the few square metres of icy pavement where she found herself penned in, jammed between tall buildings, shouting crowds and the whirr of police helicopters. She managed briefly to coincide with him over a cup of coffee in the sports centre where the alternative 'People's Summit' or KlimaForum was being held.

"Be careful, Clara," he said. "The Danish Police are for real and they're in touch with their UK counterparts. If you get arrested you'll be in trouble. Stay out of stuff."

So she had rejected invitations to help reclaim the Bella Centre and instead hung out at KlimaForum, listening to talks, attending workshops and continually checking her phone for a text from Jay. As news of the negotiations became more pessimistic and the mood became angrier Clara withdrew into herself feeling useless and superfluous. She found herself believing irrationally that when the US President flew in he would somehow save the negotiations and when of course his presence had no such effect, the collapse of hope was all the more devastating. In the bleak aftermath of the journey home Clara managed to find Jay on the ferry and presented him with the gift she had carefully chosen from the bookstall. She had inscribed it 'To dearest Jay, Christmas 2009, with all my love, Clara'. He flicked through its pages.

"*The Global Fight for Climate Justice*," he said. "Interesting. But you know I don't read."

"You could begin," she said. "If capitalism can change, so can you."

"You're very sweet," Jay said but the words sounded automatic and the sentiment hollow.

He disappeared to the Duty-Free shop and came back with a small bottle of perfume. "I don't usually do Christmas presents," he said. "Consider yourself honoured."

They said goodbye before the ferry docked, without making any arrangements to meet again.

"When will I see you?" she had asked.

"I'll text," was all he had replied, disappearing towards the car deck.

She had walked into the kitchen at home to find her mother stuffing a turkey and George slumped in a chair at the table with a glass of whisky in his hand, critically observing. Gail Fortune had looked up in surprise, a lump of grey stuffing in her hand.

"Oh Clara, you're here at last. You can tell me which end this is meant to go."

"Up its arse, Mum, up its arse," George had said. Exhausted, she had walked past them without speaking and retreated to her bedroom and the shower and some clean clothes.

When Clara had come downstairs and placed the presents she had bought at the KlimaForum bookstall beneath the Christmas tree, her mother was falsely cheerful, fiddling with the decorations. "I thought we'd make it look nice, one last time."

She seemed to think Clara had been away on a skiing trip.

"Not skiing?" she had said in surprise when Clara had corrected her. "I was sure you said skiing. Was it a field trip then?"

"Kind of," Clara had replied.

Her father was morose. "As well as can be expected," was all he said in response to her attempt to open conversation.

It was George who finally explained what had happened. He had pulled the offending newspaper from beneath the cushions of the sofa and shown her the article that had led to the suspension of her father's radio show and the cancellation of his newspaper column.

"He ain't really saying," George added "but I think there's going to be some kind of an enquiry. Professional misconduct. And if that one sticks - curtains I guess. Bye-bye career."

Clara felt a constriction at her throat. "What about Mum? How is Mum with it all?"

"Don't think she cares any more. He's only here because they thought it would be nice for us to do one last Christmas together. Don't ask me why. It all sucks as far as I can see."

The presents she had bought at the KlimaForum bookstall seemed less appropriate when opened in the overheated sitting room amongst the twinkling Christmas lights and strings of Christmas cards. Her mother had turned the pages of *Confessions of an Eco-Sinner* in puzzlement and her father had put aside *Ecopsychology* without comment. Only George had been appreciative.

"That's cool, Clar," he said flipping through the cartoon explanation of climate change. "I didn't have any money for presents this year, but I've written you a song." He picked out the melody on the piano and sang.

"My sister is the stars in the sky,
My sister is the sun on ice,
My sister is the ocean's living life
She puts herself between you and the abyss
Hers is the voice that tells you desist
Wash your oil from her hair,

Wash your coal from her skin,
Let her breathe, let us breathe, let us breathe."

"That's lovely George," Clara had said, unable to stop the tears from coursing down her cheeks. Her father had rolled his eyes and passed her a box of tissues.

"I thought children were meant to grow out of crying all the time," her mother had said.

Clara had texted Jay repeatedly but received no reply.

When Ruby came back from the Canaries they met, sitting as ever in the window seat in Clara's room at the top of the house. Except it wasn't the same as ever. Clara felt as though she was waving to Ruby through a bank of fog which only occasionally cleared, and that when briefly it did it revealed Ruby moving purposefully away from her. She could not understand Clara's devastation at the result of Copenhagen.

"There'll be another attempt won't there? Loads of negotiations take years to complete. It's not the end of the world."

"I think that's exactly what it is," Clara replied. "I do think it's the end of world – certainly as we know it, certainly as we grew up to expect it would be."

"Oh, Clar, you're such a pessimist. Tell me about something else. Tell me about this boyfriend of yours."

Clara showed Ruby the photos of Jay on her phone. "Looks a bit old," Ruby commented. And then when Clara tried to explain about polyamory Ruby exploded in disbelief. "You've got to be joking, Clar. No way."

Clara withdrew hurt and Ruby back-pedalled. "I just mean I wouldn't put up with it, that's all. If it's really what you're into I guess it's fine."

Eventually Ruby had asked about the family. "What's going on with your folks? The atmosphere down there's about minus 273°C."

Clara explained and Ruby had momentarily returned to her old warmth and compassion. "What a fuck-up. What a total and complete fuck-up. I'm so sorry Clar."

She had put her arms round her. Once more Clara could not stop the tears from running down her face and Ruby had looked at her old friend with a mixture of pity and exasperation. "Come on, Clar. Get a grip. It's crap but it's probably for the best. You'll get through it."

They had not met again and now, sitting on the train, Clara felt bleakly that Ruby was lost to her. She read the text from Jay again and again. There was no Christmas or New Year message. It just said 'Back in Sheffield. Sorry about silence. Battery problem with phone. OK to come for a few days if you want.'

Esther

The taxi dropped them at the Cemetery gates. Felix had joined them at Leeds and now Esther walked slowly up the driveway between her son and her daughter, her arms linked loosely in theirs. A low hedge of box lined the carefully manicured rose gardens and at the end of the driveway sat the anonymous, municipal Chapel of Rest. She glanced at Felix and then at Jane. Felix's dark suit hung easily on his lean frame, the only clue to his other existence the leather satchel slung across his back in which he carried his pencils, a sketch pad and probably a book. Jane, walking easily beside her looked straight ahead, her square, reassuring body speaking competence with each step. Jane's hand lay warmly on her own, Felix's sat loosely, his fingers occasionally breaking into a restless, tapping rhythm.

Esther steered them round the Chapel of Rest towards the far end of the cemetery where the neat rows of gravestones gave way to rough, unoccupied grassland. The grave which had taken her father's coffin twenty years earlier had been re-opened and the earth was heaped on each side awaiting the arrival of the funeral party. Esther nodded towards a bench some yards away.

"We can sit here."

The sky was a uniform January grey, the air still. Esther was momentarily back in the interminable meetings in the crowded room with the high windows which admitted light but kept the world out, listening to the crescendo and diminuendo of the elders' voices. It was Felix who broke the silence.

"What I still don't understand is why we couldn't go to the Church."

"Meeting Rooms," Esther said. "They don't have Churches."

"Whatever. But why aren't we invited?"

"Because we don't believe. Because they are walking in the light and we are not. They think that everything worldly is the work of the devil and they're afraid of being contaminated by us."

"So they're crazy."

"You could say that." She paused. Jane squeezed her hand. "They're also very loving. When you're not being terrified by hell or bored witless by the sermons it's a very safe place to be."

Jane shot a critical glance at her brother. "It's complicated Felix."

Esther nodded her agreement. "It's complicated because I loved them."

They heard the hearse before they saw it, the low engine rumbling in second gear, so that it kept just in front of the procession of mourners who followed, heads bowed and on foot. There were forty or fifty people, from an elderly lady pushed in a wheelchair by a muscular young man to groups of schoolchildren, toddlers and a baby carried in its mother's arms. Esther struggled to recognise anyone, gradually picking out her brothers from their privileged positions at the front. She scanned the group again and again for Ruth, eventually spotting her hurrying up the road with a small girl in tow and hearing her voice, briefly caught in the silence, "She needed the toilet."

The coffin was slid from the back of the hearse onto the shoulders of six young men. They were not undertakers' men Esther realised but Assembly members. She could not have said how she knew. Was it the haircuts? The style of the suits? The in-turned, self-sufficient demeanour? How was it after all these years that this group of people could not be anything but Assembly members?

"What happens now?" whispered Felix as the people grouped themselves around the graveside. "Is this where we get the 'ashes to ashes' stuff?"

Esther shook her head. "That's Church of England."

"What's the difference?"

"The Assembly don't have set services. Someone will speak. Someone will preach."

"Tell us who's who."

Esther picked out her brothers for them. Reuben now approaching sixty, tall and dark and still with a full head of hair, stood an imposing head above the others. Philip and David had placed themselves on either side of him, two solid pale men with the balding heads and jowly cheeks of late middle age. There was a whole generation whom she did not recognise at all, nephews and nieces, cousins and second cousins, wives and husbands and other Assembly members.

"And Ruth," Jane said "Which one is Aunt Ruth?"

Esther pointed to the drab figure at the edge of the crowd, attending to a child's snuffly nose.

Snatches of Reuben's voice were carried across to them in the still air. Esther could hear that he had started with the familiar denunciations of human nature, "It is carnal, it is lustful, it is deceitful. It craves the debauchery of its own wickedness," stirring his audience's anxiety with reminders of what awaited the sinful, "The place of unquenchable fire, the place of memory and remorse..." before comforting them with a paraphrase from St. Paul, "The mind governed by the flesh is death, but the mind governed by the Spirit is life and peace."

Esther's head dropped automatically as the assembled company spoke the Lord's Prayer and she found her lips repeating the words beneath her breath. The coffin was lowered into the grave and the young men who had carried it began to shovel the earth back in. The group began to move away from the graveside.

"Is that it?" asked Felix.

"That's it. They'll have had a longer service earlier at the Meeting Room."

"And they're not going to speak to you?"

"No. They think they'd be contaminated. They think any contact could corrupt them."

"Bollocks," Felix said. "I think it's revenge. They can't forgive you for living your own life."

The group around the grave was beginning to disperse and move down the road towards the Chapel of Rest and the exit. They left without looking towards Esther and her children and without making eye contact. Ruth, trailing the rest of the company, moved slowly, crabwise towards them, gradually putting distance between herself and her family until she stood in front of the bench where Esther, Jane and Felix sat. Esther looked up at the lined, weary face.

"Ruth," she said, standing up to embrace her sister.

"I'm glad you came Esther. I told Reuben I would speak to you."

"Thank you for letting me know."

Felix and Jane had also risen. "This is your Aunt Ruth," Esther said. "Ruth, this is my daughter Jane and my son Felix."

Jane held out her hand as she might have done at a parents' evening. "I'm delighted to meet you," she said.

Ruth took the hand tentatively. "Jane," she said wonderingly, "and Felix. How lovely."

"How are you Ruth?" Esther asked.

Ruth took a long time to reply. "It's a blessing to know that Mother is walking with the Lord," she said eventually.

Two small girls detached themselves from the dark-coated mass walking towards the gates and ran towards Ruth.

"Auntie Ruth, Auntie Ruth, we're going."

They stopped several yards away, one looking back towards the family slowly processing down the drive, the other looking at her feet in awkward embarrassment.

"The big one's Philip's granddaughter Sarah and the little one's David's granddaughter, Jessie," Ruth said.

Esther checked her surprise. Of course there would be grandchildren by now. Assembly members married young and the children arrived quickly.

Ruth smiled and waved to the little girls. "I'm just coming." She turned back to Esther. "Reuben says I can write if I want to," she said. "And you can write back. The Elders prayed about it."

Esther embraced her sister. "Dear Ruth," she said. "Dear, dear Ruth."

On the train heading South, after Felix had left them at Leeds, Jane said "Will you write?"

"I don't know," Esther replied. She was twisting a loose thread from her scarf around a finger. "After I saw my mother that last time, something changed." She hesitated, searching for the words that would not make her seem crazy. "For years I've had voices from the Bible constantly in my head. Phrases arrive, sometimes like accusations, sometimes as commentary, not because I want them there. They just float up from the unconscious and speak to me."

Jane's face spoke puzzlement but she said nothing.

"The strange thing is that since I saw Mother, they seem to have gone away. On the train coming back I had this one phrase repeatedly in my mind – 'It is finished.' It's Christ's words on the Cross. 'He said, It is finished: and he bowed his head, and gave up the ghost.' It felt sacrilegious but I couldn't get it out of my head."

Jane frowned in concentration.

"Then the next day that phrase was gone and since then, the voices seem to have gone away altogether. I don't think they've spoken to me since that visit."

"That's a good thing isn't it?"

"I think so. It feels like the Bible's not persecuting me anymore."

"How can a book persecute you?"

Esther smiled. "Oh it can, believe me, it can," she said.

They sat quietly for a moment.

"So will you write to Aunt Ruth?" Jane asked.

"I don't know."

The train surged on through the dark and it was fifty miles or so before either spoke again. Esther watched her daughter help a mother encumbered with a pushchair, toddler and baby off the train. When she returned to her seat Jane spoke again.

"'It is finished' doesn't say anything about what is finished, does it?"

"Meaning?"

"If it's the persecution that's finished, then you could write to Aunt Ruth."

Esther took her daughter's hand. "You are a good person, Jane," she said.

Thomas

Thomas spread the papers out on his desk and peered at the spreadsheets on his laptop. On his left were a pile of financial documents and on the right those about the Ethics Panel hearing. He could not make the figures on the spreadsheet balance. The mortgage on the family home, the mortgage on the London flat, his contribution to Clara's living costs and the outstanding debts on his three credit cards far exceeded his much reduced income. He scanned the letter on the top of the pile: his wife's solicitor was demanding disclosure of all his pension schemes and investments. It was pointless. They had halved in value since the 2008 crash, besides which he would have to cash them all in to get through the next few months.

He composed an email to Clara, telling her that he would be forced to suspend his payments to her at the end of the month and suggesting that she find herself a part-time job that was compatible with her studies or ask her mother for help. He could not make the email come out satisfactorily. The first version felt too impersonal, the second too apologetic, while the third was a torrent of self-pity. He gave up, deleted the drafts and wrote instead to his wife explaining that in a few weeks' time there would be no investments to disclose.

Thomas pushed this stack to one side and looked at the other. There was a formal letter from the Foundation about the hearing, with copies of the Code of Ethics and procedures for the panel hearing. They had appointed an investigator who would be assembling evidence, copies of all documents would be provided to him, he had a right to be represented at the hearing etc., etc. He flicked through the documents which he had assembled himself: a letter from his GP confirming he had been advised to take time off work due to stress, a report from a well-known psychiatrist which had cost him a lot of money but declared him fit to practice, and a letter from Esther which was less supportive than he had hoped. She had stated the facts about supervision neutrally and it was less than fulsome.

He began assembling the notes of his work with Nicole which the panel had asked to see. They were sparse with long gaps when he had recorded nothing. Using an old pad of A4 which he had found in the bottom drawer of his desk he started carefully reconstructing an account which he would be happy to submit. He was glad that he had never succumbed to the ease of an electronic record. At least this way he could present the truth as he saw it now. He put down the black biro and made the next entry in blue, pleased at this touch of authenticity.

The previous week Thomas had spent a dispiriting session with the lawyer who was being provided by his insurers. She was an abrupt, efficient woman with a sharp manner who specialised in tribunals and complaints. Thomas was relieved that she was on his side rather than the other but he did not find her encouraging. Prior to their meeting she had red-pencilled her way through Thomas's prepared statement, removing his heartfelt justifications and lengthy theoretical explanations and substituting some terse and uncontroversial facts instead. When they met face to face, she had poured cold water on Thomas' assertion that he had not been at fault due to Nicole's erotic transference to him.

"Let me give you an example," she had said. "If you were an engineer and you told me that your bridge had collapsed due to a rare but well-known flaw in the materials, that wouldn't be much of a defence. You would be expected to design your bridge to take account of that. It seems to me the erotic transference is rather the same. You're supposed to know about it, take evasive action, design it out."

"But I'm the victim here," Thomas had protested. "Nicole was manipulative. She set out to seduce me. And then when she'd got me exactly where she wanted me, she discarded me and started this conspiracy of lies."

"Let's look at the facts," the lawyer had said. "Let's look at the clauses of the Code of Ethics you are accused of breaching and the detail of what actually happened. Then we can see whether you have a case to answer, whether there are facts you will need to admit and whether there are facts we can present in mitigation – such as the power of an erotic transference."

Humiliatingly, she had taken him through the evening Nicole had spent at his flat.

"Was it after the therapy had ended or before?"

"After."

"How long after?"

"Two weeks."

"What happened when she arrived?"

"We embraced, we came through to my consulting room."

"Did you kiss?"

"Yes."

"On the lips?"

"Yes."

"Did your tongue penetrate her mouth?"

Thomas had protested again. "I don't know, I can't remember. Does it matter?"

"I'm asking you questions that you may be asked by the panel."

And so it had gone on, down to the last humiliating details of how she had knelt on the floor beside him, resting her head in his lap, while he had stroked her hair and she had fondled her way inside his clothing.

"But we didn't have sexual intercourse," he insisted. "We did not actually have sex. And it was after the therapy had ended."

The lawyer had turned the pages of the Code of Ethics. "That detail may not be pertinent," she had said. "What it says here is 'Psychotherapists should maintain appropriate boundaries with their patients. They must take care not to exploit or abuse current or former patients financially, emotionally or sexually'."

She had been equally sharp about Thomas's hope that Nicole would not make a statement - "We have to prepare on the basis that she will," - and brisk about the risks of denying that sexual contact had taken place. "If you do that it would be difficult for me to represent you given what you have put in your written statement and discussed with me today."

It was only at the end of the hour they spent together that the lawyer had advised him on how to reply to the difficult questions he would inevitably be asked and guided him to the arguments they could make in mitigation.

Esther had been kinder but equally blunt. "No-one is going to deny that there was an erotic transference in play but you will not help matters by presenting yourself as the victim. It was your job to interpret that transference, your job to deal with it."

The trouble with middle-aged women, Thomas thought bitterly, was that they had no idea what it was like to be the victim of unwanted sexual attention. Who would fancy Esther Dunn anyway?

Esther had carried smoothly on. "If you admit the mistake, show that you understand the damage you may have caused, show remorse and a desire for reparation, then there's a chance that they will only impose minimal sanctions on you."

She had got under his skin again. "Remorse? You expect me to show remorse?" he had exploded. "After what has been done to me, after what I am being put through, after the excruciating, humiliating exposure I've been subjected to – you expect me to show remorse?"

She had looked at him with one eyebrow slightly raised, as if she could not quite believe what she was hearing.

"Thomas," she had said, wearily. "These are serious matters. You have admitted to a serious breach of professional conduct. Your actions are likely to have damaged your patient. You may not be able to manage remorse but it would be appropriate."

As always with Esther he had left feeling wrong-footed. He fiddled with his phone, wondering whether to risk contacting Nicole again.

Felix

Felix found himself angry all the time. At work he was furiously productive. In seminars he was sharp and dismissive. And in activist meetings he would contemptuously condemn any faltering, ill-thought opinion. Stefan had checked him once and he had apologised, withdrawing to the back of the meeting, taking out his sketchbook and experimenting with a newfound interest in caricature.

His particular ire was reserved for prominent environmentalists with whom he disagreed.

"All these people can talk about is changing light bulbs, growing potatoes or cosying up to the establishment," he said bitterly, "while the oil companies fund think tanks which provide misinformation and lobby government. We can't even bring the banks to justice."

People agreed with him but the conversations went nowhere. The mood in meetings had changed. The excitement and sense of purpose had vanished. After the first shocked and angry outbursts no-one discussed Copenhagen. They began mechanically to make plans for next summer's Climate Camp. Felix was cheered that the target would be the financial industry but he could find no enthusiasm for the lists of tasks which they made. People were drifting away. Some claimed exhaustion. Some cited family pressures. Others simply disappeared.

He spent a weekend in Birmingham with Anusha, stamping up and down the confines of her small flat, arguing with his invisible audiences till she said, "Stop, Felix, stop," and he had sat down on the settee and put his head in his hands.

"I feel the same, Felix" she said. "There used to be this little space where I could do my work, where I could talk about climate change to people who'd never heard the words but whose beliefs make them allies."

"And it's gone."

"It's gone. People are too worried about money or their jobs, or just getting by from day to day. And I don't think it's going to get any better."

"What do you mean?"

"We didn't get the lottery funding we were hoping for." Anusha's small local project – working with the city's minority communities about climate change – was dependent on an accumulation of local authority and charitable grants. Felix pulled his attention properly towards his old friend.

"I'm sorry. I didn't know."

"The lottery are channelling all their funds to the 2012 Olympics. The charitable trusts have seen their investment income slashed by the financial crash. And the local authority have said they can't afford to renew the grant."

"So that's it?"

"That's it. I'll be out of a job in May. Me and a load of Labour MPs as well if the polls are correct."

"Who cares about them? What's the difference between one lot of neo-liberal bastards and another?"

It was Anusha's turn to be angry. "The difference between one lot of neo-liberal bastards and another lot is the space where we can do something. It's the space where you and your friends can hang off coal trucks and occupy runways. It's the space where there's funding for my project. It's also – in case you hadn't noticed - the space between poverty and destitution, the difference between feeling that you have a right to equal treatment and being treated like dirt on someone's shoe because your job's been destroyed or you happen to have a face that doesn't fit. You may not like this lot but you don't remember what the other lot were like."

"Neither do you!"

"No, but I listen to our parents. You've always rushed off without paying attention. Remember that time in Pinkerton Park – that Christmas when you got roller boots and I got a scooter..."

"Anusha, what's that got to do with anything, we were nine years old."

"...and I wanted to try your roller boots and our Mums said turn and turn about but you raced off down the hill, all the way to the river and by the time you'd got back up the hill..."

"Anusha, I couldn't stop, there's no brakes on roller boots..."

"Exactly. My point exactly. You raced off because you didn't stop to think about where you were going..."

"Anusha, Anusha, you're not being fair." She paused and looked directly at him. "Anyway," he said, "your scooter was pink."

They both collapsed in laughter. When they had collected themselves, Felix said, still a little hurt, "I don't think I'm really a selfish person."

"Agreed," she said. "You're my oldest, best-est friend. Which is why I can say these things to you. Check your privilege."

"Do you know what you're going to do?" he asked, hoping to be allowed to change the subject. She passed him the stack of books piled on the coffee table and he turned them to look at the spines and titles. They were all about economics, the subject of Anusha's degree. *Prosperity without Growth, Managing without Growth, Growth Isn't Working, Steady State Economics.*

"We know that infinite growth is impossible on a finite planet," Anusha said. "We know that the neo-liberal experiment brought capitalism to the point of collapse. This is our moment. They're on the back foot and there are two possibilities. Either they use the shock of the crash to impose austerity or we seize the moment, change the game..."

"Reading books isn't going to do that."

"Someone has to work out what an ecologically sound economy would look like."

"And you reckon it's you?" he teased.

Anusha shoved him backwards on the settee. "I'm thinking of doing a PhD," she said, "with this woman."

Felix flipped through the book she had passed him, looked at the picture of the curly-headed author on the back, and listened to Anusha's enthusiasm for a new global currency that would control carbon emissions fairly.

"Sounds amazing," he said, not entirely understanding but caught temporarily in her excitement. Anusha had always had the capacity to rise above setbacks and to see difficulties as temporary. He felt himself dull and stupid in comparison.

"What about you?" she asked. "What are you working on?"

"Oh, you know," he said. "Houses for the very rich. I suggest super-insulation. They settle on a marble bathroom and gold taps."

"Don't be cynical Felix," Anusha said. "We'll build council housing again one day. One day you'll be designing estates full of eco-homes, palaces for ordinary people."

He looked at her wearily.

She hugged him. "Please don't be cynical Felix. Please. It doesn't suit you."

Back in Sheffield, depressed now rather than angry, Felix found himself jammed at the same pub table as Clara in the aftermath of yet another dull and frustrating meeting. Other people pulled on scarfs and hats and headed for the door until only Clara and himself were left, sipping the ends of their drinks. Felix was surprised to notice that he hadn't avoided her and that he no longer felt the anguished lurch in his stomach every time he saw her. She smiled at him, a thin, shy smile and he smiled back.

"You OK?"

She nodded. "And you?"

He nodded back. "No Jay tonight?"

"He's working away. They've got a big contract that's been waiting for better weather and now they've got to catch up."

"But you're still together."

"We're still together."

He studied her freckled face and the soft curls of mousey brown hair. The feelings were still there but only as a curious gnaw in his gut. They talked awkwardly, asking conventional questions and offering conventional answers until he noticed, as he enquired how her Christmas had been, a familiar tear appear at the corner of her eye.

"What's up?"

Clara tried to brush the tear away. "Nothing."

Felix looked at her quizzically and raised one eyebrow in imitation of his mother.

"Everything's shit at home," she said. "My parents are divorcing, the house is being sold, my brother's still drinking and my father's been accused of abusing one of his patients."

Felix let his breath out slowly between his teeth, trying to think what his mother or Jane might say in response to this. Failing, he said, "That's a lot of shit. And the trial too."

"I hardly think about the trial," she said. "If I let myself, I'm terrified. I'm convinced I'm going to prison."

Felix felt on surer ground and offered reassurance. "It's a first offence. You've got a good legal team."

"That's what everyone says but I can't believe it."

More tears appeared and he offered her the red spotted handkerchief from his satchel. She looked at it doubtfully. "It's clean," he said.

Clara smiled and wiped her eyes. He walked her to her bus stop, trying to find words that might breed some of Anusha's resilience in the slight figure beside him. The bus came.

"You take care," he said as she stepped towards the lighted doors.

"And you," she replied and was gone.

Thomas

Thomas chose his clothes with care, selecting a pale ivory shirt, a charcoal grey suit and a tie which suggested membership of a Cambridge college, though he had in fact bought it in Leather Lane market. He hesitated over his cufflinks, eventually rejecting the monogrammed gold for the less ostentatious onyx and silver. He gave a last polish to a pair of handmade, dark shoes and slipped his feet into them. While at university an aristocratic acquaintance had told him that the way the upper classes identified each other was through the subtleties of their dress code. "Your shoes give you away, long before your accent," the man had laughed and ever since, Thomas had cultivated his outward appearance with care. He inspected his face in the mirror, dabbed a hint of expensive aftershave on his cheeks and adjusted the handkerchief that peeked from his top pocket. Satisfied, he slipped his best dark coat from its hanger. Brushing his hands gently across the soft wool and cashmere fabric he felt subtly comforted. Picking up his briefcase and umbrella he made his way to the tube. The hearing was scheduled for 10.30.

His lawyer was already sitting in the waiting room of the Foundation's headquarters in Merton Square. She had a look of displeasure on her face.

"They've just told me that they've received a statement from the patient. Apparently it came in late last night."

Thomas' could feel his carefully assembled composure disintegrating. He sat down heavily.

"They've suggested two options. If we wish, the hearing can be adjourned to a future date in order to give us time to consider the statement. Alternatively, we can have an hour to look at it now and the hearing proceeds as normal."

Thomas could not think above the sound of his heartbeat. Last night as he prepared for bed he had begun to think that he might be safe. Since just before Christmas he had lived in dread that Nicole would make a statement. But as January had slipped into February and he had begun to count down the days towards the hearing, he had allowed himself to feel first hopeful and then confident that he was right and that she would not do anything that might harm him. "What do you suggest?" he asked falteringly.

"If you'd like to go ahead today, we could agree on condition that anything in the statement which is not an agreed matter of fact has to be put aside for the purposes of their adjudication."

"You mean that unless I agree that what she says is true it can't be used against me?"

The woman hesitated. "These cases are so often one person's word against another's, so unless there is agreement about the facts or some external corroboration it becomes a question of plausibility, credibility."

"And she's not going to appear in person?"

"Apparently not. It seems she was unsure about whether she even wanted to make a statement and this is why it only came in at the last minute."

Thomas could imagine Nicole, havering, hesitating, sitting on the sofa with her arms around a dog and prevaricating. She would not have wanted to harm him.

"But what do you advise?"

"A lot depends on what this document says. Complainant's statements are often quite muddled – facts jumbled in with assertions and outpourings of feeling – and that could work in our favour. It would mean there wasn't much there that they could use. On the other hand, if it's precise and eloquent, you may be called on to answer direct questions that are hard to deny. Then again, asking for an adjournment won't make those questions any easier to respond to and will also give them time to hone their argument. They've only just seen this document too."

Thomas tried to imagine Nicole sitting at a computer, typing an account of their relationship. It was an unlikely scenario. Nicole struggled to spell a text message correctly.

"Could we look at it and then make up our minds?"

"We could but they've asked us to decide now. One of the panel members has come up from Brighton and they don't want to keep him hanging around."

Thomas looked through the window at the plane trees in the square. The hum of distant traffic penetrated the double glazing and the silence of his indecision. He remembered Nicole's giggle, the way she would kick off her shoes to curl up on the couch and the sound of her voice as she formed his name. She had loved him, respected him, looked up to him. She had told him explicitly that she would never do anything to harm him. He allowed himself briefly to think that her statement might even be supportive of him, that she might have used it to deny that anything sexual had taken place between them, before rapidly suppressing this as a dangerous fantasy.

"So you think we should go ahead?" he asked.

"It's your decision."

"I think," he said slowly, "that I would like to get this over with."

"Good," the lawyer said briskly. "I'll tell them."

The secretary showed them into an empty consulting room and handed them each a document. They read in silence for a few moments, the lawyer marking her paper with a highlighter pen. Thomas could feel the tremor start in his right leg. The prose was clear, succinct and damning and at the end was a log of the phone calls and text messages he had made to her phone in the aftermath of their relationship. There were twenty-four of them.

"She didn't write this. She can't have written this."

The lawyer turned the two sheets of paper over. "It's signed. It's been witnessed. It seems to be in order."

"Those people from APPA – they've got to her, they've influenced her, they've persuaded her to write this."

"It's not illegal to get professional help in writing a statement," the lawyer said drily. "Let's go through it."

She moved rapidly through the factual information about the dates of the therapy and Nicole's reasons for consulting him and settled on the second paragraph.

"We need to get this bit straight. She says 'During the first year of the therapy when I got upset he frequently sat on the couch behind me and put his arms round me to comfort me.' True?"

"Yes I did do that but not frequently. Occasionally. For therapeutic reasons. To help her talk. Not the way that's implied there."

The lawyer made a note. "Then she says, 'I could feel that he had an erection and this made me extremely uncomfortable. I didn't know what to do.' Did you have an erection?"

"I don't know...I can't remember...it's possible."

"I need you to be clear if you can."

"She's an attractive woman, I'm a normal man."

"If you can be clear it will help."

"No. No. I didn't. I'm sure I didn't. If I had I would have moved away. Of course I would. I'd have moved away."

"Paragraph three. She says 'When we said goodbye at the end of a session he would always put his arms around me, pull me close and then kiss me. Sometimes he would rub himself against me. I thought perhaps this was a normal part of therapy. I didn't want to offend him.' True or not?"

"I was trying to show her that I accepted her. She was very dissociated. The physical contact helped her feel real. It was therapeutic, not like it sounds there."

"Let's take it bit by bit."

Slowly they worked through the document. In it Nicole asserted that Thomas was the one who had suggested they form a relationship outside the consulting room. She described herself as flattered but confused, seduced by the strength of his personality and consenting to his sexual advances only because she did not know how to say no to someone she felt grateful to. She had ended contact with him as soon as she had spoken with APPA and had begun to understand what had happened. He had continued to pursue her, she wrote, and she had felt harassed by his phone calls and text messages.

The final paragraph was devastating. 'I do not know how to get over what happened in therapy. I feel betrayed and that a part of my life has been taken from me. I thought I could trust Thomas. I thought he was acting in my best interests. I believed what he said. Now I do not know what to believe or who to trust.' The document was signed in her careful, sloping hand. The witness signature was that of the chair of APPA.

"Put it to one side," the lawyer said, striking through the paragraph. "She was asked for an account of the therapy not a victim impact statement. We're looking for facts that can be agreed on."

"But she's saying that I've ruined her life."

"Put it to one side," the lawyer repeated. "Answer the panel's questions as factually and briefly as you can. I'll make sure that they follow process correctly. I'll be sitting beside you and I'll intervene if they ask anything that's not strictly relevant. OK?"

Thomas entered the hearing already exhausted.

Clara

Jay swung the van into the petrol station.

"I'm going to fill her up. I've got an early start tomorrow."

"OK."

Clara's voice was dull. Seeing her anxiety about the first court hearing, Jay had suggested they go away for the weekend but it had not gone well. She had imagined a pretty stone cottage with a cosy fireside and bright sunshine against a cold, crisp sky but Jay had chosen a cheap bed and breakfast above a pub in an unremarkable village and it had rained almost continuously. She had tried unsuccessfully to make notes for the essay that was due on Monday but her thoughts returned again and again to the trial.

"Don't fret," Jay had said curtly. "It's pointless." He had seemed distant and preoccupied. They had not argued but his familiar warmth was absent and she could not stop thinking about what would happen on Wednesday. Her defiance had all slipped away.

They had left the village earlier than planned and Jay had powered the van recklessly down the steep country lanes of the Dales, braking hard at the bends and accelerating fast out of them. Back in Sheffield the driving rain had eased but Clara looked out of the van at a depressing urban landscape of take-aways, betting shops and litter. She felt sick.

Jay reached in through the window for his jacket and wallet.

"Could you get me some mints?" she asked. "I'm feeling a bit queasy."

"There should be some in the glove compartment but I'll get you some fresh, anyway."

"Thanks."

He crossed the forecourt to pay. Clara flipped open the glove compartment and rummaged amongst the junk of old receipts, letters, parking tickets and packets of tissues. Scrabbling towards the back to feel for the mints she knocked everything onto the floor. Picking it all up again, she noticed that Jay's passport was amongst the papers. She found the mints and then flicked curiously towards the back to look at Jay's picture. The photograph was unmistakeably Jay. He was younger and his hair was amusingly short. The cut was almost military but she would have known him anywhere. It was his eyes that she loved, the way you could see the hint of a smile beginning at the corners, in defiance of the passport photographer. Remembering Jay's continued reluctance to admit to his age, she checked the date of birth and was surprised. March 1970. He was much older than the twenty-eight which she had decided was the maximum he could possibly be. He was not, she realised, much younger than her Dad and this thought produced an uneasy feeling in the pit of her stomach. Puzzled, she quickly checked the rest of the details. The surname was wrong too. Lots of people in the movement used nicknames and aliases though. She would tease him about it when he came back, call him Mr. Yeates.

She was rearranging the papers, stacking them neatly with the passport at the top, when one caught her eye. She had thought it was another speeding ticket but it wasn't. It was a payslip in the same name as the passport. She read it again and again, failing each time to make sense of it. In the top right-hand corner was a star-shaped logo surmounted by a crown. She looked back at the picture of Jay in the passport, looked again at the name in the passport and again at the name on the payslip and the date. She could not make sense of it. The payslip had been issued three months ago and the employer was given as the Metropolitan Police.

Clara looked over towards the shop. Jay was at the back of a long queue. Slowly, she took her phone from her pocket. She took a photograph of the payslip and then one of the back page of the passport. Then she placed the two documents side by side on the seat beside her, took two more pictures and replaced everything in the glove compartment. She switched off her phone, slipped it back in her pocket, got slowly out of the van and walked into the filling station shop. She waved to Jay and indicated the toilets at the back. Crouching over the pan, she was sick.

Jay was waiting in the van, tapping his fingers against the steering wheel, by the time she had bought herself a bottle of water and returned. She clambered into the front of the van and did up her seat belt, aware that her hands were trembling.

"You OK?"

"I've been sick."

He reached out a hand, pushed the hair gently away from her face and felt her forehead.

"I don't think you're running a temperature but you're very pale." His voice was concerned and she could feel tears pricking behind her eyes in response.

"Was it my driving?"

"I guess."

"I'm sorry." He stroked her hair gently. "Let's get you home."

Jay started the engine and he drove slowly through the drizzly streets. He found a space outside the student residences and turned off the engine.

"I won't come up. I think you need to get some rest and I need to get my stuff together for tomorrow. I've got to be in Basingstoke for eight 'o' clock. Will you be all right if I leave you now?"

Clara nodded and unclicked her seatbelt.

"You're winding yourself up about the trial, aren't you?" His voice was kind and his concern seemed genuine.

She let her silence pass as acquiescence.

"Listen. I'll be back Tuesday night, Wednesday morning at the latest. It's not a big job and I should be able to get away fairly quickly. I'll be waiting for you when you come out and we can go off and do something together."

"Thanks." Her voice came out as a whisper.

"It's going to be all right - really. It always is. Worst case, you'll get a Community Service Order. You're not going down. Promise." He had turned her face so she had to meet his eyes. "Believe me?"

She found herself smiling weakly and nodding. He kissed her softly on the lips and she got out of the van. She stood and watched as he pulled out into the stream of traffic, then turned and walked slowly towards the residence block and her small, cell-like room.

Once inside, she carefully unpacked her weekend bag, moving around the cramped space like an automaton. She folded and refolded the clean clothes, put the dirty ones in her laundry bag, placed her essay notes on the desk and then rearranged everything, tipping out the contents of her pencil jar and sharpening each one carefully. From time to time, the same five words forced themselves through the imposed routine: "Jay is a police officer." Finally, she got out her phone and looked at the pictures she had taken. They were quite clear. The name in the passport was Jason Anthony Yeates. The picture in the passport was Jay. The payslip was from the Metropolitan Police and was in the same name.

Clara made herself a cup of tea and tried to make sense of what she was looking at. Jay is my boyfriend. Jay loves me. Jay is an activist who has been involved in the movement for years. Everyone knows him. Everyone trusts him. Jay cannot be a police officer. There is some kind of mistake. She searched for explanations. Perhaps Jay is short for James and he has a twin brother who is in the police force and is called Jason. Perhaps he used to be a police officer and doesn't want to admit it because people in the movement would disapprove and not trust him. Perhaps he is a look-alike for the policeman in the photograph and he's somehow got hold of this guy's passport and documents so as to infiltrate the police. She was aware that each explanation was more unlikely than the last but the photographs she had taken did not make sense.

She picked up her phone and scrolled through the numbers. She did not know who to call. Helen was in Scotland with her family for the weekend and she knew from experience that their remote smallholding had no signal. Would anyone in the activist network believe her? And if they did, would they not assume that she had been complicit? Clara remembered, with another shock, how Jay had helped her set the passwords to her phone and laptop. She began to feel fearful of her friends in the movement, remembering the suspicion she had encountered when she joined and the paranoia that had circulated after the coal train action. What might they do to Jay if this was true? And what might they do to her? Eventually she dialled Ruby's number. She was surprised when Ruby picked up.

"Hey Clar. How are you doing?"

Clara could hear the noise of traffic and the clump of Ruby's high heels on a pavement. "I'm OK," she said automatically and then added, "There's something I wanted to talk to you about."

"I'm on my way to meet friends but I'm a couple of minutes away, so go for it."

"I've just found out something a bit weird about Jay."

"The polyamorous boyfriend? What else is he into that's weird?"

"Ruby...please...this is serious..."

Ruby's next words were distorted by the wind crackling across the microphone of her mobile. Clara ploughed on. "The thing is, it turns out that Jay is in the police."

"In the what?"

"The police. Jay's a police officer."

"So what's wrong with that?"

"What's wrong with it?"

"Yeah. Why shouldn't he be in the police?"

"Because...because..."

"Listen Clar, I'm two steps away from the gang and I've got to go. I'll phone you tomorrow, OK? Just chill. Get an early night."

Clara cut the call and huddled up on the bed, pulling a rug around her. She scrolled slowly through her address book again and then put the phone down, resting her head on her knees. When she looked up again it was quite dark. She reached the travelling set of Connect 4 from the shelf and laid out the counters, red on the left, blue on the right. She closed her eyes and played against herself randomly, dropping the counters into the frame one by one. "Red it's all OK, blue it's not," she whispered to herself. When she opened her eyes and looked at the pattern, she could see that she had dropped four blue counters into a row, quite early on. She realised that she was feeling sick again and that she longed to be at home. The dark city outside the window felt alien and she felt unreal.

She leant her forehead against the cold glass of the window and stared out at the city. In her confusion the only person she wanted to see was Jay. He would have an explanation, he would tell her not to be so silly. He would lift her chin so she looked into those kind, crinkly eyes and kiss her and she would apologise and he would hold her and she would cry and apologise again and he would say it was all right, it was all, all right. Clara tapped on his name but the call went straight through to voicemail. She repeated her explanations to herself again and again but each time they sounded less and less likely. She looked at the pictures again, her finger hovering momentarily on delete. Then she transferred them to her laptop, walked across to the University Library and printed them out. Back in her room she laid them out on the bed. Finally, she picked up her phone again and scrolled through to Felix's number. His voice was cool and distant, "Clara – this is a surprise."

She swallowed. "Felix, something rather odd has happened and I wondered if you could come round."

"Now?"

"Yes. It's about...it's about..." She didn't want to mention Jay's name. "It's about some security stuff and the network."

"Could it wait till tomorrow?"

"I really need to talk to someone."

"Can you tell me on the phone?"

"I'm a bit worried to."

"Because of security?"

"Yes."

"Half an hour? Would that do?"

"Thank you."

Felix hovered awkwardly just inside the tiny room. A smell of the damp outdoors clung to his coat. He wiped his glasses carefully with a red-spotted handkerchief before turning the chair from the desk so that he faced Clara and sat down.

"Well?" His voice was neutral.

"I wanted you to look at these."

Felix looked at the pictures with the same disbelief that she had felt. "Where did you get these?"

She explained, feeling betrayal with each word.

"Jay," he said. "Jay. How can it be? He's been involved for years. He's been central to everything we've done. Why would the police go to the expense of putting someone undercover with us for that amount of time?"

"You think there's another explanation?"

He picked up the photos again. "How can there be? What other explanation can there be?"

She was silent. Even the fantasy of the twin brother felt too far-fetched to mention.

"Jay," he said. "Jay. I would never have guessed. You know we used to call him Slippery Sam because he never got arrested? He'd always duck out or peel off when things got difficult. He'd never lock on – said he was too claustrophobic to risk a police cell – crap like that. And then he got into doing the transport so he'd rarely be physically at the centre of an action." He paused. "But he was always involved at the planning stages – the camps, the occupations, the logistics for everything. It was his idea to ambush the train..."

He was pacing up and down now, as much as the small room would allow. Turning he said, "You know what this means, don't you? The trial - your trial - will collapse - and there are probably a load of other unsafe convictions too. I'm calling Stefan," he said. Felix was on the phone before Clara could demur and Stefan had arrived before she had begun to ask him what they intended to do. Felix had commandeered her laptop and was searching the net for any trace of Jay under his real name.

When Stefan arrived the two men seemed huge in her tiny room. She retreated to sit hunched up in one corner of the bed. Stefan now occupied the chair and Felix leaned forward from the end of the bed, his back firmly towards her. They were re-running history, listing the actions that Jay had been involved in and his role in each one. They interrogated her.

When had she last spoken to him? When was he due back in Sheffield? What had he said about his movements? It was important she give nothing away. They listed the people who could be allowed to know, agreed who would contact the lawyers in the morning and discussed what was likely to happen in court. Then they planned how to confront him. It was simple, but they needed Clara's co-operation.

"Are you OK with that?" Felix asked.

A shadow of concern crossed Stefan's face. "This is shit for you. I can see this is shit for you. Are you sure you're OK with it?"

"It's OK," she said. She paused and then said anxiously, "What will happen to Jay?"

"Fuck Jay," Felix said.

"No-one's going to hurt him," said Stefan. "We just want to talk to him."

The two men left and Clara curled herself, still fully dressed, on the bed, her eyes wide open, staring at the wall.

Esther

The man who sat opposite Esther was not the man who had bounced into her consulting room two weeks earlier. On that occasion he had been triumphant, full of praise for the intransigence of his lawyer. He had described how Barry Fazackerly, the panel chair, had blanched beneath the lawyer's cold assertions of what should and shouldn't be admissible according to the Foundation's own Code of Ethics and guidelines for process. She had blocked their most intrusive questions, poured cold water on much of Nicole's statement and succeeded in bringing the hearing to an early close.

Now however he lowered himself silently into the chair, opened his briefcase and passed her two documents. "Read this," he said. His lips were tight and his skin was pale in the weak February sunlight that filtered into the room. Esther took the papers. The top one was a letter from the Foundation informing him that as a result of the enquiry into his fitness to practise they had found him in breach of section 3:2 of the Code of Ethics. Since it was a serious breach his membership was terminated forthwith. The rest of the letter informed him of his right to appeal, the grounds on which that could be done and asked him to supply the contact details of all his patients and supervisees as the Foundation needed to write to them informing them of its decision.

The papers beneath were a detailed account of the adjudication. Esther glanced at these briefly. The judgment found that he had failed to maintain appropriate boundaries with his patients and had abused one patient both emotionally and sexually. It listed in excruciating detail the incidents which formed the basis of this judgment – the hugs, the kisses, the embraces, the meetings outside the consulting room, the sex and the offer of relationship, the harassing phone calls and attempts to persuade Nicole to stay silent. It said nothing about the impact on Nicole personally but listed in detail the impacts that could be expected on a vulnerable patient from behaviour of this kind, emphasising the serious damage that could be done.

Finally, it noted that 'Mr Fortune has shown neither insight into his behaviour nor remorse and the Panel therefore does not think that he will be able to remedy the faults which have led to these occurrences.'

Esther handed the documents back. She had wondered at his ebullience the last time they met but it would have felt unkind to challenge the optimism that seemed to be keeping him afloat and she had stayed silent. "This must be devastating for you, Thomas," she said.

"They've destroyed me. It's envy...spite... corruption. It should have been absolutely clear to anyone with an ounce of therapeutic sense that Nicole is a borderline case – very, very difficult to deal with, prone to lies and exaggeration, devious and manipulative in the extreme. They've used this to remove me. There are always enemies - people in my position always have enemies - but I never thought they would go this far."

Esther ignored this statement. "What are you going to do?" she asked. "Do you want to appeal? Have you spoken to the lawyer again?"

"The lawyer," Thomas said bitterly, "The lawyer turns out to be as much use as a chocolate teapot. She says there are no grounds in regard to the process. Apparently it was all properly done. Apparently you can destroy a man's career with a flick of your fingers if you follow the rules..."

"And the sanction?" she asked.

"They might reduce it on appeal but what difference would that make? Five years suspension, two years suspension – my career would still be destroyed."

This was true, Esther thought. No-one would refer a patient to him again.

He continued. "And my insurers have said they won't pay for any more legal advice so I'd be on my own."

"This is a lot for you to come to terms with," Esther said. She cursed the cliché that was all that would come to her lips but he seemed oblivious to it. Her thoughts were racing around his continued insistence that he had been wronged and his inability to see the harm he had caused.

"I spent four years training," he said "ten years building my practice, five years in a well-deserved position of respect and prominence and it comes to this. After everything that I've contributed to the profession I'm being destroyed by pygmies who can't see beyond the rule book, cretins who don't understand the transference, cowards who'd rather sacrifice a colleague than defend him..."

Esther let him run on. There seemed little point in confronting him. Beneath the bluster there was a fragility that alarmed her. His angry beliefs were all that stood between him and collapse. When he eventually paused, exhausted of ideas, with the anger slowly draining from his face, she simply said "Shall we talk about what you are going to do?"

He looked at her blankly. "What can I do? There's nothing I can do."

"I meant about your patients."

"To tell you the truth, I haven't thought about them at all."

It was the first objectively true statement Thomas had made since entering the consulting room and its honesty was almost endearing. Esther felt for the first time that morning that a small part of him might be in tenuous contact with reality. She took out the list of his patients.

"Let's look at who you want to say goodbye to in person, who you will write to, who you will refer each person to," she said.

He nodded his acquiescence and they began.

Later, standing in her kitchen, Esther looked out through the patio doors at her garden. The early crocuses were open in the sunlight. She could hear the flowing notes of a blackbird singing from the top of the silver birch tree, punctuated by the distinctive two-note call of long-tailed tits in the bushes below. Buds were swelling on the roses and the forsythia was about to burst into a profusion of yellow. The promise of spring cheered her but her sense of failure was deep. She had failed to bring Thomas to a proper understanding of his counter-transference to Nicole. She had failed to challenge his distortions and misinterpretations. She might have diverted him from his fantasies of marriage to Nicole but she had failed to bring him to a realisation of the effects of his behaviour on her. Even now, he seemed to have no idea of the turmoil he would have left in her life. The revelation that he had continued to pursue Nicole with phone calls and text messages designed to silence her confirmed to Esther the extent of her own failure. She stared at the garden, blaming herself for his downfall.

All I did was witness it, she thought, just as I witness this garden arrive at spring, earlier and earlier each year. I noted his delusion just as I note that the hedgehogs have disappeared. I remarked on his lack of insight just as I remark that there are no longer clouds of insects stuck to my windscreen in the summer. I catalogued his destruction but I failed to prevent it.

She opened the patio doors. The air was sharp on her skin. The sudden contact with nature reminded her that perhaps there was a touch of grandiosity in her belief that she could have stopped Thomas Fortune. She placed a handful of mealworms on the bird table and returned to the house, watching as first a robin and then a pair of blue tits flew in from the hedge.

The doorbell rang and she walked slowly through the house to the front door and her next patient.

Clara

Jay had texted Clara on Tuesday evening, "Can't get back till tomorrow. Good luck. See you in the evening." And on Wednesday morning around eleven, Clara had texted back, "Proceedings adjourned due to legal arguments. Meet me in town at 7pm?"

Now she stood on the corner of a windy street, glancing one way and then another, uncertain how quickly news would have travelled, uncertain whether he would come. She felt hollowed out inside, a physical body without meaning or substance, but when she saw his familiar figure swinging along the pavement towards her, the life rushed back into her and she kissed him as passionately as ever, sheltering herself against the warmth of his rough jacket.

"How's my favourite activist?" he said affectionately, playing with her hair.

She surprised herself by speaking her agreed lines with conviction. "We're invited to Stefan's for supper." His presence made life seem ordinary once more and the invitation an innocent act of friendship.

"Hey, that's nice." He took her arm and steered her easily along the street. "Tell me what happened this morning."

The hollow feeling returned, alongside a terror of being discovered. "I don't really understand it," she lied. "The lawyers asked to see the judge in chambers and everything's been adjourned. Something to do with new evidence I think."

Jay was puzzled and asked questions. What new evidence? Which lawyers? The prosecution or the defence? She became confused, repeating that she didn't know, until Jay laughed his comfortable, deep chuckle and said, "You were too anxious to pay attention, weren't you? Don't worry. It'll be OK."

Stefan and Felix had assembled a small group of people whom they trusted. "We need explanations," Stefan had said. "I want to hear it from himself. I want to confront him with this."

Once inside the door, Clara's composure gave way. As Jay moved confidently through towards the kitchen, slapping shoulders and squeezing arms, she grabbed Helen. "I can't stay, Helen. I don't want to see this."

Helen pulled her upstairs to one of the bedrooms and Clara sat on the edge of the bed shaking. Helen looked at her with concern.

"I think you should go home. I'll call you later, tell you what happened. I need to get back down there."

Clara slipped out of the house and walked blindly through the dark streets back to the student residences. It was the last time she saw Jay in person.

Helen came round the following day and they sat at either end of her narrow bed, knees hunched to chins, cups of coffee cradled in their hands.

"Tell me what happened," Clara said.

"Are you sure?"

"I need to know."

Helen described how, as they'd sat squashed into Stefan's front room with bowls of rice and vegetables in their hands, Jay had suddenly noticed Clara's absence. He had been prevented from leaving to look for her by Felix on one side and Helen on the other, each placing a restraining hand on his arm. "Clara's fine," Helen had said and Stefan who was sitting opposite had spoken directly, telling him there was something they needed to talk to him about.

At first Jay had protested. He'd looked at them in astonishment, turning from one to another looking for support.

"With the police? How could you possibly think that?" he had demanded. "You all know me, you've known me for years, we're friends, we're mates, this is ridiculous."

He'd tried to pick them off one by one, reminding Felix of the time he'd dragged him from the scrum of an arrest, Sophie and Amber of the time he'd stood bail for them, Stefan of the evenings they'd spent checking equipment and packing the van.

"These aren't the actions of a police officer," he'd expostulated. "How can you possibly think I'm part of the police? How can you say this?"

Stefan had produced the photographs and passed them across to Jay. They had watched as he looked at them in silence, the expression on his face changing from hurt bravado to quiet shock. Then he had put his head in his hands and sobbed. Helen, unable to stop herself, had reached out a hand in comfort. When he raised his head his face was streaked with tears.

"So how did he explain it?" Clara asked. Helen's description of Jay's distress woke a new hope in her that there might be an innocent explanation which she had missed.

"He said he didn't know who he was anymore," Helen said. "He claimed he'd started out believing we must all be criminals but that as he got to know us, he'd started to understand things which had never crossed his radar before and he'd come to believe that what we do is valid. He said he liked us all, respected us, felt torn between what he was involved in with us and what his responsibilities were as a police officer."

"So really, he was as much part of us as part of them," Clara said hopefully.

"I don't think so, Clara. We tried to get him to talk about the unit he works for. We asked him what it was called, who he was responsible to, who authorised this kind of spying, how long it had been going on, how it was funded, whether he had colleagues who we hadn't uncovered – all that kind of thing."

"And...?"

"Nothing. He clammed up. Wouldn't say a word. That made it clear where his loyalties were. He valued his job more than he valued us, whatever he said about his sympathies for what we do. We don't know where he's from, where he's based, what his rank is, whether he's married..."

"I think he's probably married," Clara said quietly, remembering the photos of the two children Jay had claimed were his sister's kids. She sipped her coffee. Cold now, it sent a chill of isolation to her stomach. "Why did he...why did he get involved with me?" she asked.

"He didn't say."

A long silence followed and then Clara asked "Did he say anything about me?"

Helen hesitated, looked down at the patterned rug which covered the bed and then raised her eyes to meet Clara's. "No. He didn't mention you."

Clara let her eyes fall, in her turn picking out the geometric weave of red and black thread. Helen reached out a hand and said "I'm sorry Clara."

The red thread went across, down, across, up, across, down, across, up. Clara counted the repetitions in the row closest to her feet and then counted them in the row beyond.

"Clara?" Helen said.

Clara looked up. The tears that would normally have been coursing down her cheeks were quite absent. All meaning felt sucked out of the words they spoke.

"Are you OK?"

"I don't know." They sat in silence for a while and then Clara said "Why me? Why did he pick on me?"

Helen hesitated again. "Maybe he liked you. Maybe it was genuine."

Clara's finger traced the geometric pattern, across, down, across, up, across, down.

"I got him access to the youth coalition," she said. "He was too old to be part of it himself but through me he got to know everything. That's why, isn't it? You know he had my passwords?"

"No-one blames you for that."

"But that's why he..." Clara searched for the right word. "That's why he targeted me."

"He might still have cared about you. One of the things he said was that he sometimes didn't know himself when he was acting and when he really believed something. He said that when he was with us he just felt like another activist and when he went back to his colleagues he felt like a police officer. Maybe that was genuine. Maybe he really was confused about who he was."

Clara could see Jay's face in front of her, the crinkle at the corner of his eyes, and the way his face would break slowly into a smile. She could feel the roughness of his fingers and the gentleness of his touch as he caressed her cheek and tipped her face towards him. She could hear his voice and the affectionate greeting that had become part of their ritual of reunion. "How's my favourite activist?" he would say and she would reply, "How's my favourite roofer?" and they would both laugh. Then she remembered his arguments about polyamory, his unexplained absences, his irritation if she phoned when he was away, his refusal to admit his age and his secrecy about the past.

She forced her eyes to focus on the bright square of the window, tracking the aluminium frame along the top and down the side, across, up, along, down, till the shape and the view became a meaningless blur of light and colour.

"No," she said. "He knew. He picked me because I was young and stupid and naïve."

"I don't think you're stupid, Clara."

Clara said nothing. She kept her eyes half-closed so that all she saw was the square of light. Helen's voice sounded as if it was coming from underwater. There was a long, long silence and then Helen spoke again.

"Listen Clara," Helen said. "You know I'm going back up to Scotland? You know I've taken the job in Glasgow? I'll be back down if there's another court appearance but otherwise I'm gone from here."

Clara nodded in acknowledgment.

"So stay in touch. Whenever you want to talk, you've got my number. I'll call you. I'll call you often. And you call me, anytime. OK?"

"OK," Clara said. She forced a smile, they embraced and Helen left.

Two days later she received a text message from Jay which said simply, "I'm sorry." When she tried to reply, the number was no longer available.

They went to the press of course. Clara watched as the story was picked up, first by one newspaper then another. As journalists became involved, the name of the unit and the reach of its operations were revealed. Undercover officers had been used for years against a wide range of political groups. Jay was not the only police officer to have infiltrated the movement and it was revealed that a police database of so-called 'domestic extremists' included mainstream environmentalists as well as activists. The police argued that the operation had provided essential intelligence and prevented violence but the threats to civil liberties and peaceful protest were instantly taken up by voices across the media. Questions were asked in parliament and there were calls for resignations.

Paula, the woman whom Jay had lived with on and off for two years, placed herself centre stage. Furious that she hadn't been invited to the meeting where Jay had been confronted she made up for this with a series of angry interviews with the press. Clara, in contrast, lived in fear that her relationship would be made public. She had seen what press attention had done to her father and she had no wish to join him in the ignominy of exposure. When she spoke to her parents she made light of her connection to the developing scandal. The court case - which her parents had barely registered - had collapsed as predicted. Jay's centrality to the planning, organisation and execution of the action meant that there was no prospect of a safe conviction. Only George connected the face that now stared from the papers and television screens, sometimes with his trademark ponytail and earrings, sometimes in his graduation mug shot from police college, with his sister.

"Ain't he that bloke you were going out with Clara?" he demanded. "The one in the pub who gave me fifteen quid for your phone?"

"You're mistaken George," she said coldly and cut the call.

As the revelations about his sexual relationships emerged, the Metropolitan Police distanced themselves from Jay. He began to be referred to as a 'rogue officer' who had acted contrary to orders. Jay retaliated with interviews describing his double life. In one he claimed he had been suffering from Stockholm syndrome. In another he talked of how his relationships with the activists had been genuine: "They were my friends. They meant everything to me." Challenged by the interviewer, he justified the sexual relationships as necessary to maintaining his cover and claimed he had always treated the women respectfully and sensitively. Other interviews emphasised his close relationship with his handlers, how his phone had a tracking device which told them where he was at all times, how they knew exactly what he had been doing and had sanctioned every move. He accused his superiors of hanging him out to dry and destroying his life but he also spoke of his fear of being pursued by the people he had infiltrated. The article described the meeting where they had confronted him as a kangaroo court and said that he now barricaded his door at night in fear of attack. Clara felt that she was reading about a stranger.

Helen called, to try to persuade her to join the growing group of women who had been tricked into relationships with undercover police officers.

"It goes back years," Helen explained. "There's a whole group of people whose boyfriends simply disappeared. There'd be some story about being depressed, moving abroad, being transferred and the guy would just vanish. One of them even had a baby with someone. And it's all coming out. There's going to be an enquiry. There's going to be legal action. You're not alone Clara."

But Clara wanted to be alone. It was the only way she could hold any part of herself together. She found herself obsessively counting – the number of stairs on the four flights up to her room, the number of steps between lampposts, the number of cars that passed while she was waiting at traffic lights to cross the road.

Term dragged on and she found herself less and less able to study. Some days she made it to the door of a lecture theatre before turning back to the solitude of her room. Other days she faltered as she entered the main concourse or saw the throngs of students crowding the coffee bar. Seen through the glass they looked like characters in a puppet show, automata waving their arms, opening and shutting their mouths in a meaningless babel of silent shrieks. Sitting in the library she read the same sentence over and over again. She wrote not a word of the overdue essays and assignments that now crowded her in-tray and she failed to reply to the emails enquiring when they could be expected. Three days before the end of term, she stood in her tutor's office with a doctor's letter in one hand and a train ticket in the other.

"See if you can catch up over the vacation," said her tutor, perusing the letter. "If not we'll have to look at the possibility of your starting again next year."

Standing on the platform at Sheffield station Clara stared at the tracks stretching away from her. They glinted in the sunlight and she automatically began to count the number of paving slabs between herself and the track. Then she counted the number of steps, walking forward one slow step at a time across the yellow safety line, until she stood at the platform edge. She took out her phone and looked again at Jay's two-word text. 'I'm sorry,' she read and "I'm sorry," she said, half beneath her breath.

"Are you all right love?" The voice beside her spoke in a strong Yorkshire accent and it made her jump. A tall man with dreadlocks and a Rasta hat caught her arm. "Steady lass, or you'll be joining the birds." He nodded towards the sparrows, fluttering and pecking between the tracks. "Train's just coming." He stepped her back two paces.

The train hissed and whined its way into the station. Clara retrieved her bags, climbed the steps into the carriage and allowed the train to carry her southwards.

SPRING 2010

Felix

Two weeks before Jane's wedding Felix was home for the weekend, helping with last minute arrangements. He had just collected the bridesmaids' gifts from the jewellers and was on his way to speak to the florist. Stepping out in warm May sunshine he was pleased with himself for managing to talk about cheap jewellery and exotic blooms without ranting about conflict minerals or air miles. He was also glad of the distraction. The recent election had threatened to revive his despair. He had no illusions about the new government and was bracing himself for a bonfire of environmental regulation.

They had agreed that Esther would walk Jane up the aisle and that Felix would make a speech as brother of the bride. Thoughts about his family and the phrases which might express them were beginning to form in his mind. His mother had looked at him with one eyebrow slightly raised when he had suggested that he might make the speech but he had replied, quite calmly, "It's all right Mum. I'm not angry anymore." And it was true, he wasn't. When Felix had thought about his father recently it was to remember how his father had placed his stubby child's fingers around the paintbrush and watched patiently as Felix had daubed the paint in electric blue and sunshine yellow splodges across the paper. He remembered the days spent with a packet of sandwiches and a pair of binoculars, sketching in a grassy meadow while his father searched for a rare butterfly. And he remembered snatches of conversation, excerpts from long philosophical discussions about the nature of being. "Did Dad really tell us 'Life can only be understood backward but it must be lived forward'?" he had asked Jane.

"Yes," she had laughed. "Repeatedly. Every time one of us messed up."

"What's changed?" Jane had asked. "Why are you wanting to talk about Dad all of a sudden?"

"Don't know." He hadn't thought about it till Jane had asked. The image of the funeral came back to him. "Something to do with those black-suited crows and their thirty year grudge."

Crossing the market he was shocked from his reverie by coming face to face with a slight, familiar figure.

"Clara! What are you doing here?"

Clara looked up at him, equally surprised. She was thinner than ever. Her skin was an unhealthy grey colour and her usually carefully groomed hair hung untidily around her shoulders. She stammered as she replied.

"F-F-Felix. I-I didn't expect to see you here."

They looked at each other in mutual incomprehension for a moment. Then, unsure where the words came from, he said, "Time for a coffee?"

They walked in silence to the café. Sitting opposite each other Felix placed his phone and book on the table and tried to open a conversation.

"You're home for the weekend too?"

"Not exactly." She stirred her latte.

Felix tried again. "I'm here because my sister's getting married in two weeks and I'm helping sort stuff out – flowers, speeches, caterers – all that sort of thing."

Clara gave the ghost of a smile and said, "That's nice. I didn't know you had a sister."

He wanted to contradict her, remind her that she had met Jane, that first weekend when she had stayed at his mother's house, remind her that they had shared those lovers' confidences about their families, their histories and the people who mattered to them, but she seemed absent and disconnected.

"What about you? Family visit?" he said.

Clara shook her head.

"I've been home for a time," she said at last. "Since all that stuff with Jay came out. I couldn't quite hold it together in Sheffield." Felix realised that in all the rage and excitement of Jay's exposure he hadn't given a thought to Clara.

"I'm sorry Clara," he said. "I should have realised."

She shrugged his concern away. "It was just that I couldn't work. I couldn't concentrate. I missed too many deadlines to be able to sit the exams. My tutor says I could start the course again if I want."

"So you'll be back – come the autumn, you'll be back."

"I don't know. I can't imagine myself in Sheffield anymore. I can't imagine anything really."

Felix wondered for the first time what it might have been like to be so intimately tangled in the deceit of Jay's life. What might it be like to love and then lose someone who had never truly existed? How might it feel to discover that you had given yourself so totally to someone who was acting a part? Paula, the woman who had occupied the newspapers with the story of her relationship with Jay, had spoken of it as rape. Felix felt ashamed that he had given so little consideration to what Clara might have experienced.

"You sound depressed," he said.

"Probably."

There was another long silence in which he failed to find any words that might help. He watched as she traced a pattern on the table top with her finger. Along, up, across, down, along, up, across, down, until she came to the edge of the table and sat with her finger hovering over the drop to the floor. He remembered the angry words he had flung at his mother when his father had died: "He only pretended he loved us." But his father hadn't been pretending at all and Jay had.

"Are you seeing anyone? Talking to anyone?" he tried, at last.

"Therapy you mean?" Her face screwed into distaste. "Why would I want to do that?"

"Because – because - it can help, can't it?" Remembering his own reluctance to talk after his father died, he felt fraudulent in his suggestion.

"Did you hear about my Dad?"

He shook his head and she explained wearily. "My Dad got struck off for having an affair with a patient. Why would I want to go and see someone like that?"

"Because they're not all like that, surely. My Mum's not like that."

"I'm sure your Mum's a saint," she said sarcastically. "Anyway, I'm not going to be here much longer. The house is being sold and we're moving."

There was a longer silence while she stirred her latte again. Then she turned the book which he had placed on the table towards her and said, "What are you reading?"

"Gramsci."

"Who's he?"

Felix was relieved at the change of subject and began to explain Gramsci, aware that the words which spun from his lips and his analysis of how these illuminated their movement's mistakes, were falling unheard into the space between them. "There's a quote I really like," he said, "One I hang onto at the moment. 'Pessimism of the intellect, optimism of the will'."

"What does it mean?"

"I think he means you must have no illusions about how bad things are but hang in there, believe you can still do something."

Clara gave him a half smile and then said, "I'm sorry Felix. I shouldn't have said that about your Mum."

Slowly she explained. Her parents had separated. Her mother had a new job in Salisbury. Her brother would be going into rehab somewhere nearby. In a couple of weeks she'd be gone.

"Except that I don't quite fit their plans. The house Mum has bought only has two bedrooms, one for her and one for

George. Salisbury's expensive apparently and it's all she could afford."

"So what are you supposed to do?"

"My Mum says she's taking responsibility for George so my Dad should take responsibility for me. But my Dad says we're adults now so we're not their responsibility and his London flat only has one bedroom. I agree with him really. I don't want them taking responsibility for me."

"But they can't just throw you out..."

"Mum says I can stay till George gets out of rehab – it'll be about four months if he sticks it. And she says there'll be a sofa bed if I want to come in the vacations. But I don't want to go to Salisbury. Why would I want to go to Salisbury?" She paused. "Why would I want to go anywhere?"

Clara panicked him. Three months ago the tears would have been streaming down her face as she spoke. Now it was a mask, a hard, grey mask.

"Clara," he said. "You have to talk to someone. You have to let someone help you."

"There isn't anyone. And I haven't any money."

Her words were neutral and apparently factual but they were charged with silent rage. Felix remembered his pleasure at his mother's despair when he had spat words of scorn and contempt about his recently dead father. He felt helpless.

He said slowly, "Would you talk to my Mum? I don't mean for therapy. I just mean to talk to her, ask her stuff? Find out if there's some way to get free help?"

Clara said nothing.

"She used to talk to my friends sometimes when we were in sixth form – nothing heavy, just little bits of advice when they screwed up."

"I'm not the one who screwed up."

Felix was silenced again. She robbed him of words just as he had robbed his mother of words. He continued to look at her, willing her to look up and meet his gaze.

"Please Clara."

"I'm leaving in a few weeks."

"Please."

Clara looked at him properly for the first time and met his eyes. "OK," she said neutrally. "If you want."

They left the café and walked through the market. As they passed the church a middle-aged woman with dark hair and a cheerful face stopped them.

"Clara!" she said. "How nice to see you! Ruby said you were back home. I'd been wondering when you'd come and see us." She chattered on, saying she was sorry Clara had needed to come home, asking after Clara's parents and gradually coming to a standstill in the face of Clara's monosyllabic answers. "You come and see us," she finished. "I've missed your interesting conversation. And Fred's missed your games of Connect 4."

"Who's that?" Felix asked as the woman disappeared into the Saturday crowds.

"My friend Ruby's Mum. Fred's her little brother."

"She seemed nice."

"Yes." There was a hint of life in the grey cheeks.

When Felix spoke to his mother, he was taken aback by her response. By the time he had reached the sixth form he had welcomed her subtle interventions in his friends' lives and her willingness to spend half an hour encouraging one to speak to their parents and another to phone the youth counselling service.

"No," Esther said. "I can't. Absolutely not. I'm sorry, but I can't see her."

"Not for therapy, Mum. Just to chat to her. Point her to something like you used to do with my friends."

Seeing the expression on Felix's face she had apologised further. "It's just that it's not possible," she said. "It's complicated. There are professional reasons why I can't see Clara."

Felix pleaded. "Mum, she's in a terrible state. She was having a scene with Jay, the bloke who we outed as a police spy. She needs to talk to someone and I can't do it. I'm useless at that sort of thing, you know I am and anyway I'm not here."

Felix watched as his mother tapped a pencil on the kitchen table. He could see that she was upset or angry or both and that she was not going to say why. Eventually she stood up.

"Leave it with me," she said and left the room.

The following day she handed Felix a piece of paper with a name and a phone number on it. "Give that to Clara," she said. "I've asked Martin Tischbein if he'll see her and he's agreed. But she needs to make the appointment herself, Felix. It's no good if you ring for her."

"Tisch," he said wonderingly, "You've persuaded Tisch to see her."

"Yes," she said and smiled. "He owes me for all the trouble I took over his Festschrift."

"Thanks Mum."

Clara

Clara stood on the pavement outside a bungalow surrounded by a garden full of late spring flowers – aquilegia, bluebells, forget-me-nots and some dramatic dark irises. Wisteria framed the front of the house and its drooping blooms filled the air with their sweet fragrance but she was oblivious to it. Rage had left her and anxiety had returned. She checked her watch and ventured up the front path. She was surprised to see that the man who opened the door was old, though he moved easily and his voice was firm. She followed him into a quiet room of muted greys and soft browns and sat nervously in the chair he indicated to her.

Martin Tischbein settled himself in the chair opposite her and opened his hands in a gesture of encouragement. "Would you like to tell me why you have come to see me?"

Clara said nothing and the silence ticked past on the clock which sat on the table between them. She could feel his eyes on her, then realised that he had moved his gaze a little, as if sensing her discomfort. She glanced back at him with a feeling of desperation. No words would come, just a feeling that she was in the wrong place, that it was impossible to say anything, that this old man could not begin to understand anything at all about her and that she could not leave without causing offence. The minutes ticked by, three, four, five. She said nothing. He said nothing. Then he shifted in his seat and said:

"What are you thinking?"

The words left her lips before she could stop them. "That you're awfully old." She blushed deeply and she began to stutter phrases of embarrassment and apology "I mean...I'm sorry...I didn't mean..."

Martin Tischbein looked at her seriously and after a pause in which he seemed to be thinking said, "Perhaps you are afraid that I will die before you have time to get what you want from me."

She looked at him in confusion. This was not what she had expected at all. She had once listened to her father's radio show and he had asked rapid questions and then advised, cajoled and lectured till the caller expressed effusive thanks and retreated. His occasional forays into advice to George had taken a similar form, though George had not been grateful.

"Perhaps people have a habit of leaving you before you have been able to get what you need from them," Martin Tischbein continued and then as she didn't reply added, "Might that be true?"

She was quiet for a time, looking straight at him, noticing the pale grey eyes behind the glasses and thinking that there was something kind in the face that seemed to be studying her so carefully. She managed a nod and a whispered "Yes."

"So," he said. "We have begun." He spoke slowly, as if forming the sentences from somewhere deep inside himself and continued: "What you want to tell me, I think, is how afraid you are."

It was a statement but he looked at her questioningly and at last she said a quiet "Yes."

"And this..." - he imitated the pattern she had been tracing on the arm of the chair, across, up, along, down – "this is one of the things which you do when you are afraid?"

"Yes."

There was another long silence in which Clara found herself flooded with memories of all the times she had been afraid, from her first steps away from her mother at nursery to the last time she had seen Jay and the frozen knowledge that he had betrayed her. Images tumbled over each other, times she had struggled with rules she did not understand, times she had displayed confidence she did not feel, times when she had cracked with the shame of retreat and lain awake night after night, filled with the numb, nameless dread which invaded the loveless house. She noticed that her finger had momentarily stopped moving and looked up.

"If you would like to tell me more about these things," Martin Tischbein said, "I would like to hear them."

And so, gradually, Clara began to talk. She told him about her parents and George, about moving from the house with the red door in London and her terror of change. She told him how the game of Connect 4 had comforted her when she won and devastated her if she lost, how counting brought solace but only till she landed on a number designated as unlucky, and how food so often felt like ashes in her mouth and like concrete in her stomach. She spoke about her father's ebullient incomprehension and her mother's vague indifference. She described George's addictions and her father's disgrace. She talked about meeting Felix and falling out with Ruby, and finally she talked about climate change and activism, polyamory and Jay.

Martin Tischbein said little. Sometimes, as Clara skated away from something which seemed obvious to her, he would bring her back, enquiring what she had felt, quietly giving names to experiences which she had dismissed as foolish or unimportant. "You do not have a good sense of going-on-being," he said at one point and "You think you need permission to be fully alive," at another. All he said about Jay was, "This man gave you hope, I think, and you have lost that." It was true. Clara found, to her surprise, that the tears were flowing once again down her cheeks but they felt different now, tears of release not shame.

Martin Tischbein had glanced at the clock and she stopped, instantly registering his slight shift of attention. "We only have another five minutes," he said, "So we must decide what to do next." He paused and looked at her. "Would you like to come and see me again?" he asked.

"Yes," Clara said "I would."

"Good," he replied. "I think we have a lot more work to do."

Then she remembered. "But I can't," she said. "I have no money and no job and my mother is moving, and I owe you for this session. What do I owe you for this session?"

Martin Tischbein spoke again in his slow, careful way. "You do not owe me for this session," he said. "This session is for you to find out if you want to come and see me and for me to find out if I think we could work together. For this there is no charge." He paused. "You have told me a lot about being afraid and now you are panicking again which is not surprising. But you have also told me a lot about being resourceful. I think we could make another appointment and when you come you can tell me what progress you have made about these practicalities."

He wrote an appointment time on a card and a figure beside. "That is what I will charge you for each session," he said. Clara looked at the card. The amount was, she knew, much less than her father had charged his patients. She took the card, stood up and left.

Esther

Esther sat beside Meena on a large, white squashy sofa, beneath large, arched windows which looked out on a formal terrace and an expanse of lawn and shrubs which stretched away towards parkland and field. It was still light and the Western sun streamed into the room, dappling the parquet floor. The room had once been an orangery and the building had once been a stately home. It now belonged to the local authority, housed an art collection, a folk museum and the County archive and did a profitable line in conferences and weddings.

The ceremony was over, the meal was eaten and the guests were standing around in small groups as the band prepared. Esther had chatted to some of Jane's friends, exchanged pleasantries with Adam's family and spoken kindly to Jane and Felix's half-sisters, the twelve-year old twins whom Jane called the 'halves' and Felix called the 'haves'. They had arrived with Adam's mother, two identical, well-behaved girls who had explained politely that although they were missing horse-riding it was worth it to see Jane get married.

Esther watched as Adam led Jane onto the dance floor. Jane had changed from her silk, cream wedding dress into a flamboyant, full-skirted dress with red polka dots and bright red shoes. Her hair was pulled up into a ponytail and the band – a collection of Adam's old university friends – were playing rock and roll classics from the 1950s. Adam was leading Jane in an exhilarating, complex jive which sent her skirt swinging and her ponytail flying.

"She looks radiant," Meena said.

"She does," Esther agreed. It was what people always said about brides but it was true. Jane looked radiant. She had lost weight and she moved fluidly and confidently, her eyes never leaving Adam's as she stepped around, past, beside and towards him.

The wedding had gone well. Esther felt proud of both her children. Felix's speech had surprised her. He had been serious, thoughtful and confident. He had paid tribute to herself and to Jane - "the two women who have shaped my life" - speaking of how much Jane had learned from their mother and how much he had learned from Jane, of how he had learned to see adversity differently through their example, learning to find joy in unexpected places. He talked of Jane's loving nature, her tolerance, her determination, her good sense and he related it all back to their mother. He paid tribute to Adam - "a good mate I never expected to have" - and to Adam's family. He included his half-sisters, the twins Lucy and Chloe, saying how pleased Jane was to see their lively presence at her wedding. Finally Felix talked of their father. He said how sad he was that Gordon was not there to see Jane married, how sad he was that Gordon had missed so much of their lives but acknowledged that it was his absence in the last twelve years as much as his presence in the first twelve that had shaped them all as they were now. At the end he had read out the cards and good wishes which had come from those unable to attend, including one from Ruth. "Finally," he had said, "I have a card from our Aunt Ruth who writes 'May the Lord bless your union and bring you joy.' I think we can all say 'Amen' to that." Esther had smiled at Felix's ready acceptance of religious sentiment which a few months earlier would have sent him into a tirade of fury. His new-found tolerance had not yet settled into a proper discrimination she thought. Nonetheless she felt a quiet contentment that her sister had written and that Felix had welcomed her words.

Other people joined the dance floor. Felix and Anusha stumbled through a clumsy imitation of the happy couple before collapsing in breathless laughter on an identical sofa on the opposite side of the room. Felix laid his head on Anusha's shoulder. Anusha responded by tickling him and they play wrestled for a moment.

"What do you think?" Meena asked. "They are fond of each other, aren't they?"

"Like puppies," Esther replied.

"Sometimes," Meena agreed. "But they are serious together as well. I think they are coming to see more in each other than puppies do."

Felix was fumbling in the pocket of his jacket which he had discarded on the sofa beside him. They watched as he pulled out his phone, read something, moved closer to Anusha and showed it to her. She read it, looked at him, smiled and then kissed him on the cheek.

"You see?" Meena said.

"In our dreams," Esther replied.

"No," Meena protested. "It is their dreams too. You wait."

Felix was standing up with his phone in his hand. He threaded his way through the dancers and flopped down on the sofa beside Esther. Meena reached across and stroked his arm. "So Felix," she said, "Are you finished with all this hanging off diggers and ambushing trains now?"

"Not a bit of it," said Felix, smiling. "But it's a long game now. I'm studying strategy."

Meena tutted and smiled back, "Underneath, just the same Felix," she said. "You are like Anusha. You don't give up."

Felix turned to Esther. "Something to show you," he said, putting the phone in Esther's hand. "There's a message for you."

The text was from Clara. 'Dear Felix,' it said, 'I wanted to thank you for talking to me the other week and particularly I wanted to ask you to thank your Mum for putting me in touch with Martin Tischbein. I have been to see him twice now and I am not going to Salisbury with my mother. I have my old job back at the supermarket and I am going to live with Ruby's family as a kind of au pair. They have a spare room and I will be looking after her little brother Fred after school and in the holidays in exchange for rent and food. I do not know about Sheffield and my course. There is a lot to think about but I am feeling a little better. Clara, xxx.'

"I'm glad she's feeling better," Esther said neutrally, handing back the phone.

"Me too," Felix said. He got up and crossed the room.

The band had finished their set and were being replaced by a man with turntables and music with a thumping bass. Esther watched as the older people began to retreat. Adam's parents had gathered up the twins and were shaking hands and saying goodbye. Paresh, Meena's husband, reappeared from a side room where he had been playing chess with Adam's grandfather. Meena stood up.

"Time for us to go," she said.

"Indeed," Esther said and they too began their round of farewells before stepping into the fading light of the terrace and making their way home.

EPILOGUE

Esther

It was a hot day in late summer. Esther had come in from the garden to fetch a drink and was idly checking the laptop she had left open. Her news feed depressed her: drought and famine in Sahel, rivers polluted by oil sands in Alberta, floods in China. Against her better judgment she clicked on an email headed 'Good news from the world of coaching'. When she opened it she discovered that it was not spam but was addressed to her personally and came from Thomas Fortune.

'Dear Esther,' it read. 'Since we last met I have been busy putting my life back together and I wanted to let you know that I am now on the road to a new and exciting career as a life and business coach. I am beginning to make connections in the corporate world but as a relative newcomer my fees are reasonable and I am keen to establish as wide a client base as possible. Take a look at my website and do feel free to pass on the information to anyone whom you think might be able to benefit. Yours, as ever, Thomas.'

Esther didn't know whether to admire his brazen resilience or fear for his new clientele. A wave of anger swept over her and she took a long drink of iced water before stepping into the patch of warm sunlight on the flagged floor and listening determinedly to the birdsong from the apple tree. Turning back momentarily to the table she deleted the email, picked up her secateurs and returned to her garden.

Made in the USA
Monee, IL
08 January 2023

24760695R00163